EMBASSY

OF THE

EMPIRE

A James Acton Thriller

Also by J. Robert Kennedy

James Acton Thrillers

The Protocol
Brass Monkey
Broken Dove
The Templar's Relic
Flags of Sin
The Arab Fall
The Circle of Eight
The Venice Code
Pompeii's Ghosts
Amazon Burning
The Riddle
Blood Relics
Sins of the Titanic
Saint Peter's Soldiers
The Thirteenth Legion
Raging Sun
Wages of Sin
Wrath of the Gods
The Templar's Revenge
The Nazi's Engineer
Atlantis Lost
The Cylon Curse
The Viking Deception
Keepers of the Lost Ark
The Tomb of Genghis Khan
The Manila Deception
The Fourth Bible
Embassy of the Empire

Special Agent Dylan Kane Thrillers

Rogue Operator
Containment Failure
Cold Warriors
Death to America
Black Widow
The Agenda
Retribution
State Sanctioned
Extraordinary Rendition

Templar Detective Thrillers

The Templar Detective
The Parisian Adulteress
The Sergeant's Secret
The Unholy Exorcist
The Code Breaker
The Black Scourge

Kriminalinspektor Wolfgang Vogel Mysteries

The Colonel's Wife
Sins of the Child

Delta Force Unleashed Thrillers

Payback
Infidels
The Lazarus Moment
Kill Chain
Forgotten

Detective Shakespeare Mysteries

Depraved Difference
Tick Tock
The Redeemer

Zander Varga, Vampire Detective

The Turned

EMBASSY OF THE EMPIRE

A James Acton Thriller

J. ROBERT KENNEDY

ISBN: 9781990418532

First Edition

10 9 8 7 6 5 4 3 2 1

For Michael Kovrig and Michael Spavor, Canadian citizens held hostage and in violation of international law by Communist China since December 10, 2018.

EMBASSY

OF THE

EMPIRE

A James Acton Thriller

"The South China Sea islands have been China's territory since ancient times. It is the bounded duty of the Chinese government to uphold China's territorial sovereignty and legitimate maritime right and interests."

Chinese President Xi Jinping
September 2015, National University of Singapore

"The plot at the east window has been exposed."

Ancient Chinese Proverb

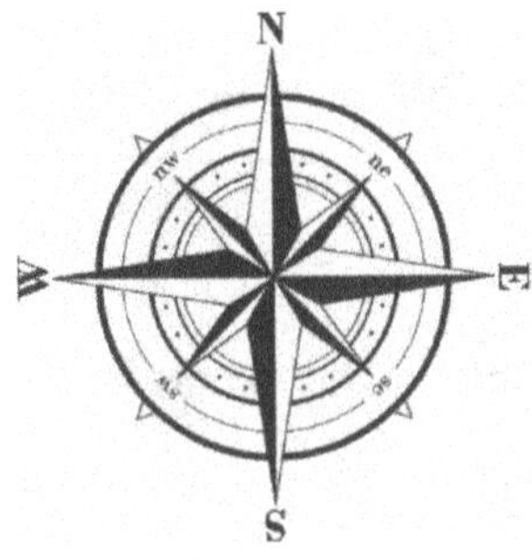

PREFACE

In 2015, the People's Republic of China began dredging activity in the South China Sea on Cuarteron Reef, in territory claimed by five other nations including the Philippines and Taiwan. Before the end of the year, the Chinese had expanded the reef into 57 acres of useable land, including helicopter pads as well as gun, radar, and missile emplacements. By 2016, photographs suggested anti-aircraft and missile defense systems had been installed.

Over the next couple of years, six other artificial islands were created by the Chinese government in the same area known as the Spratly Islands, and claims were then laid to the waters surrounding these manmade islands in contravention to international law.

In response to these illegal actions, various navies have begun Freedom of Navigation Operations through these disputed territories, to signal to China their claims are not only against international law, but are also not recognized under the Third United Nations Conference on the

Law of the Sea (UNCLOS III). Countries including Japan, Australia, France, the United Kingdom, and the United States have sailed these FONOP missions.

On September 30, 2018, the USS Decatur was forced to take evasive action to avoid the Chinese destroyer Lanzhou, which had made increasingly aggressive moves toward the American vessel, coming as close as 135 feet to the Decatur, risking collision.

The Chinese government has claimed these FONOP missions are in violation of their law, and have vowed to put an end to them, following through with increasingly aggressive actions toward vessels legally traversing through unfounded territorial claims.

It's only a matter of time before something goes horribly wrong.

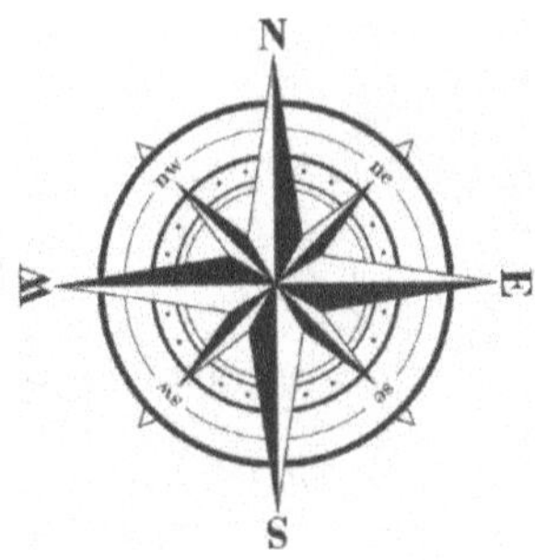

Hyatt Place Luoyang

Luoyang, China

Present Day

Special Agent Yan Shengtao's adrenaline was pegged as he climbed out of his car. The official records on his targets said they were staying at the Hyatt, so he had put two men on the hotel just in case they returned. Not ten minutes ago, he received a report that one of the targets had been seen entering the hotel alone. It was the first sighting of either of them, and the first indication that Professor Cao might be telling the truth. He was disappointed the sighting didn't include both of them, but he had little doubt that should he capture one, and have the local English media report that fact, the other would surrender.

He sprinted toward the doors, the staff pulling them open, fear in their eyes at the sight of his Ministry of State Security identity card held out in front of him, and the dozen uniformed personnel with whom he had arrived. He turned to face his team. "Nobody gets in or out. Two on this door, the rest of you find the other exits."

They split off to execute their orders as he scanned the crowd, mostly Westerners cowering in fear as they lined up at the counters, desperate to flee the country they were here to no doubt exploit, before war broke out. He shoved his way through the crowd and smashed his fist on the counter, putting the fear of the state into the young woman behind it. He held out his tablet with the screen split, showing the names and pictures of his targets. "What room are these people in?"

The woman said nothing, her entire body trembling as she tapped at her keyboard. "Seven-Twelve."

He held out his hand. "Give me a key."

She unclipped a passkey from her waist and handed it to him. He forced his way toward the elevators, and a few minutes later was inside their room. It was a suite unlike any he had ever seen outside of a movie or a television show, and it made no sense to him. There was nothing in the files he had been provided that suggested they could afford anything such as this. How they could possibly do so raised enough red flags that he now understood why the Politburo was after them. They must be criminals of some sort, perhaps stealing from his country. His government obviously hadn't been able to prove anything, and was now taking advantage of the current situation to possibly pull them in for interrogation when they previously couldn't.

But the real story was that neither of his targets were here, though there was evidence someone had been. Clothing dumped on the bed suggested whoever had been here was searching for something. His eyes widened.

Passports!

He headed from the room and pointed at one of his team. "Search the room top to bottom. Report anything unusual."

"Yes, sir."

He headed back down into the lobby to find the additional personnel he had ordered had arrived, the hotel now buttoned up. He walked over to a gathering of the unit commanders. "Search the hotel, top to bottom." He tapped a few menu items on his tablet, sending the photos of the targets to all of those within the area, including those in front of him. He indicated one of the pictures. "This one was seen entering the hotel fifteen minutes ago. I want them found."

"Yes, sir," echoed the unit commanders.

"They arrived here by vehicle, so there's a chance they might still be in the area. Have your people on the lookout." He headed for his car as there was nothing he could do here now. He was certain they were long gone, and unfortunately his mandate didn't include roadblocks that would impact the local citizenry.

The question was, where were they heading, and what was so important they would risk coming back to their hotel room? Unfortunately, for the moment, there was only one person who might provide those answers, and he sat in an interrogation room, cooperating fully, with no leverage he could use against the man to make him reveal any secrets he might be holding back.

Like why one of the 25 members of the Politburo that controlled the Communist Party of China, wanted him to arrest Professors James Acton and Laura Palmer.

At all costs.

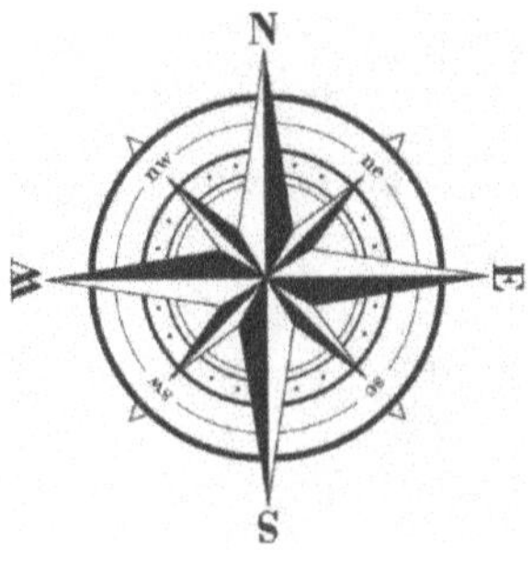

Imperial Palace

Luoyang, Han Empire

166 AD

Stunning.

That's the only word Lucius Seneca could think of as he took in everything around him. Absolutely stunning. It rivaled anything he had seen at the Imperial Palace in Rome, though he was certain anyone who hadn't witnessed the seat of the Roman Emperor before would react in much the same way he was now. It wasn't necessarily that this was more opulent than the palace back home, it was that it was different. The colors were bright and vibrant, the patterns intricate and unfamiliar, the uniforms worn by the honor guard unlike any he had seen before. It was an impressive, awe-inspiring sight, and his heart pounded with the excitement of standing here, by his father's side, facing Emperor Huan, whose throne room this was.

The journey to get here had been long and arduous. They had crossed on horseback through the farthest reaches of the Empire, then sailed by boat across seas upon which few Romans had ever ventured, then finally, their guide had brought them northward until they reached the capital of the domain this emperor they stood before claimed as his own. The journey had taken almost two years, and they had lost many. But they were finally here, and the heavy price paid would now hopefully prove worth it, though only if the man before them granted his blessing to establish the first embassy of the Roman Empire in the fabled land at the opposite end of the Silk Road.

The Han Empire.

If Emperor Huan denied them their request, there were only two possibilities. He would execute them for some perceived affront, or they would be sent home to Rome facing years more of torturous travel, with the knowledge they had failed in their mission. Emperor Marcus Aurelius had dispatched them to establish trade relations and a military alliance. It was believed the two empires had several common enemies whose territory lay between their lands, and should they form a military pact, they could attack on two fronts, thus eliminating their mutual threats, allowing the establishment of firm trade routes between the two wealthy empires.

He eyed their guide and translator, Nedum, a man found at a seaport halfway through their journey who not only spoke Latin, but also the language spoken here in the Han Empire, or at least that was what he claimed. The few people they had in Rome who had been to the Han Empire, didn't speak the language, and had only succeeded by finding translators along the way. If this man did indeed speak the language of the Han Empire, then everything would hopefully go smoothly. And all evidence suggested he did indeed, for he had managed to get them from the borders of the Empire and into the palace, though there were on occasion smirks and laughter as apparently his fluency was questionable.

Nedum took a knee and bowed deeply, waving his hand at the Roman contingent, indicating they should follow his lead. His father immediately did so, though Lucius hesitated. This man was not his emperor, and the only men he would show fealty to would be Roman. A tug on his sleeve had him glancing down at his father who glared at him.

"Take a knee now, or you walk back to Rome tonight."

He frowned, but complied.

Huan spoke and the translator did his job, though Lucius was no longer paying attention, for he had spotted something far more interesting. To the side of the throne stood a group of young women who appeared to be servants of another, ornately dressed, and more breathtaking than anything he had seen in his life. She was staring directly ahead, her face expressionless as her emperor spoke. He couldn't tear his eyes away from her. His stomach filled with butterflies as he realized this entire journey, even should it end in failure, would have been worth the effort merely for these few moments gazing upon this magnificent creature.

One of the servants whispered in her ear and she turned her head slightly, her eyes meeting his. He smiled, and his heart hammered then nearly stopped when a sliver of a smile appeared on her flawless face.

His father rose unnoticed beside him as he continued to share the mesmerizing moment with this beautiful woman. A hand grabbed his shoulder and hauled him to his feet as Huan stepped forward to greet them. His father and the others executed a salute, which he hastily delivered a moment later, his eyes darting back to the beautiful woman whose stoic expression had returned, her eyes again directed at her emperor.

"The Emperor would like to present his daughter, Princess Jieyou."

Lucius' heart leaped as the young woman stepped forward with her entourage.

Princess!

She bowed, as did his father.

"It is an honor to meet you, Princess Jieyou. May I present my son, Lucius."

Lucius bowed deeply, as did she, and as he rose, their eyes once again met, a hint of a smile appearing in the corner of her lips, and he was certain he spotted a twinkle in her eye. That he was interested in her was beyond question, and he had no doubt she had picked up on that fact. Yet princesses were spoken for, mere pawns in the game of politics their fathers played day in and day out. She was no doubt already betrothed to the son of a rival to her father that would cement some treaty—and if she weren't, it was merely because it hadn't yet been necessary.

And the sons of ambassadors from empires too far away to be of strategic importance to this empire would never be worthy of such an honor, and any hopes he might have had of getting to know this woman better were dashed upon the rocks of diplomacy the moment her identity had been revealed.

And this had his young, inexperienced heart aching with the loss of what should be his destiny.

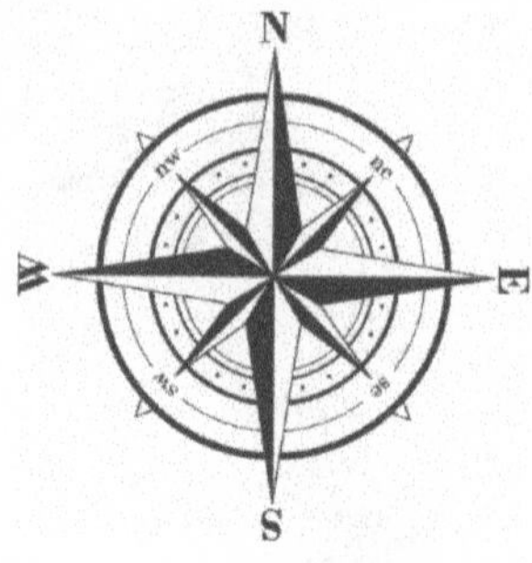

University College London

London, England

Present Day, Two Days Earlier

Terrence Mitchell stared at the test results displayed on his monitor. He had taken the samples himself, so there could be no error, yet it had to be a mistake. The genetic markers left no doubt—the sample showed that the woman was of Asian descent, with a 99% certainty that she was from a part of Asia now within modern China. Yet that was impossible, for the carbon dating results were equally conclusive, and it placed her death approximately 1800 years ago. And these two facts, along with one other critical one, made these results impossible, for her body had been unearthed only weeks ago, along with several others, in London.

How could a Chinese woman have died over 1800 years ago in England?

It was impossible, or at least it should have been. To this point, as far as he was aware, DNA tests had shown there had been bodies found in the past with some Asian DNA markers indicating children or grandchildren with a Chinese ancestor had lived here, though never before had an actual Chinese person been found.

Something had to be wrong.

His wife, Jenny, burst into the room. "You're not going to believe this."

"What?"

"I just got the results back on the other bodies, and it just doesn't make any sense."

"Let me guess. They're Chinese?"

Her eyes widened. "Yours too?"

"It has to be a mistake, right?"

She shook her head. "All of them? Impossible."

"Could there be cross-contamination? Could all of our samples have come from the same source by mistake?"

She wagged her tablet at him. "No, I checked that. They're all distinct individuals. Three women were absolutely pure Chinese, or at least from that region."

"And the others?"

"We're still running tests, but some of the others showed they were children of these women based upon mitochondrial DNA, and the Y chromosome testing we were able to do on the boys showed their fathers had the typical DNA markers you would expect from a Roman of the era."

"So, Roman men sired children with pure Chinese women?"

"Exactly."

"But how did they get here? It makes no sense."

Jenny shrugged. "Not to us, but maybe it might to someone else."

He smiled and grabbed his phone off the desk, selecting one of his contacts before putting it on speaker. It rang several times before the familiar voice of their former professor answered. "Hello, Terrence, what a pleasant surprise. How are you?"

"I'm fine, Professor Palmer. I'm here with Jenny. We've got a bit of a puzzle we'd like your opinion on. Jenny is sending you some DNA and carbon dating test results now." His wife's fingers flew over her tablet. "You should have them in your email now. The results are, to say the least, strange."

"Strange in what way?"

"I don't want to taint your opinion with ours. Please go over them then call me back and let me know what you think."

"I will. Give me a few minutes and Jim and I will take a look."

"Thank you, Professor."

"Don't you think you should be calling me Laura by now?"

"No, ma'am, it's never going to happen."

She laughed. "Very well, I'll get back to you soon."

The call ended and Jenny sat beside him. "You realize this discovery is huge?"

He nodded.

"We're going to be famous."

He gave her a look. "We're archaeologists. The next time you're out for drinks, ask one of your friends if they can name a single archaeologist. And Indiana Jones doesn't count."

She chuckled. "I suppose you're right. Now what do we do?"

"We start writing a paper on what we found."

"Or we could go get plastered."

He grinned. "I like the way you think."

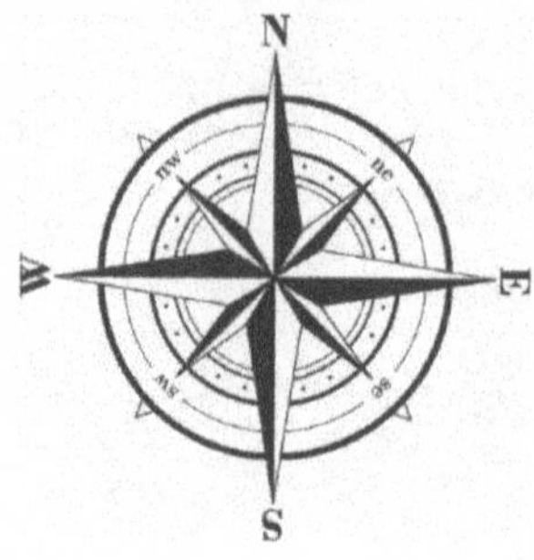

Acton/Palmer Residence

St. Paul, Maryland

Archaeology Professor James Acton stood in front of the barbeque and checked his watch. He flipped his steaks then closed the lid, returning to the patio table where his best friend and dean of the university he taught at, Gregory Milton, sat with his wife, Sandra. Acton sat, grabbed his Corona beer, and took a long swig, enjoying the bite of the lime wedge floating amidst the light brew.

"Those steaks smell incredible, Jim," said Sandra.

"Thank the cow, not me. All I do is flip 'em."

She chuckled. "Anybody can flip a steak. Only an expert knows *when* to flip a steak."

He bowed his head and toasted her observation with his beer. "Wiser words were never spoken."

Milton grunted. "Then I'd hate to hear the conversations you've been participating in lately."

Acton laughed. "My freshman class this morning certainly seemed to be high school freshmen, not college. I don't know what they're teaching kids these days, but it's certainly not what I was taught."

"Yeah, the basics seemed to have been tossed out the door."

"Maybe we just have a really shitty rowing team."

Milton snorted, spraying his beer. "Thank God we're a small institution. I'd hate to be dealing with that type of garbage right now."

"True, your time is better spent dealing with the problems I create."

Milton held his beer high. "Preach."

Both Acton and Sandra gave him the eye and Milton's shoulders slumped, beer lowered. "Yeah, even I heard it."

Acton's wife, Archaeology Professor Laura Palmer, rushed out onto the deck, shoving an iPad in his hands. "You have to see this."

Acton took it and scanned what appeared to be DNA and carbon dating results. "What am I looking at?"

"Terrence and Jenny just sent this to me."

"Give us the run-down. We have guests."

She sat. "These are DNA and carbon dating test results from their dig in London."

"What dig is that?" asked Milton.

"A few months ago, they began excavations to build a new office block and found some old ruins. The excavation was halted and a team from University College London, my old institution, were sent in to examine the rooms. My former grad student, Terrence Mitchell, is leading the team."

"Good for him."

"Yes, he's come a long way, hasn't he?"

"He has, indeed." Acton held up the tablet. "So, these are test results from bodies they found, I assume?"

"Yes."

"And what's unique about them?"

"Three of the women are Chinese."

Sandra took a drink. "So? That's possible, isn't it?"

"They died around 200 AD."

Acton's eyes shot wide, as did Milton's. His wife stared at them. "Is that significant?"

Acton explained. "It is. In 200 AD, England was part of the Roman Empire, and the Roman Empire had minimal contact with the Chinese."

Milton pointed at the barbecue and Acton jumped from his seat. "It would have been the Han Empire back then, wouldn't it?" asked Milton.

Acton removed the steaks from the grill. "It would have been the tail end of it, yeah."

"So, how did they get there?" asked Sandra.

"That's the $64,000 question."

Laura's eyes narrowed. "64,000? That's rather specific, isn't it?"

Acton patted her back as he brought the tray with the steaks to the table. "Sometimes I forget you're British." He sat and waved off Sandra as she leaned forward to eye the steaks. "Let the poor things rest!"

She rolled her eyes. "Fine, Chef Ramsay. Then answer my question."

He flashed her a toothy smile. "Of course. The question is, like you said, how did these people get there? We know there are reports that in 166 AD, I believe it was, a Roman expedition reached the capital of the

Han Empire to establish the first embassy, but nobody knows what became of it until just a few months ago. Ruins were discovered during construction in China that revealed Roman architecture in the middle of what would have been the ancient capital of the Han Empire."

Sandra shrugged. "Perhaps there was a cultural exchange, and some returned to Rome."

Laura shook her head. "That wouldn't make sense. It would if the bodies were found in Italy, but not England. You wouldn't send an ambassadorial team from the Han Empire to the Roman Empire, then send them to the farthest reaches of Roman influence. They would be in Rome. And why send women?"

"Could they have been slaves?" suggested Milton.

"That's absolutely possible, though it would be costly to transport a slave that distance. It wouldn't make economic sense."

"Sex slaves? A Chinese woman would have been considered quite exotic."

"Again, very expensive. And how would they have encountered them?"

Acton agreed. "And according to those reports Terrence and Jenny sent, there were three of them. One, I could believe, but three? No, there's something more going on here."

Laura flipped through the reports. "And the timing is too coincidental. If they died around 200 AD, and this embassy was established in 166 AD, that's only a thirty-four year gap. If a group did go from the Han Empire back to Rome, the question is, why would they have then gone on to England?"

"Could they have been exiled?" suggested Milton.

Laura nodded. "It's a possibility, though again, why wouldn't they return to their empire? Unless they find more evidence, it could be a mystery that's never solved."

Acton glanced at Laura. "Why don't you go over there and help them?"

She shook her head. "No, I couldn't do that. They would think I didn't trust their abilities. I'll provide advice if they ask it, and if they should want me there, I'll of course go, but the cord has been cut and it has to remain cut."

Acton agreed, then his eyes widened with a smile. "Then I've got another idea."

Milton groaned. "Is this going to cause me paperwork and headaches?"

Acton grinned. "Absolutely."

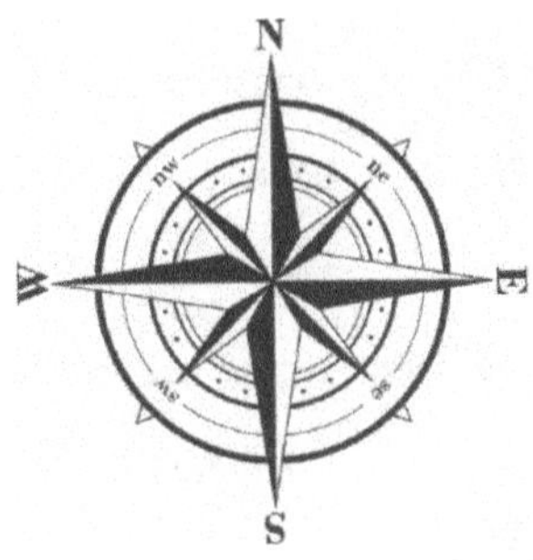

Roman Diplomatic Mission Quarters

Luoyang, Han Empire

166 AD

"I think that went rather well, don't you?"

Lucius Seneca regarded his father, Statius, sitting across from him. "I suppose. We're still alive."

His father chuckled. "Yes, that's always a good indicator the day wasn't entirely a failure. What's your impression of the Emperor?"

Lucius shrugged. "Seemed rather small to me."

"Indeed. They're all rather small, aren't they? It's hard to believe they could be formidable in battle, which makes me question how strong an ally they might be when dealing with the Parthians." He scratched his chin. "Though you can't always judge a man by size alone. From the accounts of those we've met along the way, they certainly seem to have a reputation as capable warriors." His father folded his arms. "The palace was impressive, wasn't it?"

Lucius agreed. "Quite. Very colorful."

"Yes, I noticed that too. We seem to tend toward whites and solid colors, especially reds. While I believe the contrast and its effect are impressive, the variations we saw today certainly gave the impression that this empire is very wealthy. Even if they should not prove to be effective warriors, a trade alliance might be fruitful."

"The merchants we encountered along the way certainly seemed interested in our glassware."

His father agreed. "You noticed that as well, did you?"

"It was hard to miss. If our mission weren't to establish a trade and military treaty with the Han Empire, we could have easily sold everything we brought long before we even reached here."

"Tomorrow, we will be showing what we have to offer to the Emperor and his people. It is essential in any future meetings that you follow my lead immediately. No more hesitations or distractions, like what happened earlier."

He cringed at the scolding. Until this moment, he had assumed his father had forgotten about his blunders.

His father eyed him, a slight smile creeping from the corners of his mouth. "She's quite beautiful, isn't she?"

A pit formed in his stomach and his cheeks flushed. "Sir?"

"I may be older than you, but I'm not blind. Princess Jieyou caught my eye as well."

He turned away, uncomfortable.

"But she is off-limits."

"I know, Father."

"If you were to lay even a finger on her, speak a word to her, it could mean the end of everything. All our effort, all our sacrifice, and perhaps even our lives, could be forfeit."

His pulse pounded in his ears at his father's warning. "I understand, Father."

"Good. Then off to bed with you. These quarters they've provided us appear to be quite luxurious, which I hope means they are treating us as honored guests rather than nuisances."

"Yes, Father." Lucius rose then bowed. He headed for the chambers assigned to him in the east wing, and they were as his father had described—luxurious. All of his personal items had already been laid out by his manservant brought from Rome, who stood waiting for him inside. He was helped out of his armor, then he dismissed the man, completing his nightly ablutions himself. He lay on the bed, finding it quite comfortable, though lower to the ground than he was accustomed to. He closed his eyes and drifted off.

A tap at the shuttered window had him flinching awake. He dismissed it as a tree branch blowing in the wind, or some other innocuous explanation, and closed his eyes once again. Another tap in the exact same manner as the first piqued his curiosity. He rose then stepped over to the east-facing window. He opened the shutters and his heart leaped into his throat at the sight of a beautiful woman standing just below. She handed him a piece of paper then quickly scurried off. He leaned back inside and closed the shutters, then stepped over to a lamp and unfolded the piece of paper, his eyes shooting wide at what it contained.

A map.

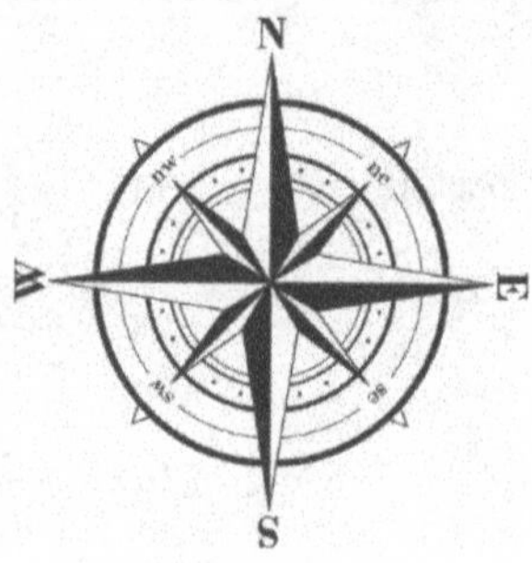

Acton/Palmer Residence

St. Paul, Maryland

Present Day

"Are you sure you want to go?"

James Acton rolled his eyes at his wife, Laura Palmer, as they both listened to Gregory Milton on speakerphone. "Of course we want to go. This is an incredible find, and could provide clues as to how Chinese women in the second century came to be living in Londinium, a Britannic settlement of the Roman Empire. We're archaeologists. This is what we live for."

"Yes, but the situation in China right now isn't good, what with all the political fighting between them and most of the world. Not to mention the rumors of something having just happened there that has the leadership spooked. I'm just questioning if now is the right time? Why not wait a few months and let things settle down?"

Acton had read some of the conspiracy theories online about the assassination of General Zhang by Muslims, and agreed with many of those who thought what was now happening there was an over-reaction if it had indeed been some lone-wolf gunman as the Chinese had claimed. Zhang had been powerful within the Communist infrastructure, but was also considered a possible rival to the current president. Acton's former student, CIA Special Agent Dylan Kane, was intimately familiar with China and its internal affairs, and he would make a point of speaking to him about it should he see him again in the near future.

He returned his attention to Milton, who had continued in his attempts to talk him out of it. Acton interrupted him. "Listen, Greg, I know you're concerned for us, and I appreciate that. But they're not going to start randomly arresting foreign nationals."

"Oh, you've never heard of the two Michaels, Kovrig and Spavor."

"Who?"

"They're two Canadian citizens that have been in a Chinese prison since 2018 under trumped up charges, all because we requested that the Canadian government arrest a Huawei executive in order to extradite her."

Acton had no clue who they were. "Sorry, you've got me there. I guess it's a good thing I'm not Canadian."

"Yeah, and I'm sure the Canadians thought the same thing about us. You have to remember that the Chinese are a brutal communist dictatorship that imprisons millions and murders thousands every year. Their military is belligerent and growing in power, and through coordinated intellectual property theft, they dominate technology sectors they have no business being in. International laws don't apply to them, they don't care about anybody but themselves, and you can be sure that when they do appear to, it's only because they have some ulterior motives behind their charity. If you go there now, during these heightened political tensions between our two countries and whatever other internal matters that have made them more paranoid than ever, you could become a pawn in whatever game they're playing."

Acton sighed. His friend was genuinely concerned for their safety, yet his friend also had a history of being in a constant state of paranoia, and always trying to talk him out of any foreign dig.

Yet he had been right about Peru, though for all the wrong reasons.

"We'll be fine, but I promise the moment there's any hint of trouble, we'll leave, okay?"

"There's no talking you out of this, is there?"

He glanced at Laura who waved her hands, removing herself from the discussion, not wanting to get between two best friends. "No," he replied.

"And you have all your paperwork?"

"We do. Laura's travel agent has taken care of all the visas and our charter has been booked. We're leaving tomorrow."

"Fine. I've made some calls and had the two of you officially attached to the archaeological team that's there now. That should give you a little bit of protection since you'll be more than just tourists."

Acton smiled slightly at the phone. "Thanks, Greg. That should help put all of our minds at ease a little."

"So, then you *are* concerned."

Acton tossed his head back, groaning. "I was only saying that to be nice!"

Greg laughed. "I know, and I was only saying that to get a rise out of you. Just keep me updated regularly, okay?"

Acton laughed. "Okay, Dad, I promise."

"Hey, just because half my head is gray, it doesn't mean I'm old enough to be your father."

Acton leaned over the phone. "Goodbye, Daddy." He tapped the screen to end the call.

Laura looked up from her tablet. "He *is* a worrywart, isn't he?"

"He is that, and he's become worse since Peru. I guess I can't blame him. I wasn't the only one to lose students that day."

"Are you concerned?"

Acton glanced at her. "Not at all. It's China. We've been there before."

"Yeah, and look what happened."

Acton laughed. "Yeah. Actually, I almost forgot about that. We've been through so much crap over the past few years, it's hard to keep track where we've been shot at."

"How can you forget a Chinese coup that we were caught in the middle of?"

He shrugged. "Just an average day for us."

It was her turn to laugh. "I don't know whether I should be more concerned that I'm laughing at that, or that it's true. Obviously, with it being China, we'll have to be careful and be on our best behavior, but I doubt we have to really worry about anything. Let's just stick to the dig site and our hotel, and never go out alone."

He reached out and took her hand. "Do you honestly think I'd ever let you out of my sight for a minute?"

She gave him the stink eye. "I can take care of myself, thank you very much."

He grinned. "I wasn't talking about that."

She gave him a seductive look. "Just what do you have on your mind, Mister?"

"Nothing they'll be playing on Disney Plus." He dove at her and she squealed.

Luoyang, Han Empire

166 AD

Lucius had never been more terrified or excited in his entire life, and that life included numerous battles for the Empire and a voyage that would have curdled the blood of Hercules himself. He had quickly determined that the map showed his current location and then a destination. He had doused his lamps then exited the room through his window, the drop to the ground not very far, and hopefully it wouldn't prove a challenge when he returned.

He had kept to the shadows, few out at this hour beyond guards, the capital city heavily patrolled. But with each step, he realized his ultimate destination was the Imperial Palace, and the very notion terrified him. If he were caught alone at this hour in the streets, he might be forgiven for merely being curious, but on the grounds of the palace itself, it might mean immediate death for them all.

This entire endeavor was foolish. He had no idea who the woman was who had delivered him the map, and no idea what was at the end of it beyond the red X marking his destination. Was it something he was supposed to see? Take? Or was it some person he was supposed to meet? And was it an innocent meeting, or was it a trap? Perhaps death awaited him when he reached this red X, or perhaps he would be kidnapped and held as a bargaining chip against his father, against the Roman Empire itself.

Whatever it was, he had no doubt no good could come of it, yet he was compelled to continue forward. Perhaps it was the impetuousness of youth, or perhaps it was his faint, irrational hope that at the end of this map was something that would have made worthwhile this entire infernal journey foisted upon him by his father in a bid to make him a man. He had been forced to leave the only home he had ever known, along with all of his family and friends, only to make his home here, years away from civilization. He had never wanted this, and he needed a reason, a purpose, that would give it all meaning.

He was about to step out from between two buildings when he heard voices. He fell back, pressing against the wall, and forced himself to steady his breathing as four guards walked by, marching swiftly as had most of the other patrols he had encountered. It was clear to him these men weren't searching for anything. They were merely a deterrent. The pace at which they marched and the noise they made precluded them from detecting any ne'er-do-wells, and from what he had seen, he was the only one in the city worth apprehending.

The guard passed and he cocked an ear, hearing no one else. He darted across the street, the Imperial Palace ahead, though the map thankfully didn't lead him to the main gate. He continued in the shadows along the front wall, then rounded the corner, left of the gate. The line tracing the route he should follow ended halfway along the wall, then continued on the other side. He spotted a reinforced door, and though no guards were evident, an untold number could lie on the other side.

He pressed an ear against the wood but heard nothing. He tried the handle to find it locked. He pushed against the door to no avail, then looked around, pondering what to do next.

The lock clicked.

His heart skipped several beats as he reached for his sword. He stopped. If he were to engage in battle, it would mean the death of the entire ambassadorial mission. He could still plead ignorance. He could still claim he had gone out to explore the city and gotten lost, and the only landmark he had recognized was the palace where he thought he might find help. The door opened and every muscle in his body tensed.

Then he sighed in relief at who stood there to greet him.

It was the woman who had delivered the map.

She beckoned him inside, and with furtive glances over both shoulders, he entered. She closed the door then locked it. He was now inside the Imperial Palace, alone with a woman whom he had no idea of her status or motives. He was a foreigner in a foreign land, who had no right or reason for being where he was, and if caught, all the blood spilled would be on his hands. He could still leave, he could still turn around and compel her to unlock the door, yet her demeanor suggested there was nothing to fear here. She was smiling at him, beckoning him to follow her, and he found he couldn't resist her urgings.

Yet it was clear she, too, didn't want them caught. She stuck to the shadows, listening for what he assumed were patrols, but moments later they were inside a building, and the instant she closed the door, she visibly relaxed. Her smile broadened in the torch-lit hallway, and he was led, this time at a casual pace, toward a room at the far end. She knocked and a woman replied, saying something in their native tongue. She opened the door and stepped aside, tilting her head, indicating he should enter. He hesitated and she urged him again, her smile widening.

He stepped through the door, his hand on the hilt of his sword, still uncertain as to what he might be about to face. But when he stepped inside, his wildest imaginings couldn't have prepared him for what he saw.

It was Princess Jieyou, standing by the fire, her head bowed.

He immediately took a knee as his father would have wanted him to, but was uncertain as to what to say, for he spoke none of her language.

"You may rise."

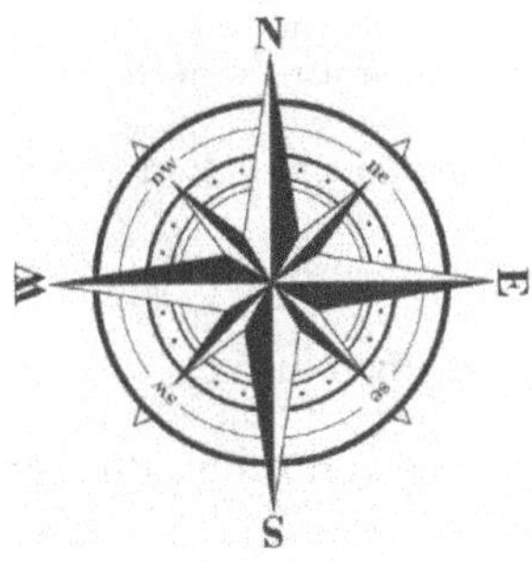

Roman Embassy Dig Site

Luoyang, China

Present Day

Professor Cao Zhengsheng stood at the edge of the pit, staring down at the excavation below, imagining what had stood here almost 2000 years ago. One of his students had begun conceptual drawings and, while mostly guesswork, they were impressive even in their most modest configurations. It was a testament to Roman design, intentionally meant to remind anyone who would see it that this was a piece of Rome in their midst. As far as they could tell, it had been surrounded by traditional Chinese structures, though with those mostly built of wood at the time, there was little left of them beyond the outline of their foundations. This structure, however, had been constructed from stone, meant to last for centuries if not longer, though all evidence so far suggested the building had been intentionally knocked down and buried shortly after its construction.

Most historians familiar with the period were aware of the reports of the first official Roman delegation sent to the Han Empire, and the dynasty's own records showed they had arrived in 166 AD by the Gregorian Calendar, yet there were few details beyond that. There were no reports of any treaties, of any return trips, of any reciprocal exchanges. There were other delegations and other attempts at formal relations a century later, yet this particular expedition had almost been forgotten by history beyond a few brief mentions.

What had been discovered only months ago, was the first physical proof of a significant Roman presence in the capital city of the Han Empire, one of the most powerful empires in the region at the time. This wasn't just a delegation that had come here to discuss a possible treaty then leave. One didn't build a significant structure such as this if that were the intention. These Romans had meant to stay, and to stay permanently. Yet after all the effort of constructing the building, it had been knocked down, the Roman presence for some reason erased from the Far East.

He checked his watch, an old friend of his, James Acton, and his wife whom he had never met though knew by reputation, Laura Palmer, were due to arrive shortly. He was eager to see them and discuss what his team had so far discovered. There was nothing he enjoyed more than conversing with friends about history and archaeology, and Acton was second to none in his field, as was his wife.

His phone vibrated in his hand and he glanced at the breaking news alert.

Incident in South China Sea between US and Chinese Navy.

He groaned.

What now?

But didn't bother tapping to read the report, instead heading for his car to pick up his old friend.

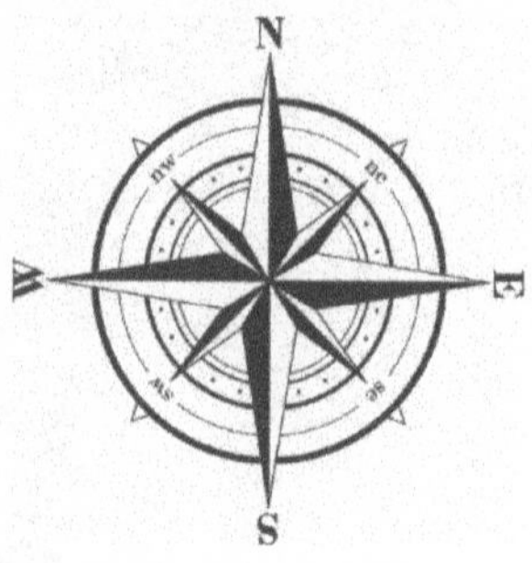

South China Sea

Hospital Corpsman First Class Doc Kidd stared up at the listing hull of the Chinese frigate they had apparently just rammed. He hadn't seen what happened. He had been below deck, manning his station after General Quarters had been sounded. The USS Somerset was a monster compared to this Chinese vessel, and wasn't capable of turning on a dime—in a game of chicken, it would always be the last to turn.

And the Chinese captain should have known that.

Yet according to the bits and pieces he had overheard from those who had been topside, the frigate had set a collision course then turned too late to avoid it, its captain misjudging his own vessel's capabilities.

He stared back at his own ship, repair crews already in action. They were taking on water, though the hole didn't seem too bad in his inexpert opinion. But the Chinese ship was another matter. A massive gash was torn through her side and below the waterline. They were taking on huge amounts of water, and the ship was rapidly sinking.

Yet none of the crew had abandoned ship.

As they approached in their Rigid-Hull Inflatable Boats, it appeared, for the moment, they had no one to save. It made no sense. The Chinese crew couldn't possibly hope to save their ship, and in situations like this, seconds could count. Why the order to abandon ship hadn't been given, he had no idea, though if he had to hazard a guess, it had everything to do with its incompetent captain.

In the US Navy, quite often promotions were given because of who you knew, but it was rare anyone would want to attach themselves to someone genuinely incompetent. He never doubted that whoever his captain was, it was someone capable of doing the job. Were they the best? That wasn't for him to decide, but he trusted in his leadership, and knew they would never intentionally risk his life unless there was a very good reason to do so.

And because of that trust, he wouldn't hesitate to do whatever was necessary.

But the Chinese Navy was an entirely different animal. China was a communist dictatorship, and while he was no expert, he loved his Tom Clancy novels, and knew enough to be aware that any position of importance within the communist state went to the best-connected individual, rather than the most qualified. It was policies like that, that led to situations like this—an incompetent captain who didn't know his ship's capabilities, deciding to intimidate the United States Navy.

Unsuccessfully.

According to the briefing they had all received before their mission, in a show of force, China was attempting to lay claim to vast swaths of the South China Sea. They were even building artificial islands to then occupy and claim the territorial waters surrounding these manmade structures. It was a blatant violation of international law, but according to his father, the Chinese never obeyed the law. And now here they were on the high seas with other Chinese vessels steaming into the area, and jets from the USS Ronald Reagan flying Combat Air Patrol overhead.

This could quickly get out of hand.

Gunfire erupted and he ducked as the coxswain of the RHIB swerved.

"Who's shooting?" cried Kidd.

"It's the damn Chinese!" replied the coxswain.

"Back off! Back off!" ordered someone.

The coxswain steered hard to port, the engine gunning as they skipped across the waves, heading back toward their home vessel as the gunfire continued. He couldn't tell if they were warning shots or if they were taking fire—he just kept his head down as he had been trained, and listened for any injuries among his crewmates. He was a corpsman. It was his job to save lives, not take them. And he never would have imagined that he'd be taking fire from the Chinese during a rescue operation.

An explosion ripped through the chaos behind them and he risked raising his head and staring back. One of the RHIBs had been hit, its fuel tanks erupting, its crew flung from the vessel, now bobbing among the waves and debris.

"We have to go back for them!" he yelled at the coxswain, who shook his head.

"My orders are to return."

Kidd made a split-second decision, then sat up and rolled over the side of the RHIB, determined to perform his sworn duty.

Leave no man behind.

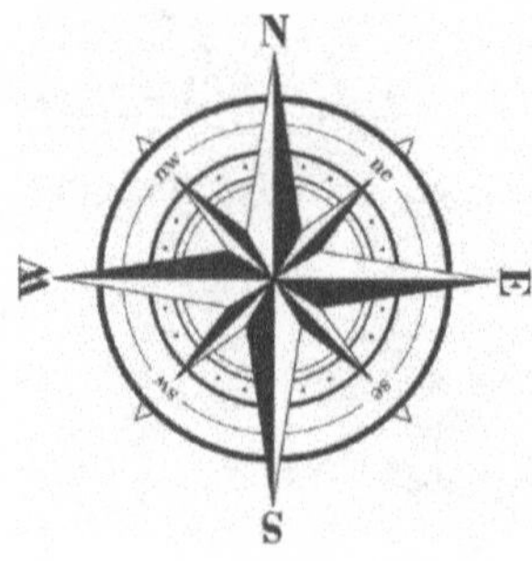

Luoyang Beijao Airport

Luoyang, China

Acton stepped down from their private jet, part of a lease-share network that Laura had joined years ago. He held out a hand and she took it as he steadied her down the small set of steps and onto the tarmac of the private terminal. He wasn't certain if he'd ever get used to the fact he was married to an extremely wealthy woman. Her brother had been a tech entrepreneur years ago and had sold his company at a massive profit. When he had died on one of her digs in Syria, he had left her everything, and through her wise stewardship of what he had left behind, she—and now, he supposed, they—were worth almost half a billion dollars.

Though you'd never find them on any Forbes Magazine list.

Everything was privately held, therefore not required to be reported publicly. And they didn't flaunt their wealth, though perhaps that wasn't entirely true. The Gulfstream behind them was certainly not an example of flying coach. They lived in his home bought before they had even met, she kept her flat in London bought before her brother had died, and other than that, they used their money to travel in comfort, to support their digs and their students, and various charities. All anonymously. Neither of them wanted the limelight, though sometimes the limelight was forced upon them.

They stepped into the terminal to clear customs, the Chinese officials appearing to pay them more attention than usual. He had been through scores of airports over the years, and over the past several traveling on his wife's private jets, this was the most intense scrutiny he had experienced in a private charter terminal where typically everything was very lax. The Chinese, like most countries, were reluctant to inconvenience the rich, for the rich were usually there either to spend large sums while vacationing, or invest in the Chinese economy.

The rich typically weren't there to blow up buildings or cause political dissent.

Yet today, he felt as if a cavity search were about to happen. He said nothing, though did exchange a glance with Laura, and from her expression, it was clear she had picked up on the unusually thorough examination.

They finally cleared customs and headed out into the arrivals area. He smiled when he spotted his old friend, Professor Cao Zhengsheng.

"Jim, over here!"

Acton waved and headed toward his friend whom he hadn't seen in at least five years. They had met on his first dig in Columbia almost 20 years ago, and though they saw each other rarely, they had exchanged letters when they were still in style, then emails almost every month, keeping each other up to date on not only their academic endeavors, but their personal lives as well.

"Jim, it's so good to see you!"

Acton gave the man a thumping hug, then stepped back. "May I present Archaeology Professor Laura Palmer."

Cao smiled. "Ah, the woman who finally made an honest man of my friend." He shook her hand vigorously then stepped back. "Where's your luggage? Are you not planning on staying?"

Acton chuckled. "One advantage of flying private charter is you never worry about your luggage. It's already being taken to the hotel."

Cao laughed. "I had heard rumors that you were now wealthy, and the only explanation I could come up with was that you had somehow found something of significance, like the Ark of the Covenant, and melted it down then sold it."

Acton exchanged a knowing glance with his wife. "I'm sure if we had found the Ark, somebody would have heard about it."

"Not unless you stole it."

"The truth of the matter is, I married very well, and she had money too!"

"Oh, James, stop it." Laura turned to Cao. "You didn't have to pick us up. We could have met you at the dig site."

"And miss seeing my friend for the first time in years, and meeting his lovely new wife who clearly could have done much better than him? Not coming was never an option. Now, I assume you'd like to go to your hotel first?"

Acton sniffed a pit. "Yeah. Even though it was a private jet, I still always like to freshen up."

"Fine, I'll drop you off there, then you can let me know when you're ready. I'll come pick you up and take you to the dig."

"Oh, that's not necessary. We've arranged a rental. It's waiting for us at the hotel. When you insisted on meeting us here, we had our travel agent rearrange the pick-up."

Cao shook his head gently. "Ahh, to be rich."

Acton grinned. "It does have its perks."

Cao jabbed a finger into Acton's chest. "You're paying for all of our dinners."

Acton laughed. "You have a deal, as long as we get that private tour."

"My friend, I'll have you down on your hands and knees digging in the dirt with the rest of us."

Acton smiled. "I wouldn't have it any other way."

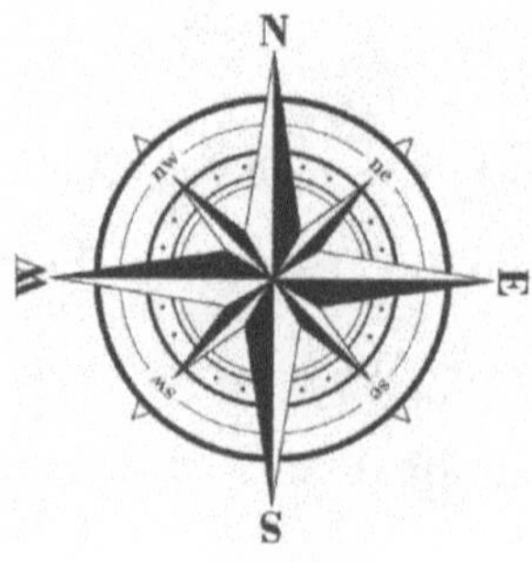

South China Sea

Corpsman Kidd swam toward the survivors, their life jackets doing their jobs, though to classify them as survivors might have been premature. Some were definitely alive, though others he wasn't certain, as they merely floated in the water, unmoving. He reached the first and grabbed the man by the shoulder, turning him over, and gasped. The face revealed was charred from the explosion, a piece of shrapnel embedded in the forehead. He checked for a pulse, knowing it was of no use, yet he had to be sure, and as he had feared, found none.

Gunfire continued to erupt in sporadic bursts, though none for the moment appeared aimed at him. All of the RHIBs sent for the rescue mission, from what he could tell, were now out of the area, and the gunfire was directed at the waters between the two ships, likely to act as a deterrent from sending any more. As he swam toward the next possible survivor, the Chinese ship continued to sink, yet the crew still remained on board.

"Help me! Somebody, help me!"

He reached the moaning victim floating on his back, his life jacket saving him from slipping under the waves. "I've got you, buddy." He came up to the man's side and the survivor reached toward his voice. Kidd suppressed the urge to gag. The man's eyes were burned shut. Kidd took his hand and squeezed it. "I'm here. You're going to be okay."

"I can't see!"

"Don't worry about that right now. You've got some burns, but you'll be fine. What's your name?"

"Seaman Scott."

"What's your first name?"

"Jay-Jason."

"Nice to meet you, Jason. I'm Doc Kidd. I'm a corpsman. I'm here to help you. How's your breathing?"

Scott inhaled then nodded. "I-I think I'm good."

"That's great news. Okay, Jason, your life jacket is in good shape, so you're going to float here no problem. Does it hurt anywhere besides your eyes?"

"No, I don't think so."

"Lift your left hand for me and wiggle your fingers." Scott did and Kidd had him repeat the process with his other hand then kick both legs. "Good, you're in good shape. You're going to be fine. I'm going to leave you now and check on your buddies, okay?"

"Okay."

Kidd scanned the water, spotting another body floating nearby. He swam toward it and gunfire erupted once again, tearing up the water in front of him. He shrugged out of his life jacket to dive below the surface when the 30mm Bushmaster II cannons of the USS Somerset opened fire. Lead tore into the side of the Chinese vessel, engaging whatever gun crew was firing upon him.

And as he slipped below the waves, he was forced to ask if his foolish act, one that had forced his crewmates to defend him, had just started a war.

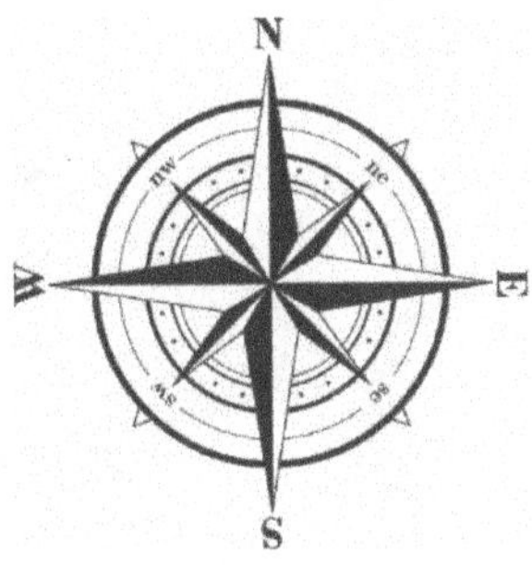

Hyatt Place Luoyang

Luoyang, China

Acton toweled dry as Laura showered. Normally he would have joined her, however a stern finger and a tapping of her watch had put an end to any hanky-panky he might have desired. His phone vibrated with a news alert about an incident in the South China Sea. He stepped into the bedroom of their suite and turned on the television, tuning it to CNN International where he could always be sure to get one side of the news.

Four talking heads greeted him, and they were soon replaced by a map of the South China Sea. Apparently, there was an ongoing incident between a US Navy vessel and a Chinese one. Details were sketchy, though that never stopped the bobble heads from making up the relevant facts. He switched over to BBC World News where at least the reporting was more balanced than anything he had found back home, and found no mention beyond a headline on the scroll.

In other words, nobody knew anything yet, so why waste the viewer's time with opinion.

His phone vibrated with a text message from Milton.

Check the news.

Acton chuckled, firing off a reply.

Is that your way of saying I told you so?

His phone immediately vibrated.

I'd tell you to get back on the plane right now, but I know you're going to ignore me. Just be careful.

Acton replied.

Always.

The shower turned off and he tossed his phone on the bed as he dressed. "Greg just texted me. He's in a tizzy."

"Why?"

"Apparently, there's some incident between the Americans and the Chinese in the South China Sea."

"Oh? What happened?"

"Not sure. It looks like nobody really knows yet, but of course our news back home is reporting all the spun facts until they can correct them later."

"Let me guess, Greg wants us to turn around and come back?"

"Yep."

"What do you think?"

"I think until we know more about what's going on, we continue with our plans. Something tells me we're not going to war yet."

She chuckled. "That's the twenty-four-hour news cycle for you. They sensationalize everything, including a stubbed toe, just to fill the time."

"Yep, the day CNN launched was the death of true journalism."

She poked her head out the bathroom door, giving him a look. "You don't just blame them, do you? They're all guilty of it."

He slipped on his pants. "No, of course not. I just blame the advent of the all-day news channel, not CNN specifically. There used to be a time when you'd sit down and watch Sam Donaldson or Tom Brokaw or the other guy, get your news in thirty minutes in the evening, and then read about it in detail in the morning paper. It was all boiled down to the facts, and any opinion was left for the editorial pages. Now, because they're trying to fill twenty-four hours and there isn't enough news to do that, they fill it with opinion, and then over the past decade, blurred the lines to the point you can't tell what's fact and what's opinion. You can't have reporters giving opinions. You should have reporters reporting, and pundits opining. What we've got now is ridiculous. And with the major networks making editorial decisions based upon political leanings, they've helped divide our country like no one ever has since probably McCarthyism."

She groaned. "I knew I shouldn't have asked."

He laughed. "You know me. Get me on a rant with a captive audience, and there's no stopping me."

She stepped out of the bathroom as naked as the day she was born. "Does this help take your mind off problems with our media?"

He grinned as he undid his pants. "Absolutely."

She wagged a finger. “Good, but don’t get any ideas. Cao is waiting for us.”

Acton groaned, staring down at the half-mast that had sprung up. “Sorry, buddy, denied again.”

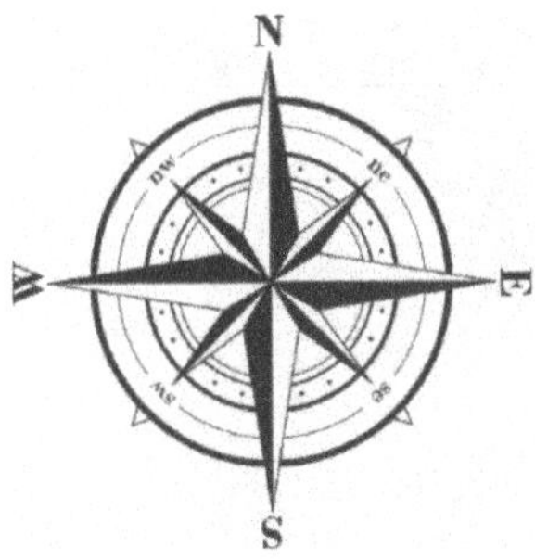

South China Sea

Kidd continued to drop below the surface of the water as the men and women of the USS Somerset opened fire, shredding the gun positions of the Chinese vessel. His lungs protested and he was forced to kick to the surface, grabbing the life jacket he had freed himself from only moments before. He threw a fist in the air and cheered as the guns on the Chinese ship fell silent, the weapons now smoking wrecks. His crewmates had his back, allowing him to ignore the threat that continued to sink so close by, and he fit his life jacket back in place to resume his efforts.

He heard something behind him and turned, spotting several RHIBs rushing back toward his position. With the guns silent, he heard someone call for help on the other side of the wreckage of the destroyed RHIB. He swam around it, finding a woman floating in the water, one arm raised in the air, burned beyond recognition. He reached her and took her undamaged hand, squeezing it. She turned her trembling face toward him, her eyes wide as she slipped into shock.

"Just hang on, help is on the way."

She barely acknowledged him. "Why did they shoot at us? We were trying to help them."

"I don't know, but don't worry about them anymore, our guys took care of them."

"But I just wanted to help. Why did they shoot at us?"

It was clear there was nothing he could do for her that couldn't be done in the next five minutes, the RHIBs all upon them. He heard screams and shouts from the Chinese ship and turned as the final death gasp of the stricken vessel groaned through the lonely seas. The crew finally ignored whatever ridiculous orders they had been given and leaped into the chop as the frigate slipped under the waves, leaving behind nothing but a furious gurgling in the water and a massive belch as the last of the air was forced out of its innards and sought freedom above the ocean waves.

And he had no sympathy for them whatsoever.

They had caused this. They had rammed his ship. They had fired upon those helping them. As far as he was concerned, every single one of them deserved to die, though if they did, there would be no witnesses from their side as to what had indeed happened here today. And with the state of relations between his country and theirs, the paranoid communist regime would never believe the truth, and would claim any proof the Americans produced was fake, as their corrupt regime wouldn't hesitate to do the same.

He waved as the first RHIB reached him. The engine throttled down and half a dozen of the crew rolled over the side, joining him in the water as the other boats spread out around the wreckage, retrieving the wounded and dead. He was hauled into the RHIB and he flopped on the deck, gasping for breath for several moments before sitting upright and returning to his job. All around him the living and dead were being retrieved, and he turned to see the Chinese crew that had survived swimming toward them. The coxswain gunned his motor, turning them back toward the USS Somerset.

"What about the Chinese?" asked Kidd.

"Screw the Chinese."

"We're just leaving them?"

"We're not. We're saving our people, then we're coming back for them."

Kidd nodded, agreeing with the decision that wasn't his to question, then turned his attention to the woman with the burned arm, and wondered what the coming days might bring after the most serious act of violence between America and China since the Korean War.

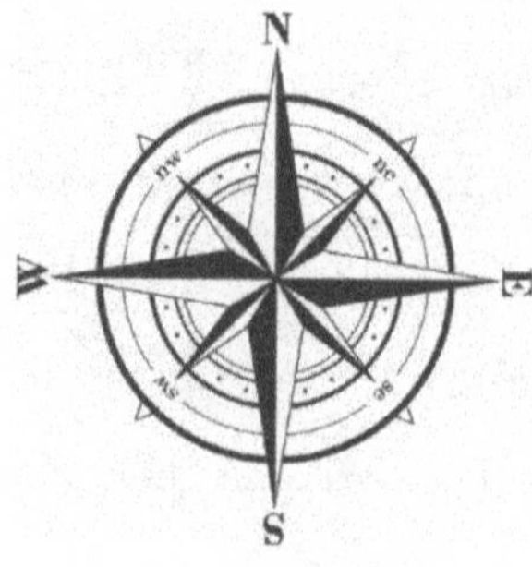

Imperial Palace

Luoyang, Han Empire

166 AD

Lucius' eyes shot wide as his head darted up and he stared at the princess that had dominated his thoughts since the moment he had laid eyes upon her. "You speak Latin?"

Jieyou smiled slightly. "This surprises you?"

"Frankly, it stuns me."

"We have been preparing for your arrival for years. I was chosen among the family to learn your language should a union between our two empires become necessary." She waved her hand, indicating for him to rise, and he did so.

"If that is the case, then I am the wrong person to be meeting with. I am but the son of the ambassador, and of no importance. If you would like, I can arrange a meeting with my father."

She sat and pointed at the other end of the couch. He perched on the edge of it, his heart still hammering, still uncertain as to why he was here. "If I had wanted to meet your father, I would have had my lady-in-waiting bring him instead."

His cheeks flushed. "Why did you ask that I come?"

"Because I wanted to meet you."

"Why?"

"I caught you staring at me, and you intrigued me."

His stomach flipped. "But surely you would get in trouble, just as I would, should we be caught."

She leaned closer to him, her face brightening. "Yes, and that makes it all the more exciting, doesn't it?"

He smiled slightly. "Yes, I suppose it does. But I doubt you would face the same consequences I would."

"And what consequences do you think you would face?"

He frowned. "I have little doubt your father would have me killed if I were caught here alone with you."

"Yes, I have no doubt he would."

"And yet you would still have me brought here, knowing the fate I might face?"

"I had assumed you were willing to face such a fate, considering the display you put on today at the reception with my father."

He eyed her. "What do you mean?"

"It is forbidden to look at a princess unless invited to do so."

He gulped, averting his eyes. "I'm sorry, I was unaware of that."

"And if you had been, would you have still looked?"

He met her gaze again, his pulse pounding as it had never before for a woman. She was exotic. She was lovely. She was everything he hadn't realized he wanted until this very day. "Yes."

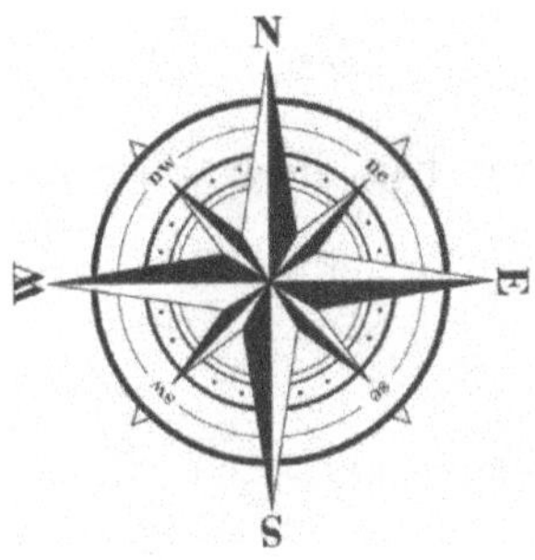

Embassy Dig Site

Luoyang, China

Present Day

The GPS indicated they had finally arrived, and Acton found an available parking spot just down the street from the dig site. "That took a little longer than I expected."

Laura climbed out and joined him on the sidewalk. "Chinese traffic seems to be every bit as bad as LA."

"Yeah, but LA doesn't have this pollution. My God! No wonder so many people here wear face masks." He took her hand, and they walked over to the fenced-in area. They peered through the chain link and he spotted Professor Cao down below. He whistled and Cao looked up, smiling. He pointed to their left and Acton spotted a gate. They walked over to it and the guard waved them through, a guard who didn't appear to be private security, instead official Chinese. Acton flashed the man a smile, but none was returned.

He didn't take it personally, as he had made an ass of himself in London attempting to get a rise out of the Queen's Guards outside Buckingham Palace. He had been unsuccessful, and Laura had admonished him for his efforts, then showed him some video of when the guards did react.

And he was thankful he hadn't been provided the opportunity to piss his pants.

"Use the ladder," called Cao, pointing. Acton spotted it and he quickly climbed down into the pit, then held it steady while Laura descended the rickety contraption that had seen better days. He took a moment to survey their surroundings, his expert eye roaming over every piece of excavated stone, every indicator of the walls that once were, and how competent those working the site appeared to be. He had no doubts about Cao's abilities. His friend was as competent as any archaeologist he had met, though sometimes good help was hard to find.

This site, discovered just a few months ago, was the talk of the archaeological world, and few had seen it beyond pictures. The last ones he had seen showed barely any of the progress since made. Remarkable, large stone columns, still intact, lay on their sides. Walls only a few feet high marked the layout of the structure, and while it was breathtaking, what had him even more excited was what he could only get a glimpse of in a large tent set up to his left.

Artifacts.

Buildings were buildings, and fascinating in themselves, though Roman architecture was similar depending upon the period in which it had been built. This appeared to be very typical of second-century

Roman architecture, which was confirmed by not only carbon dating tests of artifacts found here, but the few written accounts of the embassy's creation from the documents of the Han Dynasty.

But artifacts were something different. They were personal. They gave insight into the culture and the individuals who once occupied this structure. These were the things that genuinely excited archaeologists. The news always misunderstood when a new site was discovered. They focused on where it was found and what culture had built it, then gushed about the architecture. But what was more exciting was what the media ignored. It was what was within that building, within that structure—the artifacts. Whether statues or carvings, or things as simple as utensils, they gave insight into their ancestors that no building could ever hope to provide. The Egyptian ruins were impressive, but told little of their purpose. It wasn't until they got inside and discovered the artifacts, that the truth was revealed. It was the mummified remains. The sarcophagi. The hieroglyphics. The treasures buried along with the pharaohs. Those were what revealed ancient Egyptian culture.

And here, today, he was surrounded by a time capsule of Ancient Rome, in the middle of a city where it should never be, and his entire body was covered in goosebumps.

He slowly completed his survey when he finally noticed Laura staring up at him, a smile on her face. "What?"

"I love it when you get like that."

"Get like what?"

"Lost in the moment."

He chuckled. "Sorry about that. It's just so amazing that we're standing in the first embassy of the Roman Empire in what would become China."

She leaned against him. "I wonder what happened here."

He wrapped an arm around her shoulders. "Let's go find out."

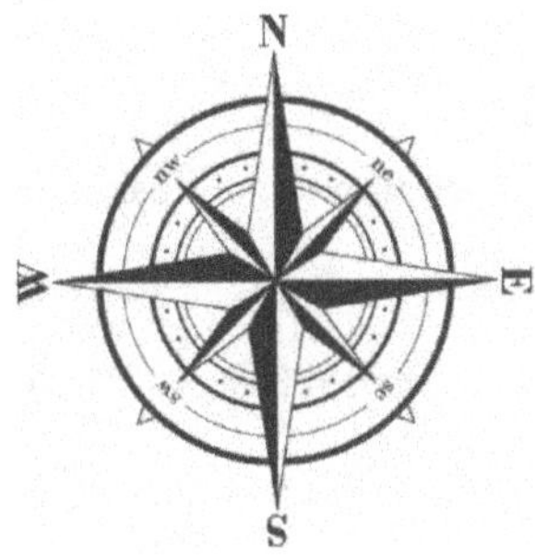

USS Somerset

South China Sea

Kidd ignored the alarm as GQ was once again sounded, and reached out to steady himself as the engines surged. What was going on above decks, he had no idea. Right now, his only concern was tending to the wounded. Two were dead, but the rest had survived. So far. With all the foot pounding in the passageways and the shouts heard through the bulkheads, he feared those two dead would be but the first of many. He checked the IV bag on one of the burn victims, his brain on autopilot, performing his duty as he had been trained to do.

Yet it had all been just that.

Training.

In his entire short career, the only wounded he had ever dealt with were those wounded during an exercise or in just a simple accident. He had never dealt with people wounded in combat. He had never struggled to keep the lifeblood flowing in someone he had personally rescued.

And never before in his life had he been under fire.

During training, there was always a risk of death or injury, though the exercises were designed to minimize the possibility. Sometimes they were so realistic his heart would pound and his adrenaline would rush through his veins, causing him to shake in terror if he lost himself in the moment and forgot that those commanding him weren't trying to kill him.

But today, America's greatest enemy had attempted just that. And as that realization set in, his heart once again hammered and his hands shook. He thought of his parents, he thought of his sister, and he thought of his nephew that he hadn't yet met, born only a week ago. Next week, he was supposed to be on two weeks' leave. His plan had been to fly home, see the family, and be introduced to its new addition.

He doubted that would be happening any time soon.

The ship leaned hard to port, sending him tumbling to the deck, snapping him back to reality. Sirens wailed, and the distinctive flutter of the Bushmaster cannons could be heard along with the launching of several RIM-116 Rolling Airframe Missiles, suggesting they were under aerial attack, either by plane or anti-ship cruise missile.

And that fact could mean only one thing.

War.

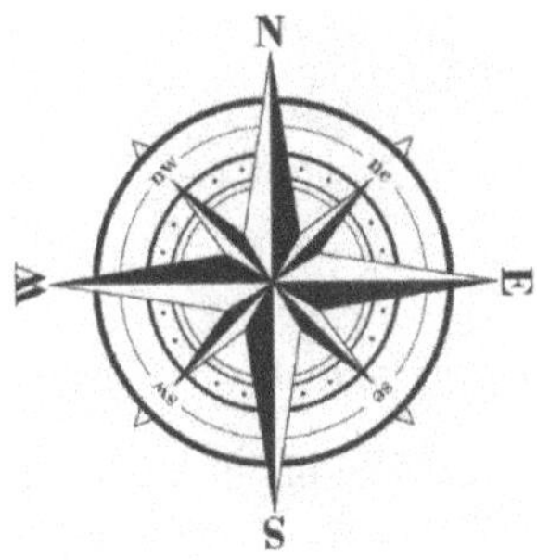

Embassy Dig Site

Luoyang, China

Acton strolled through the tent with Laura, Cao describing each of the items laid out before them, the tour invigorating both physically and mentally.

"And this is merely the tip of the proverbial iceberg. We have many more items back at the university. This is just what we found in the past several days. Tomorrow, I'll take you to see the rest."

Acton grinned at Cao. "That will be fantastic." He jabbed a finger at the contents of the table in front of them. "*This* is why I got into archaeology." He picked up an intricately carved dagger made of bronze. He drew the blade, the metal still pristine thanks to its millennia-old sheath. He held it out gently, laid flat in his palms. "This is why I love this job. Who did this belong to? It's clearly Roman, but"—he pointed at some lettering—"this swears allegiance to Emperor Hadrian, which places its creation possibly half a century before this embassy was supposed to have been built."

"So, it's not standard issue," said Cao.

Acton shook his head. "No. And no regular soldier is issued something like this. It's too valuable." He pointed at another blade nearby, a basic design. "A regular soldier would be issued something such as that, utilitarian, simple. This"—he held up the ornate dagger—"this is a family heirloom, and wouldn't have been owned by a simple soldier. This was the weapon of an officer." His mind raced with the possibilities. "Did it belong to the head of the guard? Or perhaps to the ambassador himself?"

Laura leaned in to examine the blade. "It's likely we'll never know."

"No, we never will, but it's a hell of a lot of fun to speculate."

Cao chuckled. "Now *that's* the Jim Acton I remember and am happy to see is still there. Too many of us lose the thrill of the discovery with age." He tilted his head toward Laura. "And I wonder how much of that has to do with this beautiful young lady."

Acton winked at Laura. "I'd say she's played a small part." His phone vibrated in his pocket and he fished it out, his eyes popping at the alert.

Laura sensed his concern. "What is it?"

"It's an emergency alert from the Embassy."

"What does it say?" asked Cao.

Acton tapped it and the alert opened. "It says there's been an incident between the US and Chinese navies that has escalated. All American citizens in China are advised to remain indoors at the address registered with the Embassy if possible, and await further instructions."

Laura took his hand, squeezing it tight, and he could see the concern in her eyes. And he shared it.

Cao dismissed the warning with a bat of his hand. "I'm sure it's nothing. Somebody's joking with you. Phones are getting hacked all the time."

Laura's phone vibrated and she shook her head as she read the message. "The British Embassy just issued the same warning."

A young woman with bronzed skin and bright blond hair stepped inside the tent, holding out her phone. "Professor Cao, what does this mean?" Her Australian accent was unmistakable, and it was clear all Americans and their allies were receiving the same warning. He could think of only two things that could mean.

Either war was imminent, or they were already at war.

"How many foreigners do you have here?" he asked Cao.

"Just two Australians, Kyle Rapp, and of course Amelia here, Amelia Robinson." He indicated the young woman. "Everyone else is either from China or Hong Kong."

A young man walked into the tent, evidently the other Australian, Kyle. His face was ashen, and he held up his glowing phone gripped in his hand. "I just checked the CNN website. They say there's a naval battle in the South China Sea between the Americans and the Chinese."

Cao's jaw dropped, clearly no longer convinced this was a hoax. He turned to Acton. "I don't know…I don't know what to do."

Acton saved his friend from the responsibility. "There's nothing you can do. You're Chinese. If you help any of us, they might arrest you or worse."

The thought apparently had never occurred to Cao, as his eyes widened and his face paled. Then he stumbled. Acton sprung forward and grabbed the man under his arm, steadying him. He pointed at a bottle of water sitting nearby, and Laura grabbed it. Cao took several sips then handed it back.

"I'm all right, thank you." He drew a deep breath and exhaled loudly. "They're my responsibility. They're here because of me. I can't just abandon them."

"And you won't be."

"What do you mean?"

Acton glanced at Laura who nodded almost imperceptibly. "They're coming with us."

USS Somerset

South China Sea

The Bushmaster cannons continued to thunder as RAM missiles roared from their launchers, rumbling explosions that sounded as if they were from outside of the ship, signaling their success. The cheers were also a good indication. Whatever was going on wasn't his concern, only his duty was, though knowing a battle was occurring topside that could end his life was distracting, to say the least.

Kidd looked up as a lieutenant stumbled into the infirmary with a gash on his arm. The Doc glanced over at him and decided it wasn't worth his attention.

"Corpsman, take care of that."

Kidd led the lieutenant to a nearby chair then grabbed a wound kit. He set to work, cleaning and dressing the cut. "Sir, can you tell us what's going on?"

The lieutenant winced. "It's the Chinese. They've sent every ship in the area toward us, and launched anti-ship missiles and drones, probably surveillance. We managed to take them out so far, and more Super Hornets have just arrived from the Ronald Reagan. The Chinese aircraft have bugged out, but once their navy arrives, we're going to be in for a hell of a fight if somebody doesn't calm this down. Elements of the Seventh Fleet are already heading for us, but the Chinese will be here ahead of them."

"Can we hold out?"

The lieutenant, a man likely the same age as him, obviously heard the fear in his voice. The young officer squared his jaw in an attempt to convey confidence, yet failed. "The Captain is a good man. He'll get us through this. Just follow your training and you'll survive."

Kidd nodded and turned his attention back to the wound, struggling to steady his hand and failing, for the words meant nothing, the widened eyes and the unsteady timbre of the lieutenant's voice everything.

He had just been told they were all going to die.

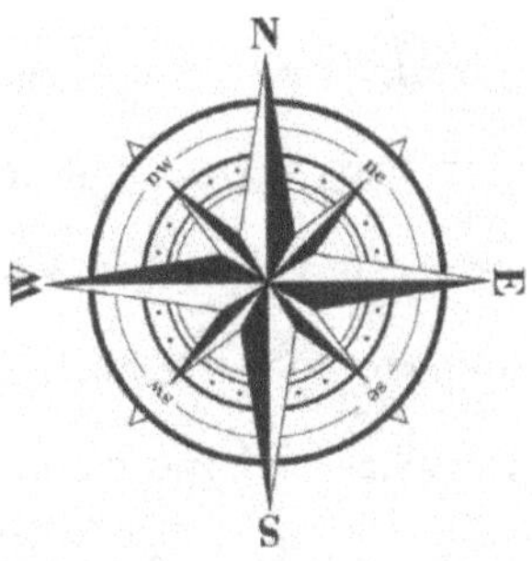

Ministry of State Security

Luoyang, China

Special Agent Yan sat behind his desk, racked with worry as he listened to the radio delivering the official government reports on what was unfolding in the South China Sea. The imperialist Americans were once again aggressors toward his country. As the news reports had clearly explained, the entire area was Chinese territory and always had been. Why countries like the Philippines, Taiwan, and especially the United States were interfering was beyond him. He agreed with one of the commentators that had just been on, when she said these other countries were jealous of China's success, and were now attempting to stifle their economic progress and hem them into land borders drawn not by the Chinese people, but their past oppressors.

He had no doubt the world was indeed jealous of what they had achieved in such a short time, just as he was certain the world was terrified that given another 20 years, China would be far more powerful than even the United States. It was this fear, however, that he couldn't understand. Why did the world fear China? What had they ever done to hurt anyone? After China had thrown out its oppressors and the Communist regime had been established, China had never attacked first. The Korean War had nothing to do with China. China merely stepped in to help their North Korean allies, and, more importantly, to prevent the United States from overreaching and establishing military forces on China's border.

Yes, there were border skirmishes with India and Pakistan, and moves to liberate oppressed peoples such as in Tibet, but China had never invaded anyone. That was a European thing. China was now investing billions upon billions of dollars through the Belt and Road Initiative, aiding poorer countries by building infrastructure that they desperately needed, including roads, ports, bridges, and more, yet he had heard that people in the West were questioning their motives. It made no sense to him. Even when China did something good, they were accused of having ulterior motives. Why was it wrong to expect allegiance to a country that had just spent billions helping out yours?

Yet the worry he felt at this moment had nothing to do with his country, and everything to do with his brother. While he had pursued a career in law enforcement, eventually joining the Ministry of State Security, his brother had joined the Navy, and the last message he had from him was that he was on board the Frigate Yueyang in the South China Sea. Its captain, in his former command before a demotion to the smaller ship, had once before challenged the Americans in a game of what his brother had called chicken. To him, it had sounded more like seeing who the smaller mouse was.

It was idiotic.

The official reports last year had been that the Americans were to blame, but his brother, while on leave, had told him the truth. And now that there were reports the Americans had intentionally rammed then opened fire on a Chinese vessel that subsequently sank, he had to wonder whether his brother's ship with its new captain was involved, and whether his brother was even alive.

His door opened without a knock and he leaped to his feet, snapping to attention before he knew who was entering, for only someone senior to him would dare breach protocol like this.

It was his supervisor, Deputy Bureau Chief Wei Zhen.

"Sir, how may I be of service?"

A tablet computer was handed over. "We're rounding up persons of interest during the crisis. These two have been problems in the past, and happened to have arrived just a few hours ago."

He glanced at the pictures. "Fortuitous timing, sir."

"Indeed. Their current location is in the file. I want them picked up and brought in."

"Right away, sir."

"And don't screw this up. This came directly from the Politburo."

Yan's eyes widened at the implications. The 25 members of the Politburo controlled the Communist Party, and by extension, the country. If the orders were coming from them, these people must be true enemies of the state. "You can count on me, sir."

"Good." Wei took the tablet back and tapped the screen several times. "Everything you need is in your secure directory. Report back to me as soon as you have them."

"Yes, sir."

Wei left and Yan brought up the files on his computer then transferred them to his tablet. He read everything included, hoping for some hint as to why the Politburo itself would be after what appeared to be academics, yet no hint was given, and the lack of information spoke volumes. It was likely a state security matter, though if it was, why they had been allowed in the country today made no sense.

A pit formed in his stomach as he realized exactly what was going on. This was a personal vendetta from someone in the Politburo taking advantage of the current situation. And it meant if he failed, then his career and perhaps his life could be forfeit, depending on whom the Politburo member decided was to blame.

He rose and strode out of his office, snapping orders as he headed for the elevators. He pressed the button as his team assembled around him.

"What are our orders, sir?" asked his second-in-command, Shen Dao.

"We're detaining two academics."

"What are the charges?"

"None that I'm aware of. The orders come from the Politburo itself."

Everyone paused for a moment, and he could sense the fear.

"What are their names?" asked Shen.

He held up the tablet. "Professors James Acton and Laura Palmer.

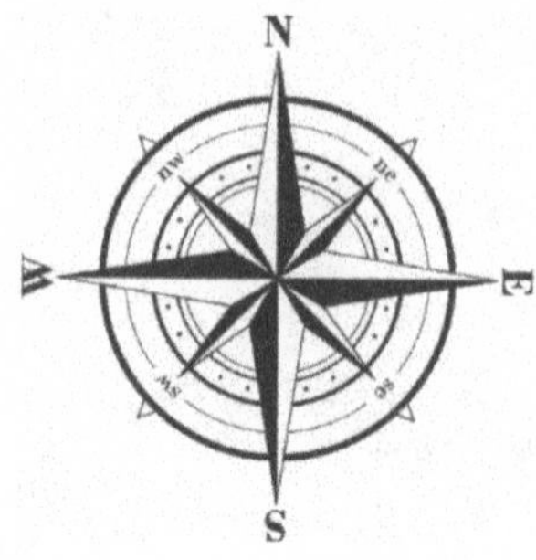

Embassy of the Roman Empire

Luoyang, Han Empire

166 AD

It had been months since they arrived, and construction of the embassy was nearly complete, the massive number of Chinese laborers, directed by the Roman architect Lucius' father had brought with them, efficient and hard working. Emperor Huan had been impressed with the goods they had brought with them, and he, like the others they had encountered earlier, was particularly interested in their glassware. He was eager to learn more of the Roman Empire, yet hadn't revealed all he knew, for Lucius was the only person still aware that his daughter spoke their language. He wanted to warn his father of this fact, for far too often discussions they thought were in private in the Emperor's Court, spoken in Latin and believed to be understood by no one else beyond their translator, were fully comprehended by the princess, and likely others hidden in the room that had taught her the language.

Yet the only way he could reveal that truth was by telling his father how he had discovered it. And though he and the princess had continued their clandestine meetings several nights a week since the first without being caught, if he informed his father of this fact, he would be placed in chains, never to see the light of day again.

So far, nothing untoward had happened, and the love he felt for Jieyou and the love he was certain she felt for him, had him confident that if something were said her father should be aware of, it wouldn't come from her lips—it would come from one of the people hidden in the court.

A stirring in his loins at the thought of her had him shifting slightly, and he forced himself to focus on the memories of the rough seas they had endured on their trip here, the days and weeks spent leaning over the deck and vomiting into the heavy seas successfully wrangling his overactive libido.

He stared up at the large building, standing out among the traditional architecture surrounding it, a testament to the might of the Roman Empire. Nobody could rival the structures they built, with the possible exception of the Egyptians, though most of theirs served no purpose. The Colosseum in Rome was the greatest building man had ever constructed that had a functional purpose. Thousands upon thousands of people filled it during the games, and half of its utility was buried beneath the stands, something of which the public was unaware. He had seen nothing here that could possibly rival it, and was proud that here, so far away from the home he knew, now stood something familiar, something substantial, something tangible he could hold on to that would remind him of what he had left behind. This was now their home, and he would likely spend the rest of his life here.

And it was something he was content with, for he had never been happier.

Yet this happiness would be fleeting. He and Jieyou would eventually be found out, and he might be put to death along with the others, or worse, she would be married off to someone else, perhaps even someone Roman, which would be a crushing blow, for he was certain he could never love anyone again the way he loved this woman.

His father stepped up beside him, his hands on his hips. "Impressive, isn't it?"

He had to agree. "If I stare just at it, I can almost imagine I'm back home."

His father put an arm over his shoulders, giving him a squeeze. "It does make one miss it, doesn't it?"

"It does."

"Soon we'll be sending a small contingent home to deliver an update to our Emperor, along with, the gods willing, the completed treaty we've been working on. If you want, you can go with them as commander, and then I'll leave it up to you to decide whether you return."

Lucius shook his head, stunning not only his father but himself as well. "No, I'd like to stay."

His father stared at him, his eyes narrow. "I must admit, I'm surprised."

Lucius shrugged. "I'm starting to like it here. And besides, you need me. I'm the only family you have."

His father regarded him. “Yet that isn’t the reason, is it?”

“What do you mean?”

“It’s not for me to say, for if I say what I believe, then it becomes truth, and then consequences become necessary.”

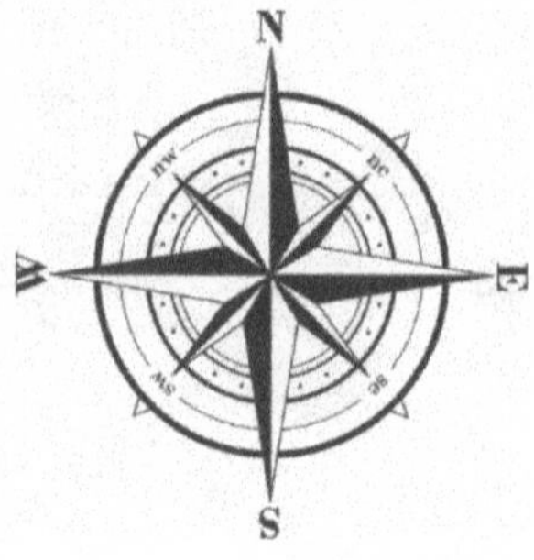

En Route to Hyatt Place Luoyang

Luoyang, China

Present Day

Acton followed the GPS directions back toward their hotel. They had an English station playing on the radio, but he turned it off in disgust. The channel was clearly Chinese propaganda, its jingoistic tone reminding him of Tokyo Rose type broadcasts by the Japanese in World War II. The communist propaganda machine was in full swing, and it sickened him. He might believe American media had become a disgrace, but they were nothing compared to the Chinese state broadcasters.

"Do you think it's wise to return to our hotel?" asked Laura.

"It's what the alert said to do. We're going to have to trust that our governments know what they're doing."

She gave him a look. "Are you serious?"

He laughed. "Yeah, I guess you're right. What would you suggest?"

"Maybe we should call for help. Dylan might be able to give us better advice."

"That's a good idea. Do it."

Laura quickly sent an encrypted message through an app that Acton's former student and now CIA operative, Dylan Kane, had installed on their phones for just this purpose. She put the phone down. "Done."

"What did you say?"

"I said, 'We're in China. What should we do?'"

He chuckled. "Nice and succinct."

"Yes, but when will he see it?"

He sighed. "That's the question, isn't it? Hopefully soon, because if the shit hits the fan, they're likely to shut down all cellular and Internet access." He snapped his fingers. "Call Tommy. See if there's a way around that, just in case."

She dialed the phone and put it on speaker. It rang several times before it was finally answered.

"Hello?"

Acton leaned closer to the phone. "Hi, Tommy, this is Jim Acton."

"Oh, Professor Acton, aren't you in China?"

"We are."

"Have you heard what's going on?"

"Yes, that's why we're calling. I'm here with Laura and two Australian students. We're heading to our hotel now on the advice of an emergency alert from the US Embassy."

"Is that wise? I mean, won't that mean they just know where to round you up?"

Acton tensed at the concern in Tommy's voice, suggesting the situation was perhaps worse than he thought. Laura placed a hand on his thigh, squeezing, clearly as concerned as he was. "Why? How bad is it?"

"It's pretty bad. Apparently, the Chinese are firing missiles at one of our ships, and we shot some planes out of the air and sank one of their ships. Both countries' fleets are less than a day apart. By this time tomorrow, we could be in a full-scale war. I just heard a report that we're at DEFCON 3, but I think the news is just making shit up. You know how they are."

Acton's chest tightened at Tommy's update. "Question for you. If they shut down communications here, is there any way to bypass it?"

"Not with cellular. They control that completely, but they can't touch satellite. Do you have a satphone with you?"

Laura held the phone a little closer to her. "We have a satphone back in the hotel room. I didn't bring it with us because I didn't think we would need it."

"Well, if you can get the satphone, then you can still reach the outside world."

Acton cursed. "Well, that means we have to go back to the hotel for sure." He glanced at the GPS. "We're maybe ten minutes away. How far apart did you say those ships were?"

"About half a day if the news is to be trusted."

"Then by tomorrow morning, all hell is going to break loose."

"I'm going to contact Chris Leroux at the CIA, and see if there's anything he can do," said Tommy.

Tommy's pipeline into the CIA was an excellent idea. "You do that. We've sent a message to Dylan, but I have no idea when he's going to see it. It might be too late if he's on an op somewhere."

"Well, if he's reachable, then Leroux will be able to get to him. I'm sure he has contacts in China that can help you as well."

"Let's hope. I'll call you back as soon as we get the satphone."

"Okay. And can I give you a piece of advice?"

"What?"

"You might want to shut off your phones and remove the batteries. Right now, you're completely trackable, and you're using foreign-registered phones. If the Chinese decide to crack down, they're going after those Maryland phone numbers first."

Acton cursed. "Okay, here's what we're going to do. At the top of each hour, if we need to communicate, we'll turn on one of our phones and call you. Understood?"

"Yes, sir."

"And call Greg. Tell him what's going on, and tell him he was right, and to savor that moment, because it's the last damn time I'm going to say it. We'll talk to you soon."

Laura ended the call and Acton handed her his phone then glanced in the rearview mirror. "Okay, everybody. Phones out, turn them off, and remove the batteries."

Laura frowned. "Umm, ours are iPhones. We can't remove them."

He frowned. "Just turn them off. Hopefully, that's enough." The two students in the rear seat held up their phones and batteries, both apparently non-Apple devices.

Amelia Robinson stared at them wide-eyed. "Who the hell are you guys?"

Acton smiled. "Archaeology professors, just like you want to be."

Her counterpart Kyle Rapp shook his head. "I've never heard of archaeology professors who have friends at the CIA."

Acton exchanged a grin with Laura. "That's just because you haven't been on the job long enough."

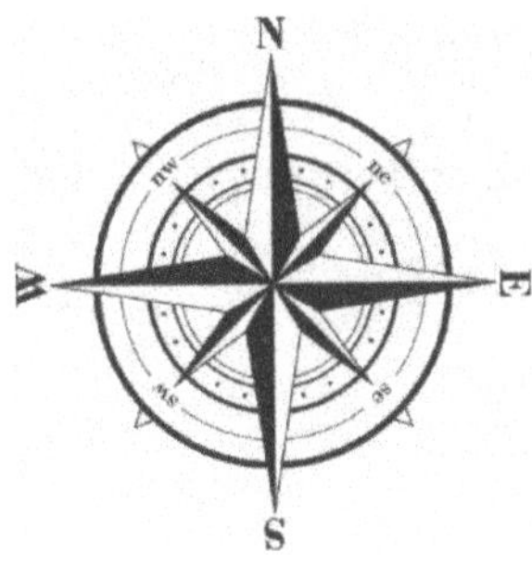

Trinh/Granger Residence

St. Paul, Maryland

Tommy Granger pulled up the number for his contact at the CIA, Chris Leroux. He dialed it and got the disconnected message that he now knew was merely a ruse. Leroux would be notified that he had called and would get back to him, hopefully in short order. He leaned back on the couch, his phone clutched in his lap, and stared at the television screen with the continuing coverage of the unfolding crisis.

His girlfriend, Mai Trinh, emerged from their bedroom, towel-drying her hair. "What's wrong?"

He waved at the television screen.

"Oh, I wouldn't worry about that. Cooler heads will prevail, I'm sure."

"I'm sure they will, but before they do, it could spell trouble."

She eyed him. "What's going on? You weren't this upset when I got in the shower. Has something else happened?"

He wagged his phone at her. "Professor Acton just called."

A quick inhalation of breath was followed by her hand darting to her chest. "Oh, no, I forgot they were in China! Are they okay?"

"They've just been told by the embassy to go back to their hotel and await further instructions."

"That sounds wise."

"Perhaps, but if the Chinese decide to start rounding up Americans, they're going to hit the hotels first."

Mai plunked down beside him on the couch. "I never thought of that. What are they going to do?"

"They said they reached out to Dylan for his advice, but they're concerned that if the shit hits the fan, the cellphones and Internet might be turned off, and then they'll lose all communications."

"But don't they normally travel with a satphone?"

"They do, but they left it at the hotel."

"Why would they do that?"

"Because they're in the middle of a modern Chinese city with excellent cellphone coverage."

"Oh, right." Mai chewed her cheek for a moment. "Is there anything we can do to help?"

"I just contacted Leroux. Hopefully, he'll get back to me shortly." The phone vibrated with an unknown caller. "This might be him." Tommy tapped to take the call.

"Hello?"

"Hi, Tommy. It's Chris. This better be important. In case you're not aware, we're kind of in the middle of something here."

"If it's the China situation, then yes, I've been watching the news. I just got a call from Professor Acton."

Leroux groaned. "Please tell me he's not in China."

"He is, sir, along with his wife, and apparently they have two Australian university students with them."

"Where exactly are they?"

Tommy put the call on speaker so Mai could listen, then grabbed his laptop, bringing up the email with the travel details. "They went to a city called Luoyang."

"Never heard of it. Where are they heading now?"

"They said the embassy has advised all Americans to return to their hotels."

"That's probably the smartest thing they can do at the moment."

"But won't the Chinese know exactly where to go if they decide to start rounding up Americans?"

There was a pause. "Yes." Leroux cursed. "And with their files, they'd be prime targets. I have no doubt the Chinese are aware of their involvement in the coup attempt a few years back. They would likely be priority targets if things were to go bad."

"Is there anything you can do?"

"I assume they have their cellphones with them?"

"Yes, but I advised them to turn them off because they could be tracked. If they need to call, they're going to call at the top of each hour."

"Smart. I'm texting you a number now. If they contact you, have them call it."

"Will do. They said they sent a message to Kane, but I don't know if he got it."

"He won't. He's deep undercover right now. Even I can't reach him."

"What about Delta?"

"This is China. Delta can't just stroll in there. Besides, this is happening now, and depending on where they are, it could take hours or even a day to get into position, and by then, it'll be too late."

"How bad is it? The news makes it look pretty bad."

"It's bad. Things are in the works in the background, but it's going to get worse before it gets better."

"Are we in any danger?"

Leroux chuckled. "No, not unless this goes nuclear, which it never will. The only people in danger at the moment are the men and women on the frontlines, and anyone unfortunate enough to be in China at this time. I have to let you go. I'll see what I can do. Just give them that number if they happen to call."

"Will do, thank you." The call ended and Tommy leaned back, exhaling in relief. "I'm getting too old for this shit."

Mai eyed him. "You're not even twenty-five."

"I know, but those two have put me through so much stress, that I feel like I'm fifty-five."

Mai shrugged. "You look pretty darn good for fifty-five."

He grunted. "With the stress my poor heart's been under the past couple of years, I doubt I'm going to *see* fifty-five."

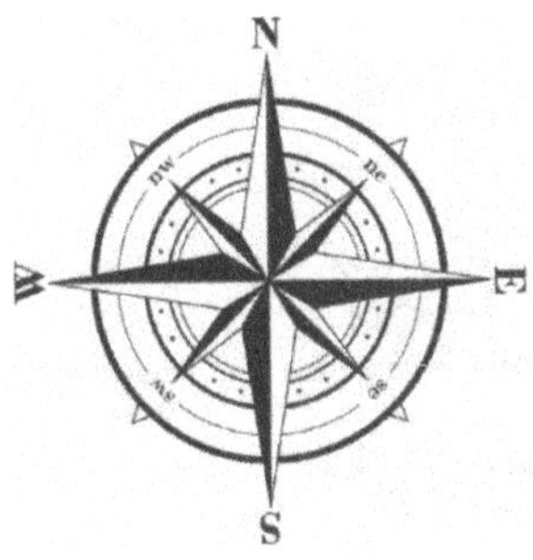

Approaching Hyatt Place Luoyang

Luoyang, China

A lump formed in Acton's throat as he checked his rearview mirror. The two Australian students were holding each other, their eyes wide with terror as they stared out the windows, whimpering every time they heard a siren or saw a government vehicle race by. His own heart rate had ticked up, and he was forcing himself to relax as best he could, and not panic every time he saw flashing lights or the police.

This was China. This was a Communist dictatorship that subjugated its population on a daily basis. Seeing police and military vehicles was completely normal here, and if he let every sighting get to him, he wouldn't be able to function.

He glanced at the GPS. They were almost at the hotel, and he hadn't yet decided what the best course of action would be.

"I'll go in."

He glanced at Laura. "I don't think so."

"Right now, we have to assume that if they're going to show an interest in any of us, it's going to be you. They're Australian, and I'm British."

He frowned, for she was correct. Everything they had heard indicated hostilities had broken out between his country and China, not any of theirs. Even the warnings they had received on their phones from their own embassies indicated the same.

"Maybe we don't need the satphone. Maybe there's another option," he suggested, though as the words came out of his mouth, he knew they were merely a desperate attempt to keep her from heading off on her own.

She firmly shook her head. "You know as well as I do that we need that phone. It could be our only lifeline."

Acton had another thought. "If they were only going to go after me, then perhaps the best thing to do is for you to go to the hotel and stay there, and for me to drop the kids off wherever they're staying."

Again, Laura shook her head. "Bollocks. There's no way we're separating. I don't care if they're only after you. And besides, you and I both know that if war does break out, my country and theirs are going to be drawn into it. And the Chinese will assume anybody with white skin is a spy regardless." She turned in her seat to face the Australian students. "But it's entirely up to you what you want to do. We'll take you to wherever you're staying if you want. But if you want to stay with us, you're welcome."

"Nup, we're staying with you guys!" yelped Amelia without a moment's hesitation, and Kyle, who appeared more terrified than her, barely nodded, his eyes filled with tears.

Laura reached out and squeezed his arm, providing a modicum of comfort, then returned her attention to the task at hand. "I don't think we should go to the hotel."

"Isn't that what I've just been saying?"

"That's not what I mean. I mean, park somewhere close by, and I'll walk the rest of the way."

Acton grunted. "Yeah, that's probably a good idea." He pointed at the GPS. "We're almost there, but I don't see where I could park." He stared at the street ahead. "I don't see any parking spots either."

"Then just drop me off and circle around."

He spotted a gas station and pointed. "Actually, this might be a good option." He pulled in and up to the pump. "I'm going to fill us up. You go to the hotel. We'll meet you here." He indicated some free parking spots in front of the small store. "If we're not here, it's because I felt it wasn't safe. I'll circle around and keep circling until you come out."

She opened the door. "But if I'm not back in thirty minutes, you go without me."

His voice cracked as he responded. "If you're not back in thirty minutes, I'm going in after you."

She leaned over and gave him a kiss, and neither of them said anything, though the look they exchanged spoke volumes. She gave him one last smile then stepped out of their car, closing the door. He watched as she rushed toward the hotel, and prayed this wasn't the last time he saw the only woman he had ever truly loved.

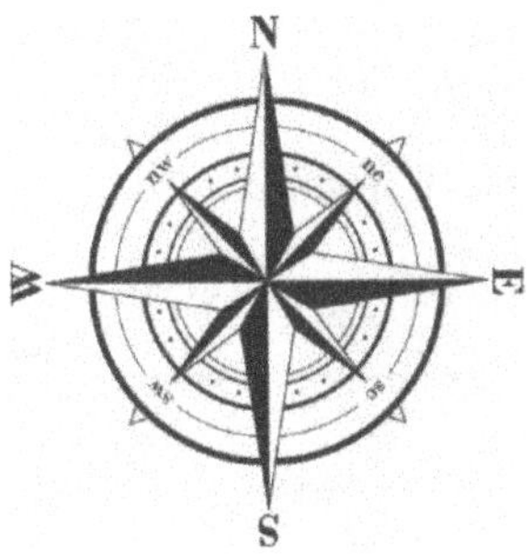

Embassy Dig Site

Luoyang, China

Professor Cao sat in his trailer at the bottom of the dig site, staring blankly at the news reports carefully filtered by his government-controlled media. Little was being said beyond the fact Americans had attacked a Chinese vessel unprovoked in international waters, however he had traveled the world enough to know facts were always in question when it came to his government. He loved his country, was loyal to it, though he yearned for the freedom so much of the world enjoyed, including his friend Professor Acton. It was always a thrill to visit a dig somewhere else on the globe, and spend weeks or months there forgetting the problems of the world he lived in, and instead discovering what challenges people hundreds or thousands of years ago faced. Sometimes, it made him envious of them, and a little more often than not, it made him feel a little bit better about his life despite the country into which he had been born.

Today, something was going on that wouldn't affect him too much unless things went seriously wrong. Little things such as this always cropped up, and cooler heads usually prevailed. But until they did, Acton and his wife, and his two Australian students, might be in danger, and it had him on edge. He wanted to send everyone home, though that would be unwise. His government hadn't directed him to do so, and it was never smart to display fear or doubt in your government's ability to control any situation.

"Professor Cao?"

There was a knock at the door of the trailer, and he recognized the voice of one of his students, Wenjun. "What is it?"

"There are police here, sir."

Cao's ears pounded with the news. His hands gripped the arms of his chair before he willed them to let go so he could stand. He stepped outside and Wenjun pointed up at the road above the dig site. The flashing from the lights of the police could be seen in the dusk, though the vehicles were out of sight. "Did they say what they wanted?"

Wenjun shook his head. "No, I just saw the lights. A few of them are at the gate now."

Cao shifted his gaze and spotted several police officers talking to a guard assigned by the government. The guard stared down into the pit then pointed directly at him, sending his heart racing anew. He struggled to steady his breathing as he headed for the ladder, repeating to himself that he had done nothing wrong, therefore had nothing to fear.

If only that were true.

In America or England, or pretty much anywhere else the people he associated with in academia lived, that would be true. But in a communist dictatorship, one never knew when one's government would come for them.

He reached the top of the ladder and walked over to the gate. "May I be of assistance?"

"Are you Professor Cao?" asked one of the men in a suit, not a uniform.

Cao's eyes darted to the left and right. Half a dozen police vehicles were visible and at least a dozen officers, a curious show of force for an archaeological site, even in China.

"I am. "

"I'm Special Agent Yan from the Ministry of State Security."

Bile filled Cao's mouth at the mention of one of the most feared agencies in the country, but he had little time to react. A tablet computer was shoved in his face, a picture of Acton displayed. "We are looking for this man." The screen was swiped, revealing Laura Palmer. "And this woman. Our records show they should be here."

The strength left Cao's body and he forced himself to take a breath before he passed out. The MSS was looking for Acton and his wife, and the omission of the Australian students made it clear this wasn't a sweep of Westerners, but a hunt specifically for his friends.

"They were here," he finally managed to say. "But they left when the warnings were issued by their embassies."

"Where did they go?"

"The instructions were to return to their hotel, so my understanding was that's where they went."

"And what hotel are they staying at?"

For a brief moment, Cao thought he might help his friends by giving the wrong hotel, then quickly shoved that thought aside, as the government would already know from their entry records. "Hyatt Place. It's on—"

"I know where it is. Do you have numbers where they can be reached?"

"I do, in my trailer. I can get them for you if you want."

"Do that."

Cao checked his watch. "The late shift is about to end. Is it okay if I dismiss the team now, or do you need to speak with them?"

Yan eyed him. "Who is funding this dig?"

"A combination of organizations."

"Are any of those Chinese?"

"Yes."

"Then you'll work your full day. Your country isn't paying you to leave work early."

Cao should've known better. He wasn't thinking clearly, and if he weren't careful, he could get not only himself in trouble, but everyone here. He bowed in deference to a man half his age. "You are correct, of course. Let me go get those numbers for you."

"You do that, and have any other foreigners that may be here report to me."

"They've all left. There were only the professors and two Australian students who left for their hotel at the same time. I'm sure you'll find everyone where they're supposed to be."

Yan said nothing, instead pointing at the pit.

Cao headed for the ladder and slid down its rails, then rushed to his trailer. He stepped inside and closed the door. He grabbed his phone and jotted down the two phone numbers he had for Acton and his wife, and stared at his computer. He desperately wanted to send an email to Acton's emergency contact to tell him what was going on, yet knew full well that any message he sent could be read.

He eyed his desk drawer where he kept a phone used only when he was out of the country. He yanked open the drawer and grabbed the device, intentionally selected for not being of Chinese manufacture. He turned it on, but to his dismay, found the battery dead. He jabbed the end of the charger into the phone, his heart hammering dangerously now, before the device finally showed any signs of life. He waited for it to finish loading then sent a text message to Dean Gregory Milton. He watched for it to go through then deleted it, unplugged the phone, and stuffed it in the back of the drawer, and prayed the message went through.

And that he hadn't just signed his own death warrant.

Somebody pounded the door of his trailer and he shoved the desk drawer closed then plugged the charger into the bottom of his Chinese-registered phone. Yan threw open the door, stepping inside, glaring at him. "What's taking you so long?"

Cao forced a smile and pointed at his phone. "Sorry, the battery was dead. I had to let it charge for a minute." He handed him the piece of paper with the numbers. "These are the two cellphone numbers I have for them."

Yan snatched the page from Cao's hands and pulled out his own cellphone. He dialed the first number, then the second, the intensity on his face growing as each moment passed. "They're both going directly to voicemail."

Cao shrugged. "I'm sorry, I have no explanation for that. All I know is that those are their numbers."

Yan looked about the trailer, picking up the charging phone before tossing it back on the desk. He stepped out of the trailer and indicated Cao should follow. "You're under arrest."

Cao's eyes bulged and he felt faint as he followed. Several of his students and other staff were mumbling with concern, and he decided it was in their best interest that he say nothing more that might provoke a response, even if only verbal, from someone on his team.

"I'm sure there's no need to arrest me. I'll come with you voluntarily. It's my duty to assist you in locating these two foreigners."

Yan's facial muscles relaxed noticeably, and his demeanor changed, bowing slightly to his elder before holding out a hand toward the ladder. "You are correct, of course. Please come with us, and we'll clear this matter up at our office."

Cao turned to the others and tapped his watch. "The day is over in ten minutes. Please finish out the day, and then return to your homes and await instructions from your government. If you hear nothing to the contrary, I expect you all here tomorrow morning on time, even if I'm not here."

Everyone bowed, but no one said anything, understanding precisely the motive behind his words.

He headed for the ladder, and as he climbed each rung, leaving the confines of the dig site, he took one last look at not only his team, but the history that lay below, and the mystery of what happened here almost 2000 years ago that remained unsolved. And at that moment, he realized how genuinely unimportant he was, how little he had ever accomplished in his life, and how in 2000 years, no one would ever find anything that would suggest he had ever existed. He said a silent goodbye to what was to have been his life's work, then was shown into the back of a police car, his reality as he knew it likely over if this international crisis escalated.

For he had agreed to add the professors to his official team roster, so he was associated with their visas, and if the MSS was specifically searching for them, then he could end up accused of aiding them in whatever nefarious activity the government might accuse them of, genuine or not.

He said a silent prayer as he closed his eyes, picturing his wife and daughter, horror-stricken at the thought of the lies that would be told about him over the coming days.

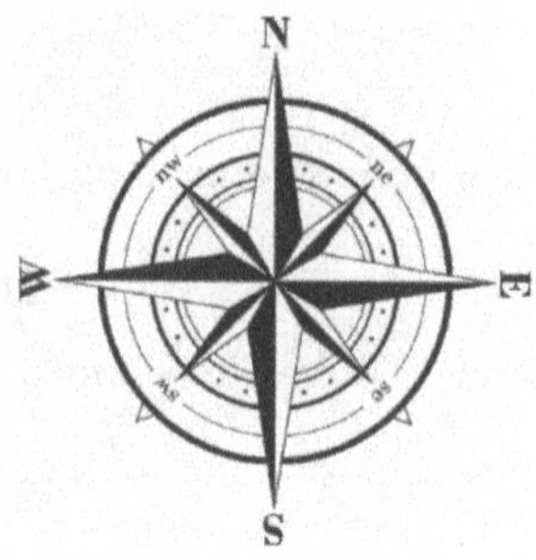

Approaching Hyatt Place Luoyang
Luoyang, China

Laura flipped her collar up and raised her shoulders as she lowered her head as much as she could. She shoved her hands into her jacket pockets and fell in behind two young women who were laughing as if the world weren't falling apart around them. But they were Chinese, and likely had no clue what was going on. And they were young, so even if they had the option of knowing the truth, unless they received it from social media, they probably wouldn't care about it or believe it. But their casual, comfortable display, made her less conspicuous.

The hotel was just ahead now, and she scrutinized her surroundings as she continued her approach. There was a government vehicle across the street, its lights flashing, two men occupying the front seats. It could be routine, and two people certainly weren't a worry considering the size of the hotel. She continued to the front entrance. The doorman bowed and opened the door for her, which she took as a good sign.

She fished her keycard out of her clutch, never one to hand it in when leaving a hotel for the day, and stepped onto an elevator with half a dozen other people, mostly Westerners, all nervous, no one saying anything to anyone. She stepped off the elevator and walked as calmly as she could toward her room, as there were surveillance cameras everywhere—this was China, and privacy was never a concern, let alone an option.

She entered the room, grabbed the satphone and its charger, then opened the safe and retrieved the cash they had locked up earlier, only having brought what they would need for the day. She stared at their luggage then made a quick decision. She grabbed her carry-on and dumped its contents on the bed, then quickly packed two changes of clothes for her and James, and two sets of the same for the students, who appeared to be similar sizes to them. Sirens wailed on the street below, but she didn't bother looking, for if it were of concern, then the seconds wasted to confirm what might be, could seal her fate.

She zipped up the carry-on, extended the handle, then left the room. She reached the elevator and pressed the button, then waited impatiently as another thought occurred to her. The hotel had their passports. When they had checked in, the hotel had been backed up, and had promised to return them within an hour, but they had left as soon as they had showered and changed. They might need them if they had any hope of escape.

She chewed her cheek as she debated what to do. James having his might not necessarily be a good thing, but having hers could be, for it would prove she was a British citizen and not an American. Not having them could prove problematic, yet getting them could mean a risky delay.

The gentle chime indicating the elevator had arrived, set her heart racing. The doors opened and she stepped inside. A Caucasian family stood there with their luggage at their feet, the kids sniffling, their eyes and cheeks red. Their father firmly held them against him as the mother's lip trembled.

They were terrified.

The doors closed, and moments later, they opened to the lobby, revealing chaos. The front desk was jammed with tourists who clearly had no intention of heeding their embassy's warning to stay inside their hotel, and were instead heading for the nearest airport to try and escape the country entirely.

And she didn't blame them.

Though, if things did turn sour, there was no way gathering all the foreigners in one place wouldn't simply aid the Chinese in their cause.

But their panic meant she had no hope of retrieving their passports.

She spotted a staff member rushing in her direction. She reached out and blocked him. "Do you speak English?"

"Yes, ma'am."

She pressed enough bills into his palm to pay six months' rent. "Get me the passports for room Seven-One-Two."

The man stared at the cash, his eyes bulging. "Yes, ma'am!" He rushed toward the desk and disappeared from sight as she checked her watch. It had been ten minutes.

Too long.

Lights suddenly flashed through the glass doors of the luxury hotel, sending her pulse racing as police cars pulled up outside.

This is it.

She involuntarily stepped backward, away from the police rushing the door. Somebody grabbed her by the shoulder and she flinched, about to cry out in shock, when she turned her head. It was the staff member. He slipped the passports into her hand.

"Follow me."

She didn't bother questioning why, for the only other option available to her was possible arrest. She followed him away from the doors and past the elevators. Moments later, they were through a staff door and into a corridor few guests likely ever saw. He was running and she was struggling to keep up, dragging her carry-on behind her, thankful this had all gone down while they were at a dig site, rather than a dinner out—the shoes she wore were more appropriate for fleeing the authorities than a pair of high heels. He pushed open a door at the end of the hallway and an alarm sounded, a light flashing. He urged her through. "Go left, away from the front."

She nodded. "Thank you."

He said nothing as he closed the door. She found herself in an alleyway filled with refuse. The street where the police were was to her right, but she wasted no time confirming that. She headed left as instructed, sprinting to the end of the alleyway, and moments later was on another busy street. She headed right, blending in with the pedestrians as she struggled to catch her breath and keep control of her carry-on.

The police presence seemed light on this street, all focus apparently on the one where she needed to be. She headed in the direction of the gas station, keeping her head down in an attempt to be as inconspicuous as possible. A vehicle screeched to a halt beside her and her heart leaped into her throat as one of its doors opened.

"Professor Palmer!"

Her head spun and she sighed in relief at the sight of Kyle with one foot out the rear door. She stepped toward the vehicle and handed him the carry-on bag, which he took and hauled inside with him as she climbed into the front seat. The doors slammed shut and James hammered on the gas, blending back in with the traffic.

"Thank God we spotted you," he said.

She put on her seatbelt then leaned back against the headrest and closed her eyes as she steadied her pounding chest. "You have no idea how happy I am to see you."

"Why? What happened?"

"The police, or military, or somebody raided the hotel just as I was about to leave."

"How did you get away?"

She held up their passports. "I bribed a staff member to get our passports. He helped me escape."

He took his and stuffed it into an inside pocket. "Good thinking. What do we do now? Did you get the satphone?"

"I did." She turned around and pointed at the carry-on. "It's in the outer pouch. Grab it and the charger."

Kyle unzipped the compartment and fished out the satphone and the charger, handing them forward. Laura plugged the charger into the car's USB port then attached it to the satphone—there was no way of knowing when they'd get a chance to charge it again.

"Let's call Tommy and see if he has any news," suggested James.

She was about to dial when she realized she had no idea what his number was. "Do you remember his number?"

"No." He cursed. "We're going to have to turn on one of our cellphones. Use yours since you're a Brit."

"Yeah, but my phone is still registered in Maryland."

"It's the safest option."

"Mine's registered in Australia," offered Kyle.

Laura smiled. "Do you know Thomas Granger?"

"No."

"Then you wouldn't have his number in your phone, would you?"

Kyle's shoulders slumped and his cheeks flushed with embarrassment. "Oh yeah."

James suppressed a chuckle. Nobody was thinking clearly. "Turn it on, put it in airplane mode, get the number, turn it off."

Laura quickly did so, every second of nothing but the Apple logo driving her heart rate faster. It finally unlocked and she swiped up, the phone automatically unlocking. Another swipe, and she disabled all the communications features, then tapped to bring up the contacts list. She pulled up Tommy's phone number and typed it into the satphone, then turned off her iPhone.

"Did you get it?"

She held up a finger as she rested against the seatback, drawing in long, slow breaths through her nose, and exhaling heavily through her mouth, her pulse slowly steadying. "Okay, I've officially never been that terrified just getting a number from a phone before."

James laughed and she noted that his knuckles were white as he gripped the steering wheel. "Call him."

She did and put it on speaker. It rang twice before being answered.

"Hello?"

"Hi, Tommy, it's Laura and Jim. Any news?"

"Oh, thank God it's you. I take it you got the satphone?"

"Yes, we did."

"Good. I highly recommend you toss those cellphones. According to the news, the Chinese have begun arresting American tourists."

"Are we at war?"

"No, not yet, at least not that I know of. As far as I can tell, the two navies aren't close enough yet to engage directly. The President is saying we won't attack first, but we won't hesitate to defend ourselves. The Chinese are demanding satisfaction for sinking one of their vessels, and don't appear to be backing down. The news is saying they've begun rounding up foreign nationals to use as bargaining chips."

"Well, they almost got me, but I managed to get away with the help of a local, so I don't know if they've got the support of their population at the moment. But that's irrelevant. Have you heard from Dylan?"

"No, and we won't. I talked to Leroux, and he said that he's unreachable."

"What about Delta?"

"Same thing. They won't be able to help because there's no way they can go into China. Leroux gave me a phone number. He wants you to call him immediately."

Laura grabbed a pen from her purse and jotted down the number.

"Is there anything we can do to help?" asked Mai, the concern in her voice evident. The young woman was like a daughter to them, and Laura's heart broke, as any mother's would, at the fear in her child's voice.

"No, just sit tight, and don't worry about us. We're going to call Leroux right now and he'll tell us what to do. You guys stay safe. Just remember that we love you, and if anything happens, reach out to Greg and Sandra." Mai crying had her own tears flowing, and she struggled to convey strength. "We'll talk to you soon."

Their replies were muted, as it was clear the two young adults were certain they were saying their final goodbyes.

And the sight of a column of military vehicles approaching had her certain they were right.

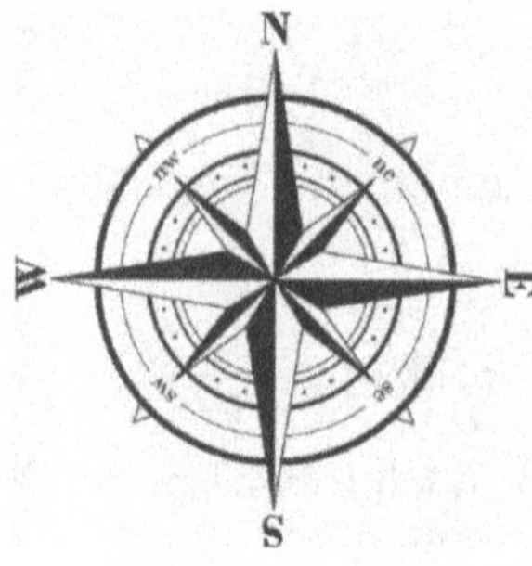

Operations Center 3, CIA Headquarters
Langley, Virginia

CIA Analyst Supervisor Chris Leroux stood at the center of the technological wonder that was Operations Center 3 at CIA Headquarters in Langley, Virginia. He headed a team of a dozen highly trained analysts and technicians, and though they dealt with life and death situations on a routine basis, everyone was on edge today with the situation developing in the South China Sea. Even Randy Child, their tech wunderkind, was nervous, the young man, barely sporting pubes, usually spinning in his chair nonchalantly whenever he was waiting for something to be processed on his terminal. Instead, he sat still, a finger nervously tapping on his knee.

He finally stopped. "Don't we have footage?"

Leroux glanced at him. "What do you mean?"

"I mean, don't we have footage of the collision?"

"I'm sure we do."

"Then why the hell aren't we releasing it? It would prove that the Chinese rammed us, that it was their own damn fault."

Sonya Tong, the second most senior in the room, turned in her chair to face Child. "Did it ever occur to you that maybe that's not what happened?"

Child's eyes bugged out. "What do you mean?

"Well, maybe we rammed them."

"You're only saying that because you're Chinese."

Leroux spun on him, jabbing a finger, spotting Tong's shocked and betrayed expression, the woman's feelings genuinely hurt as her loyalty to her country was questioned because of who her ancestors were. "Apologize now, or you're off my team!"

Child's cheeks flushed and tears filled his eyes. He turned to Tong. "I'm so sorry, Sonya. I don't know why I said that. I guess I'm just scared." The tears erupted and his shoulders shook. "I don't know why I said that, I'm so sorry, I don't know why, I don't know why I said that!"

Tong rose, her own eyes welling up with tears, and she stepped over to his station and knelt down, giving him a hug. "It's okay, I forgive you. We're all scared."

Child clung to her, and they held each other. Leroux glanced at the others in the room, finding too many with glistening eyes. They had all been through a lot together, but their operations were usually limited in scope. This time, their country could be going to war with a nuclear power, and though he had absolutely no doubt America would prevail if it went full-scale, the death toll could be staggering.

He decided something must be said.

He walked to the front of the sloping room, standing in front of the massive curved displays that stretched from one end to the other, then turned to face his team. A few short years ago, what he was doing right now would have terrified him more than the potential of war. He was an introvert, painfully so, that had been slowly coaxed out of his shell by his girlfriend, Sherrie White, a CIA operative, and his best friend, Dylan Kane, yet even though he had been pried from the closed world that had been his life for almost 30 years, situations such as this were still not his comfort zone.

"Okay, everyone, I know we're all scared, we're all tense, we're all on edge, but let's use all this anxiety to keep us sharp. We need to channel all this extra energy and put it to good use. What's the one thing we know that's true the world over?"

Tong let go of Child and returned to her seat. "That the average person is an idiot?"

Leroux chuckled. "Compared to the minds in this room, I would wholeheartedly agree, though that wasn't exactly what I was going for. Think a little bit more real world. Think social media, think Millennials. What's the average Millennial desperate for when it comes to social media?"

Child shrugged. "Content?"

"Exactly. They want to have that one unique moment that no one else has. They want to record anything that could make them famous, even if it's just for that proverbial fifteen minutes."

Child's eyes widened. "You think somebody recorded the collision?"

"What are navies the world over filled with? Young sailors. It wouldn't surprise me one bit if somebody out there on either side recorded this and posted it."

"But the Chinese ship sank."

"Yes, but remember, they didn't abandon ship, they stayed on until the very last minute, likely under orders. So, if you're eighteen and scared, and your captain has just announced you're not allowed to abandon your post, and if you jump in the water you're going to be shot, what do you do if you've got the proof in your hand that the asshole on the bridge is responsible for killing you?"

"I upload my proof."

"Exactly."

"Do the Chinese ships even have Internet?"

"They do, but it's strictly controlled. However, somebody might have had a contraband satphone or somebody in the comms center of the ship might have decided to upload the video they had taken while on the bridge, or that a buddy had just handed him, as a last 'screw you' to his captain that just got him killed. There are a million possibilities. Or it could have been one of our guys. We don't know. But let's start looking. Scour everything, see if we can find some footage, and start reviewing satellite footage. See if the cameras got lucky. We need to get the proof that might just stop the war."

Tong cleared her throat. "But won't the Pentagon already be doing this?"

Leroux eyed her. "Do you really want to leave the fate of our country in their hands?"

She smiled sheepishly. "No, I suppose not."

"Good. This room has the best damn team of analysts anywhere in the world, and there's no way in hell I'm just going to sit here, hoping someone else saves us."

Tong held up a finger. "I've got Professor Acton on the phone for you, sir."

Leroux grabbed his headset from his console and fit it in place, then nodded to Tong to put the call through. "Professor Acton, this is Chris Leroux."

"Good to hear your voice, Chris. Do you have any advice for us beyond kiss our asses goodbye?"

Leroux chuckled. "All I can say is this time, you're probably going to have to save your own skins. Dylan's deep undercover, and there's no way Bravo Team will be allowed into China."

A burst of static came through his headset as Acton sighed. "I had a feeling you were going to say that. Listen, I've got two Australian nationals with us, students from the archaeological team. What do you recommend we do?"

"Where are you now?"

"We're in Luoyang. It's about eight hours southwest of Beijing."

"I would tell you to sit tight, but I don't think that's necessarily a good idea."

"Neither do I. The embassy is advising everyone to stay in the hotels, but when Laura was retrieving our satphone, they raided it."

"If you were anybody else, I would say the best thing for you to do is to let yourself get arrested. The Chinese are just playing a game right now, and they're using American tourists and businesspeople as pawns in that game. Because of your history, you're priority targets. I have no doubt once they review who they actually have in the country, they're going to be specifically looking for you. You interfered in their affairs too many times, including in the Amazon and that coup attempt. You need to find someplace to hole up and ride this out."

"I wouldn't even know where to begin."

"It's too bad you're not in Beijing. I would recommend you go to the embassy, but in Luoyang, there's really nowhere you can go."

"Could we get to Beijing?"

Leroux stared at a map Tong had brought up for him, never ceasing to be amazed at how she could always anticipate his needs. "It's a possibility. It depends on how much of a lockdown they want to bring in. Right now, our reports are that they're hitting the hotels. We haven't heard any reports of roadblocks or checkpoints yet. If you get out of the city, you should have a straight shot to Beijing. Do you have a GPS in your vehicle?"

"We do."

"How are you for gas?

"We can make it. I just filled up."

"Then I suggest you start driving, Professor Acton. Head north, then make sure you take the G5512 and not the G30, otherwise you're going to hit Zhengzhou. That's about ten million people. If you take the G5512 then the G4 straight to Beijing, you should be able to avoid any major cities. Keep a low profile and make sure to keep this phone charged if you can."

"We can."

"Good. Call us every thirty minutes with an update as to your location. We'll work out a plan on this end. Just get yourselves to Beijing."

"Copy that."

"Good luck, Professors."

"Thanks! We're going to need it."

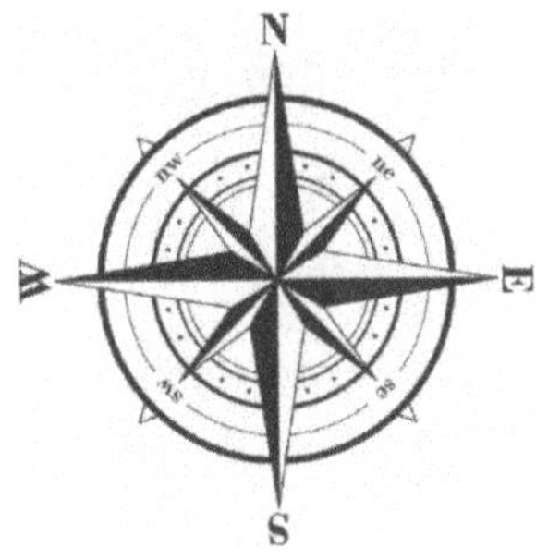

Fort Bragg, North Carolina

Sergeant Carl "Niner" Sung squeezed off the last round then ejected the spent magazine, slamming home a fresh one in less than half a second, before returning the loaded Glock to its holster. He pressed the button to retrieve his target as Sergeant Leon "Atlas" James emptied his mag in the next stall. Niner grabbed his paper target and grinned as Atlas retrieved his own, holding it up.

"Beat that, little man," rumbled the impossibly muscled Atlas. It was a perfect result, all headshots and double-tap chest shots with good groups. More than enough to put him in the 99th percentile, as any member of their unit should. They were 1st Special Forces Operational Detachment—Delta, commonly referred to by the public as Delta Force, and the best trained operators the world had ever known.

But they weren't simply soldiers—Niner also considered himself an artiste.

He held his up, a perfect smiley face shot into the target's chest, and a single ragged hole in the crotch from the remaining shots delivered for good measure.

Atlas groaned. "Who do you think you are? Martin Riggs?"

"If I'm Riggs, that makes you Murtaugh, so I guess you're too old for this shit."

"I'm too old to be putting up with your shit, pipsqueak."

Niner feigned mock hurt. "One of these days, you're going to say something that will truly drive me away, and you'll be sorry."

Atlas eyed him. "If you happen to know what that thing might be, let me know."

"You know, sticks and stones may break my bones, but your words, you huggable lunk, will always be a dagger to my heart."

Atlas groaned and turned to Command Sergeant Major Burt "Big Dog" Dawson. "We really need to find him a new team. I don't know how much more I can take of him."

Niner dropped the target sheet and leaped through the air, wrapping his legs around the massive Atlas' waist and his arms around his thick neck. "I'll never let you get rid of me." He started sport-humping Atlas' stomach and the big man grabbed him by the chest and hurled him away. Niner skidded across the floor, the other members of Bravo Team pissing themselves laughing.

Sergeant Will "Spock" Lightman cocked an eyebrow, shaking his head. "Why do I feel that David Attenborough should have been narrating that scene?"

Sergeant Gerry "Jimmy Olsen" Hudson put on a fake British accent. "And now the Korean-American special operative attempts to mate with the alpha of the group, but the alpha is having none of it." He laughed too hard to finish.

Niner picked himself up off the floor, wiping away mock tears. "One of these days, you really are going to break my heart, and you won't be seeing this anymore." He slapped his ass with one hand.

Atlas raised a boot. "The only time I ever want to see that narrow little thing is if my boot is firmly planted in it."

Niner rubbed the other ass cheek. "You already did that in Spain. My once perfect ass still has a mark." He pointed at his target. "But I think I win. You're buying the beer."

"I call it a tie."

Spock shook his head. "You two trying to settle things on the firing range is pointless. You're both too good."

Niner and Atlas both bowed. "Why thank you," they echoed before grinning at each other and exchanging fist bumps.

Jimmy's eyes rolled. "Sometimes I think you two were separated at birth."

Niner eyed Atlas, easily twice his size. "Why do I think we were just cast in the reboot of Twins?"

Atlas grinned. "Dibs on Arnold. You're DeVito."

Dawson's phone rang and he answered it, holding up a finger, silencing the frivolity. "Go ahead." Words were said on the other end, their team lead's face growing grim. "Roger that." He ended the call and returned the phone to his pocket.

"What's up?" asked Niner, all business.

"We might be going to war."

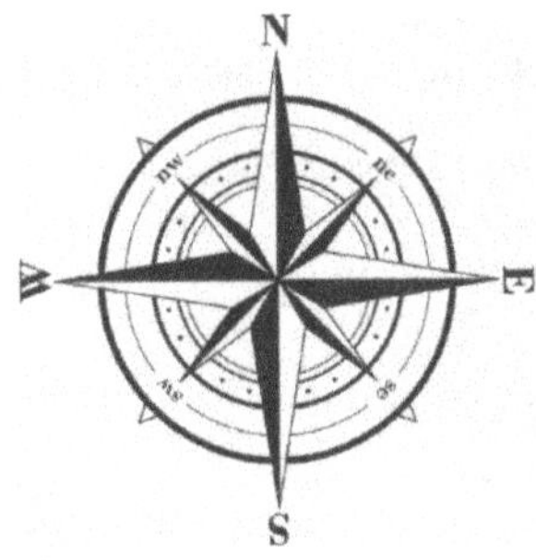

Imperial Palace

Luoyang, Han Empire

166 AD

Lucius lay in bed, Jieyou beside him, her head resting on his chest, an arm and leg draped over his naked body as they both caught their breath. Everything about this relationship was wrong, everything was dangerous, and everything was perfect. Their love was pure, and talk had turned to how they might have a future together. And one thought had occurred to him in the throes of passion that he decided must be discussed now, before he became distracted again and forgot it. He turned over onto his side and stared into her piercing eyes. He brushed the hair from her face. "I had a thought."

"And just what was this thought, my love?"

"I may have figured out a way for us to be together."

Her eyes flared with hope. "Really? How?"

"I was speaking with my father, and he said we would be sending a mission back to Rome to deliver messages to the Emperor along with the finalized treaty. He said I could command the mission."

Her eyes widened and she pulled away. "You mean you're leaving me?"

He reached out for her. "No, not at all. The mission would be under my command if I went, which means the men wouldn't question anything."

"Question what?"

"Why you were with me."

She eyed him in disbelief. "But that's impossible! As much as I'd love to go with you and live in Rome, my father would never allow it."

"No, he never would. Nor would mine. But if you were to sneak out of the palace, then meet me along our route, no one would know. And once we're clear of your empire, no one would stop us. We could return to Rome, be married, and live the rest of our lives together."

Her face brightened. "Do you really think it's possible?"

"If you're willing, absolutely."

She grabbed him and held him tight. "I could think of nothing I would rather do."

"Then we must begin to plan, and no one can know."

"It will be our secret."

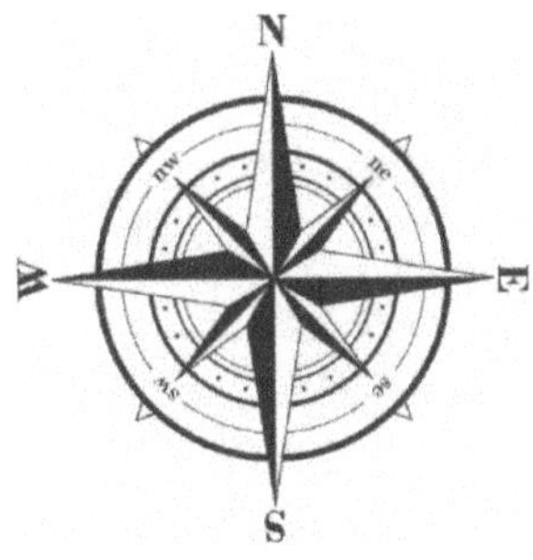

Milton Residence

St. Paul, Maryland

Present Day

Milton sat on his couch, glued to the television set. His daughter was playing on the floor, quietly humming as Sandra busied herself making breakfast in the kitchen. He reached behind his back and rubbed at the pain, his body still not fully recovered from the beating he had received a few months before.

His phone beeped, indicating a message. He retrieved it off the end table and his eyes shot wide at the text.

Chinese authorities looking specifically for Acton and Palmer. Do not respond.

He checked the number but didn't recognize it. He pulled up his email software then entered the number in the search bar and hit Enter. An email chain was displayed a moment later. The number was a backup for Professor Cao. Milton desperately wanted to respond to ask for more information, yet the message had been clear.

Do not respond.

"What's wrong, dear?"

He glanced over his shoulder at Sandra, who had stopped chopping the vegetables for their omelets. "I just got a message from Professor Cao."

"Who's that?"

"He's in charge of the dig in China that Jim and Laura went to."

"Oh, why would he be contacting you?"

His chest ached and his voice cracked. "He says the Chinese are after Jim and Laura."

Sandra's jaw dropped and the knife clattered onto the cutting board. She grabbed her tea towel and dried her hands as she rushed from the kitchen. "What does that mean? Why would they be after them?"

He gestured at the television screen. "You would think it has something to do with what's going on right now, but the wording of his message makes me think it's something more."

Sandra dropped into a chair next to him. "But she's British, and they aren't involved in this yet. Why would they be after her?"

"I don't know. All the reports are that only Americans are being confined to their hotels. Other foreign nationals have just been advised to be ready to leave if notified, but only Americans are now being advised to leave the country immediately if it's safe to do so."

"We need to let somebody know, don't we?"

"According to Tommy, they've already notified Dylan, so if he's able to help, I'm sure he's already doing so."

"Yes, but he might not know about this."

Milton frowned. "That's true."

"Didn't Tommy say he's got a contact at the CIA that he reached out to?"

"Yes, that's right!" Milton dialed Tommy's number and put it on speaker.

"Hello, Dean Milton," answered a groggy Tommy.

"Hi, Tommy, sorry to wake you, but I just received a message from Professor Cao. He's the man in charge of the dig in China. It reads, and I quote: Chinese authorities looking specifically for Acton and Palmer. Do not respond."

"Why would they specifically be looking for them?"

"Any number of reasons. They've pissed off the Chinese at least a couple of times that I can think of. Can you pass that message on to your CIA contacts, and I'll try to pass it on to Dylan?"

"Don't bother with Dylan, sir, he's deep undercover and won't be able to help. I'll pass this on to my CIA contact right away."

"Okay, you do that. Keep me posted."

"Yes, sir."

The call ended and Milton collapsed in his chair, his back aching as every muscle in his body had tensed with the message. Sandra rose and stood behind him, beginning to deliver a massage. He groaned.

"Why don't we go to the bedroom and I'll give you a proper massage?"

He shook his head. "No, I want to make sure I don't miss anything."

"Okay, but the offer's there." She continued expertly working on his back, his wife having taken lessons after he'd been shot, and as the stress in his muscles eased, his mind continued to race with worry over his best friends.

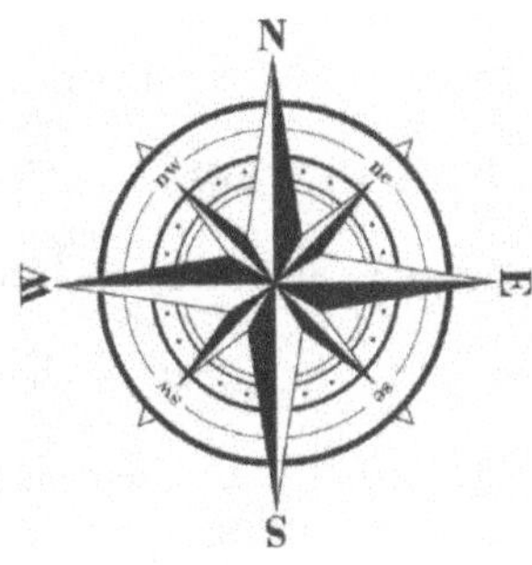

Operations Center 3, CIA Headquarters

Langley, Virginia

Leroux fit his headset in place then nodded at Tong, who tapped at her keyboard then gave a thumbs up. The phone rang and it was answered moments later.

"Hello?"

"Hello, is this Gregory Milton?"

"Yes, it is. Who's this?"

"This is Chris Leroux."

"Oh, hello. I assume you got my message through Tommy?"

"I did, and I just wanted to confirm the exact wording. I need you to read it back to me."

As Milton read the message, Tong typed it, sending it to the main display for everyone to see.

Chinese authorities looking specifically for Acton and Palmer. Do not respond.

Leroux read the message several times, little doubt possible as to its specific meaning. “And you’re sure this came from Professor Cao?”

There was a pause. “Actually, I guess I can’t be certain. I have the number that sent the message in an email chain indicating it belongs to him, though I guess it could be faked. But to what end?”

Leroux had to agree. What would be the point of sending a warning that would only bring more attention to the professors? It would make no sense. He dismissed the notion, instead working under the assumption it was genuine. “When was it sent?”

“Less than half an hour ago.”

“What was the exact time?”

“7:48 AM Eastern.”

“Okay, and I assume you didn’t reply?”

“No, like it says, he didn’t want me to, and I assume he had his reasons. “

“Good, make sure you don’t, because he likely sent this risking his own life to let us know. If he were to get a reply and it was intercepted, it could be very unfortunate for him.”

“That’s what I was thinking as well. Are you going to be able to help Jim and Laura?”

“Until this moment, they were just any other tourist or worker legally within China. Helping them wasn’t an option, because then we’d have to help everyone, and our current estimates suggest there are almost one-hundred-thousand Americans living within China’s borders legally, and at least that number on tourist visas. However, if the Chinese are specifically targeting them, then I might be able to get the green light to help them."

A burst of static erupted through the headset. "Then let's pray you get that green light."

"Yes, sir. If I have any news, I'll let you know."

"Likewise, thank you."

The call ended and Leroux tossed his headset onto his workstation then headed for the door. "I'm going to go brief the Chief, and see if we can get that green light."

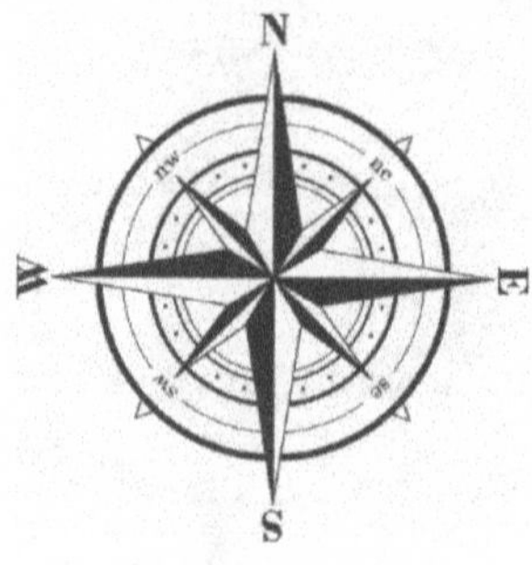

1st Special Forces Operational Detachment—Delta HQ

Fort Bragg, North Carolina

A.k.a. "The Unit"

Command Sergeant Major Burt "Big Dog" Dawson winked at his fiancé, Maggie Harris, as he entered his commanding officer's outer office. She pressed a button on the intercom. "Sergeant Major Dawson is here to see you, sir."

"Send him in."

She tilted her head toward Clancy's door. "Go on in, sexy."

Dawson grinned as she hooked a finger in her blouse, revealing just a hint of extra cleavage. He made a show of wiping his brow. "What are you trying to do? Get me all randy before I walk in there?"

She shrugged and held her hands up, the picture of innocence. "I have no idea what you're talking about. I was merely scratching an itch."

"Uh-huh."

He stepped into Clancy's office and his commanding officer pointed at Dawson's crotch. "You better keep Randy in your pants when you're in my presence, Sergeant Major." Dawson's cheeks flushed with embarrassment, uncertain as to what to say. Clancy roared in laughter and pointed at one of the chairs in front of his desk. "You two do realize that the walls here are thin, especially that door?"

Dawson sat. "I guess I'll have to keep that in mind in the future, sir."

"You do that." Clancy became all business. "Have you heard about what's going on in the South China Sea?"

"A little, sir. Nothing beyond what the news is saying."

"The facts they're reporting are accurate though incomplete. Unfortunately, the other 90% of what the news is saying is merely conjecture or opinion."

"That's why I don't watch it, sir. If it's important, you'll tell me."

Clancy chuckled. "Bucking for a promotion, Sergeant Major?"

"I don't think I could go any higher without taking a commission. And you and I both know I'd never make a good officer."

"No, you'd be busted down to lieutenant after you slugged your commanding officer for being stupid."

"I've never slugged you, sir."

"And I'm grateful for it, Sergeant Major. I've been punched many a time in my day, and there's only one man that scares me more than you do, should one of you decide I need a good beating."

"And who's that, sir?"

"Atlas."

Dawson chuckled. "Yeah, even I'm afraid of him."

"Small moons are afraid of him."

"Are we being called up, sir?"

"Yes, though nothing specific for the moment. We're just pre-positioning units around the conflict zone. We're sending you to South Korea, just in case you're needed."

Dawson eyed Clancy for a moment. "Normally something like that doesn't merit the personal briefing, sir. Is there something else going on?"

"You tell me."

Dawson's eyes widened slightly. "Sir?"

"You're telling me you haven't heard?"

"Heard what, sir?"

"About the professors?"

Dawson paused, suddenly concerned. "No, I haven't, sir. Let me guess, they were on the Chinese ship?"

Clancy laughed. "No, but they *are* in China. I got a courtesy call from our CIA friend, Leroux, just a few minutes ago, letting us know what's going on with them. They haven't contacted you?"

"No, they haven't."

"Well, they reached out to Kane and then to one of their students here who reached out to the CIA. It's probably only a matter of time before you get a call from somebody."

"And I assume you've called me here to tell me that I'm not allowed to go into China and help them?"

"I would say that should go without saying. However, you have a habit of taking interesting vacations."

Dawson stared at Clancy's commendations on the wall. "I'm sure I don't know what you mean."

"Uh-huh. I'm pre-positioning your team in the area not to help them, but to make sure you're on duty for the next seventy-two hours."

"And if the professors are in trouble?"

"Then they'll be treated like any other American citizen. Understood?"

"Absolutely, sir."

"Let me make it clear. If the Chinese begin rounding up American citizens and other foreign nationals, we can't be showing the professors any special treatment just because we know them."

"I understand, sir. I've dealt with them quite a bit, and they're resourceful. I'm sure they'll figure a way out of this on their own."

"Your plane leaves in an hour." Clancy tapped a file on his desk. "These are your orders."

Dawson took the file and headed out the door, and as he closed it, Clancy called after him. "And don't forget, I can hear you, Sergeant Major and Miss Harris."

Dawson flashed him a grin and closed the door to find Maggie behind her desk, her cheeks flushed, her hand on her chest, clearly embarrassed.

"I had no idea!" she hissed.

He cringed. "Neither did I." He leaned over the desk and gave her a kiss and then raised his voice slightly. "Do you think he hears us when we're having sex out here?"

Maggie's eyes shot wider and her jaw dropped. "BD! Oh my God, sir, he's just joking!"

"He better be," rumbled Clancy's voice through the wall.

She hit Dawson on the arm. "Get out of here before you get me fired."

Dawson laughed, shaking the file. "I'll be gone for at least a few days. Don't wait up."

She reached out and took his hand. "Be careful."

"You know me."

"Yes, I do know you, that's why I'm telling you to be careful."

He kissed her hand. "I will be. Love you."

"Love you too."

He headed back into the hallway and quickly scanned his orders, surprised to see the entire team had been called up. He pulled out his phone and dialed his second-in-command and best friend, Master Sergeant Mike "Red" Belme. "We've been called up, leaving in an hour. Notify the team."

"Dealer's choice?"

"Nope. Full deck."

"Everyone? Interesting. Are we having Chinese for dinner?"

Dawson chuckled at the coded reference. "There's a possibility. Right now, they just want us near the restaurant."

"Okay, I'll start the calls."

Dawson hung up and headed out into the parking lot to find Niner, Atlas, and Spock milling about his 1964½ Mustang convertible in original poppy red.

"So, what's up, BD?" asked Niner.

"We've been called up."

"Who?"

"All of us."

"Really? Been a while. What's the mission?"

"We're being pre-positioned in Korea, just in case things head south with the Chinese."

"Any further intel on what's actually going on over there?"

Dawson waved the file. "I've got some here, but it's thin. I'll brief everyone once we get on the plane. Wheels up in one hour. Go do what you need to do, and we'll meet back at the Unit."

"Yes, Sergeant Major," echoed his three comrades.

Everyone broke off into their separate vehicles, and Dawson climbed into the Mustang he had inherited from his father. He fired up the engine, revving it a little, loving the roar erupting from the tailpipes, then pulled out of the parking lot, his jaw square with concern, not for the mission, but for his friends who might be trapped in what could soon be a warzone.

And unfortunately, his orders were clear.

The professors were on their own this time.

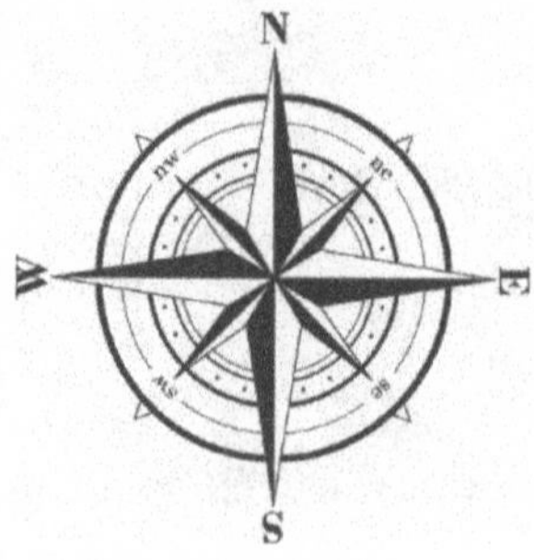

USS Somerset

South China Sea

Kidd leaned against the railing, staring out the wash deck at the rear of the ship. They had stood down from GQ about fifteen minutes ago, and the Doc had ordered him to grab some rack time, but he was too wired. Instead, he now stood decompressing in one of his favorite corners of the ship he had discovered. He closed his burning eyes and breathed in the familiar fumes, a combination of metals, fuels, and sea air that he found intoxicating.

He had no idea why he had joined the Navy. He was a landlubber who could barely swim, but for some reason, when he had joined the military out of high school, the Navy had proven irresistible. Perhaps it was all those great war movies he used to watch with his father when he was a kid. Midway, Tora! Tora! Tora!—the classics. It wasn't that life at sea appeared glamorous. If anything, those movies proved it wasn't. It was the camaraderie, the close quarters, the fact you were forced to rely on your crewmates. If the ship went down, you all went down, therefore everyone was counting on you to do your job and do it well.

And should the man beside you falter, his as well.

Never for a moment had he regretted the decision he had made, even today. He loved the Navy, he loved the military, he loved everything about it. This was the life he had chosen.

He just prayed it didn't end too soon.

The GQ alarm sounded yet again and the ship banked hard to port. The Bushmaster cannons opened fire, the sound deafening, and as the ship leaned at a dramatic angle, he gripped the railing, struggling to maintain his balance. He spotted one of their choppers angling to position itself directly at their bow, half a klick out, and it had him wondering what was going on. The ship stabilized, the engines roaring as they left the chopper behind. The cannons continued to fire then suddenly fell silent, the tracers disappearing as the chopper edged forward, deploying chaff.

Kidd turned to head for his station when another alarm sounded, then a warning was issued.

"Brace for impact!"

His pulse hammered in his ears as he gripped onto the railing with both hands, his knuckles white as he stared out the wash deck, suddenly realizing exactly what was happening. He spotted the missile racing toward them, its propellant a small bright light in the darkened sky, and he gasped out a warning to those on the helicopter. "Look out!"

But there was no way they could hear him, and even if they could, they were there by choice. The USS Somerset was never designed to repel anti-ship missiles, and this mission to maintain international navigation rights through the disputed South China Sea should never have required the capability, otherwise a ship equipped with an AEGIS Ballistic Missile Defense System would have accompanied them.

The Captain was working with what he had to save his crew.

The pilot positioned the chopper perpendicular to the bow of the ship, providing the largest target for the missile, sacrificing himself to save them all. For a moment, he swore he could hear the scream of the missile, though it was probably the screams in his head. A fireball lit the night sky as it slammed into the chopper, the airframe collapsing to the waves below in a cacophony of screeching metal and belching fuel, secondary explosions from the onboard ordnance crackling the night sky as the debris smacked onto the water, slowly dragging it and its crew to the bottom of the sea.

Kidd leaned over the rail and vomited, his eyes filled with tears at the bravery just demonstrated, and wondered if he could do the same if so ordered.

And was certain he would come up short.

Leaving Luoyang, China

Acton breathed a sigh of relief as they left behind the city that was once the ancient capital of the Han Empire. The police and military presence had definitely increased, yet there was still no evidence of roadblocks. He had turned the Chinese-controlled English broadcast back on, as it should match fairly closely with what the Chinese population was being told. And for now, the official line was that a Chinese naval vessel had been attacked without provocation by the US Navy, and that a security operation was underway to ensure the safety of American tourists within China.

There was no mention of any special instructions or restrictions for the local population, which suggested the Chinese authorities weren't prepared to set up roadblocks as of yet. That would inconvenience their citizens, and indicate the security operation now underway was more serious than they claimed. So far, that was working to their advantage.

He checked the clock on the dash then gestured at it. "I think it's been half an hour."

Laura checked. "Two more minutes. How exactly do you think he meant?"

Acton shrugged. "I don't know. He's CIA, so I'm assuming pretty exact."

"Me too." Laura turned in her seat to face their Aussie charges. "How are you two holding up?"

Amelia sniffed. "Better than earlier, I guess. I'll be right."

"Me too," said Kyle. "I think the adrenaline is starting to wear off."

Laura smiled. "That's good. We've got a long drive ahead of us, so if either you feel like you want to nod off, go ahead. We'll be in Beijing before you know it."

Amelia shook her head. "I don't think I'll ever sleep again after that."

Acton chuckled. "Trust me, when this is all over, you're going to sleep like you've never slept before."

Kyle gave him a look. "What, with one eye open, gripping my pillow tight?"

Acton roared with laughter. "A Metallica reference from a Millennial! I think I'm going to like you!" He tapped the display with the clock. "That's two minutes."

Laura dialed Leroux's number then put it on speaker.

A woman answered. "Hello?"

Laura exchanged a puzzled glance with Acton. "Umm, I was calling for Chris Leroux?"

"Identify yourself."

"Laura Palmer and James Acton."

"Hello, Professor, my name is Sonya, and I work for Mr. Leroux. He's unavailable right now. Do you have an update for us?"

"We just cleared Luoyang and are heading north. We're less than half an hour from our turnoff for the G5512. We're still roughly eight hours from Beijing."

"Did you encounter any problems?"

"No. So far, there don't appear to be any roadblocks."

"That's good. That confirms the information at our end. As far as we can tell, the Chinese are focusing on the hotels at the moment, and keeping everyone contained rather than interning them at another location."

Laura shrugged at Acton. "I suppose that's good news."

"With respect to the overall situation, perhaps. I have important information for you. I assume you know Professor Cao?"

"Of course, he's James' friend in charge of the dig site."

"Well, Gregory Milton received a text message from him a short while ago. I'll read it to you verbatim: 'Chinese authorities looking specifically for Acton and Palmer. Do not respond.'"

Acton tensed. "What's your interpretation of that?"

"Our opinion is that he is warning us that the Chinese are looking for you two specifically, not because you, Professor Acton, are an American, but because of who you specifically are. With your involvement, however involuntary it may have been, in the coup attempt several years ago, and in effectively destroying a highly lucrative mining operation in the

Amazon belonging to the Chinese, you both were always high-priority targets."

Laura stared at the phone. "Then why would they have even issued us the visas? If they're afraid of us, why let us into the country?"

"Because they're not afraid of you, at least not within China. The likelihood of you doing anything that would put their interests at risk is slim within their borders, but should they decide they need a pawn, two public figures like yourselves can prove very valuable. And while within their borders, they can arrest you with impunity."

Laura slumped in her seat. "Lovely. I don't think we'll be coming back to China again."

"It's probably not wise, though worrying about that is for another day. What this does mean, though, is that every police officer and government official in the country likely has your photos and are looking for you. And don't forget facial recognition. They have cameras everywhere."

"Any suggestions on how to defeat those?" asked Acton.

"It's dark there now, so keep your cabin lights out, keep your sun visors down to reduce the available angles for their cameras, and if you have hats and sunglasses, wear them. Anything that restricts a camera picking up your facial features. Feigning sleep for three of the four of you is the best way to do it."

Kyle leaned forward. "Are they looking for us?"

"Who's this?" asked the CIA contact.

"Kyle Rapp. I'm an Australian student working at the dig site."

"No, there's no evidence that they're specifically looking for you or Ms. Robinson."

Kyle shrugged. "Then the solution seems rather obvious, doesn't it?"

Acton eyed him, the solution not at all apparent. "What do you mean?"

"Let me take the wheel."

Acton smiled. "That just might be the smartest thing I've heard all day. What do you think, Sonya?"

"I agree, the three of you can pretend to be asleep with your heads covered, and Mr. Rapp wouldn't be required to take any precautions that might raise suspicions. We're tracking your satphone right now. Is your GPS set for miles or kilometers?"

"Kilometers."

"Then in exactly three-point-two kilometers, there's a dead spot in the highway cameras. Pull over there and switch, then contact us again in thirty minutes."

"Will do." Acton ended the call then checked the GPS, and after 3.2 kilometers, pulled over. They all switched seats, he and Laura now in the back with the two Australians in the front, and were underway in less than a minute.

He wedged into the corner, bundling up his jacket as a combination pillow and blind. Laura leaned on his chest and curled up her legs, then covered her face with her coat. "How do we look?" he asked.

Amelia glanced back. "Snug as a bug, and there's no way any camera can see your faces."

He gave a thumbs up. "Wake me in thirty minutes."

"You're actually going to be able to sleep?"

He grunted. "This isn't my first rodeo."

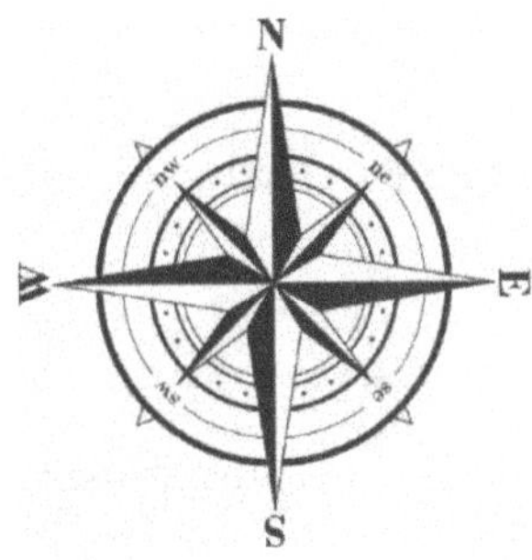

Embassy of the Roman Empire

Luoyang, Han Empire

166 AD

"I think I've changed my mind."

Lucius' father glanced up from his plate filled with local delicacies, many of which Lucius hadn't yet learned to stomach. They had long since run out of any foodstuffs they had brought with them from Rome, though they still had a supply of wine. Several of the dishes he had grown to love, and would miss them once he returned to Rome. "You've changed your mind about what?"

"About going to Rome to deliver the treaty to the Emperor."

His father leaned back. "And what has brought upon this change of heart?"

Lucius shrugged. "I'm not sure. I've just begun to feel homesick. Don't worry, I'll come back with the Emperor's reply, but I have this overwhelming sense that I need to see home at least one more time in my life."

"You'll have plenty of time to see Rome, but if you persevere, you'll be returning as the ambassador."

He eyed his father. "Are you planning on retiring?"

His father laughed. "No, but eventually I will, and by then you'll have the experience and the knowledge of this land that none in Rome can hope to have. You would be my recommendation to replace me, and the only logical choice. It would be a position of honor that could eventually lead to the Senate."

"I find that hard to believe."

"That's because you don't think far enough ahead. I volunteered us for this mission so that our family could regain its honor, its rightful place in Roman society. The shame my grandfather brought to our family has been mostly forgotten."

"It may have been forgotten, but has it been forgiven?"

"There's nothing to forgive when something is no longer remembered. All that is remembered now is that our family doesn't hold the station it once did. This mission, to establish relations with the Han Empire, will change all of that, but only if we succeed."

"Have we not succeeded?"

"Not yet. The formal negotiations of a treaty have been completed. However, without the Emperor signing off on what we've agreed to, there is no treaty. If you are indeed to return to Rome, then it will be your responsibility to bring him a copy, convince him to sign it as is, then return here with the document. Only then can the cooperation between our two empires begin."

"So, this is an important mission?"

"Absolutely."

"And you trust me with it?"

"Of course I trust you, you're my son. If I had any doubts, I wouldn't let you go."

Guilt crept in at the misplaced faith his father was putting in him. He had betrayed him for months, and now was planning the ultimate treachery, all for the love of a woman he had no place being with. Once the princess was discovered missing, he had little doubt blame would fall on his father and the Roman contingent, and it could mean their deaths.

And that was something he couldn't live with, just to satisfy his own selfish desires.

"What's wrong?"

He shook his head, forcing a smile as he realized gloom was the mask he now wore. "Nothing. I'm just thinking of home."

"The family will be happy to see you. I'll give you personal letters to bring to them."

"If only Mother were here."

It was his father's turn for gloom. "Yes, if only."

His mother had died only months before his father had agreed to this journey, a journey he had little doubt the purpose of which went far beyond reclaiming the family's glory. More likely, the primary reason was to escape the memories forged by decades spent with his mother. If he were to abandon his father for the love of a woman, he would need to find a way to shift any possible blame from the Roman contingent.

Otherwise, his plan could not proceed.

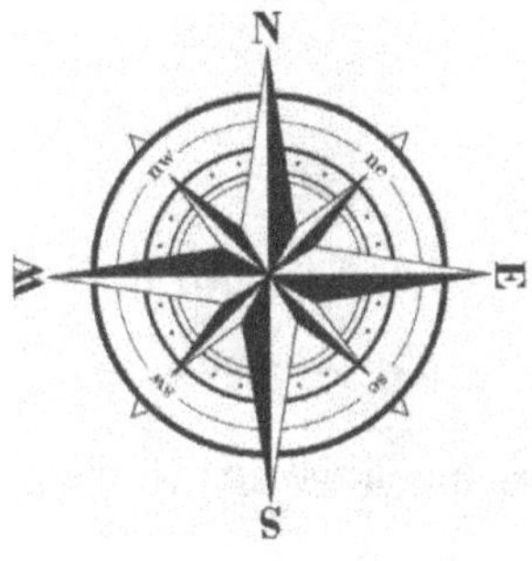

USS Somerset

South China Sea

Present Day

Kidd changed out of his salt-encrusted clothes, finally getting an opportunity to do so after diving into the water. He was exhausted. Not from a lack of sleep, but from the adrenaline pumping through him since the incident began.

Once everyone had been stabilized and the injuries treated, they had stood down from GQ, allowing the Doc to send some of them for much-needed downtime. He had protested, wanting to stay working beside his crewmates, but even they had insisted he be among the first to rest, for right now, he was a bit of a hero for having gone back to try and save the others. And while he appreciated the slaps on the back and the high-fives and fist bumps, he had no doubt a reprimand was in his future for having disobeyed orders. However, that didn't bother him. What did bother him was whether he was responsible for the escalation that had taken place.

Were the Chinese targeting him, or were they targeting the survivors, and he just happened to be among them? If he had never rolled over the side of that RHIB, would they have still opened fire? If the Chinese guns had remained silent after the initial attack, then there would have been no need for the USS Somerset to open fire. Yet the ship would have still sunk, and the real question was what the Chinese response would be as a result of that? Unfortunately, with the USS Somerset's guns opening up only minutes before the ship finally sank, the last reports the Chinese would have received from her captain would likely have been that they were taking fire, and any open mic would have heard the sound.

He soaked his head under the shower as he washed the saltwater off, his mind battling itself as it played out every scenario. And each time, no matter how irrational, he was convinced war was coming, and it was his fault. He squeezed his eyes shut as he collapsed to his knees, and the only images he could conjure were those of the dead and wounded floating in the ocean, their faces and bodies charred, not asking him for help, but instead asking him why he had disobeyed orders and started a war that would kill millions.

And it was too much. He fell to his side and curled into a ball as his entire body was racked with sobs, the water from the shower unrelentingly pelting him. Somebody rushed toward him and grabbed him.

"Hey, Kidd, you okay?"

But the words didn't register. All that did were the images of the bodies, the burning flesh, the graves of the damned.

And a voice he barely recognized as his own, repeating, "I'm sorry, I'm so sorry!"

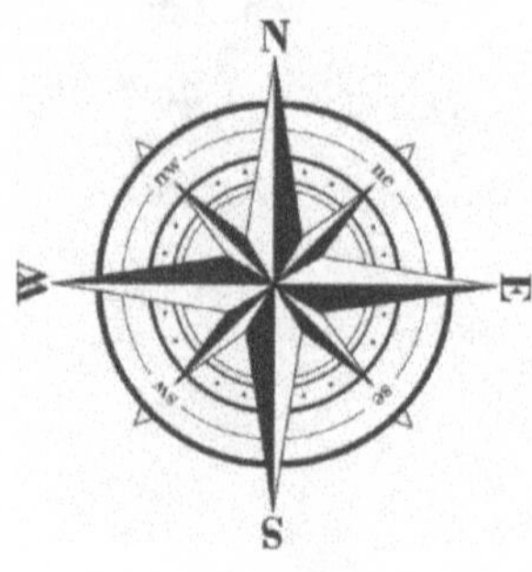

Director Morrison's Office, CIA Headquarters

Langley, Virginia

National Clandestine Service Chief for the CIA, Leif Morrison, waved Leroux into his office and pointed at a chair. Leroux sat but said nothing as Morrison read something on his laptop. Finished, he leaned back and turned his attention to Leroux. "What have you got for me?"

"I've got my team searching for any type of footage that might show what happened in the South China Sea, as well as reviewing satellite footage that might have caught something."

Morrison folded his arms. "Why? You don't trust the Pentagon?"

"Do you?"

Morrison chuckled. "Not for a second. But that's not why you're here, is it?"

"No. You'll never guess who's in China right now."

Morrison's eyes narrowed. "I have a few guesses. Let's save some time."

"Professors Acton and Palmer."

Morrison groaned, leaning back. "Are you kidding me? What is it with those two?"

"They're just unlucky, I guess."

"Please tell me they haven't somehow managed to get themselves on one of those ships."

Leroux laughed. "No, even they aren't that unlucky. From what we can gather, they just arrived at a dig site in a city called Luoyang, about eight hours southwest of Beijing. They arrived at the same time as the events were unfolding in the South China Sea, and now appear to be in trouble."

Morrison frowned. "Let me guess, they reached out to Dylan?"

"They did, however he's deep undercover so isn't even aware that the message has been sent."

"Then how did you find out?"

"Tommy Granger contacted me."

Morrison's head bobbed. "Tommy Granger. Good kid. We might have to look into bringing him on board."

"I agree."

Morrison chewed his cheek a moment. "Well, the professors are just an American and a Brit in China in the middle of an international crisis. They don't merit any special help from us. Please tell me their Delta friends aren't galivanting off on their own."

"No, I gave Colonel Clancy a courtesy call, and he said he'd be heading off any last-minute vacations. He's sending them to South

Korea, though that was a matter of routine. A lot of assets are being redeployed at the moment."

"True." Morrison eyed him. "None of what you've said explains why you're in my office right now."

"Just a few minutes ago, we received intel through Mr. Granger that the professor in charge of the dig site in China sent a text message to Dean Gregory Milton." He held up his tablet with the text of the message and read it. "Chinese authorities looking specifically for Acton and Palmer. Do not respond."

Morrison leaned forward, placing his elbows on his desk, resting his chin on his clasped hands. "Now, that's interesting, and it changes everything, doesn't it?"

Leroux agreed. "That's my assessment as well. If the Chinese are specifically targeting them, then perhaps we need to get involved."

"Agreed. What's our level of involvement at the moment?"

"All we've been doing is advising them. They have a satphone with them, and are using that to contact us every thirty minutes. Sonya should have taken a call from them just a few minutes ago."

Morrison pursed his lips, thinking, then came to a decision. "Okay, you're authorized to provide intel to them. However, I don't want any assets involved just yet. Let's see how this plays out. What's their current objective?"

"Our recommendation at the moment is that they attempt to get to their respective embassies in Beijing. There's an added complication in that they have two Australian students with them."

"Well, the Chinese aren't after the Aussies yet, but they will be soon enough if this escalates. If we treat all four of them equally, then I would recommend they get the Aussies to their embassy first, because that should be the easiest thing to accomplish, then Professor Palmer to the British Embassy, and Professor Acton to ours. Though if the Chinese are truly targeting the Professors specifically, they'll have eyes on those embassies, so we might have to come up with some way to get them inside."

"Yes, sir, my team is already working on a plan."

"Good. Keep me posted, and try not to get me called onto the carpet at the next daily briefing."

Leroux chuckled. "I'll do my best, sir."

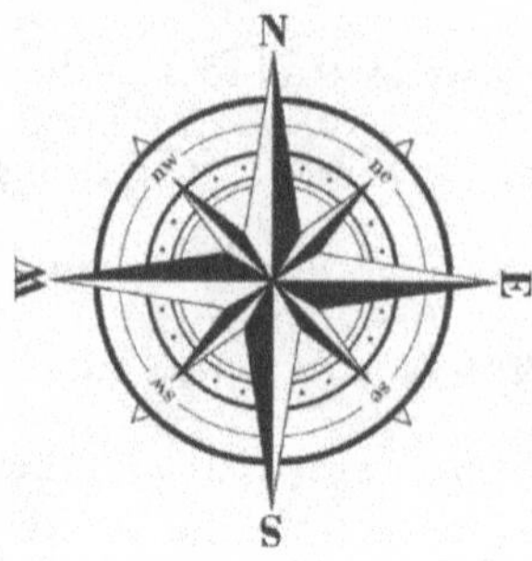

Milton Residence

St. Paul, Maryland

Milton lay on the massage table sporting nothing but his underwear as Sandra expertly massaged him. The situation had him so tense that every muscle in his lower back had screamed for a reprieve, forcing him to finally give in to her offer. His head rested in the cushioned hole, and he moaned in relief. "That's the spot right there."

Sandra kneaded her thumbs into the bundle of knotted muscles. "Yeah, I can feel it. You've done a number on yourself once again."

"I swear Jim and Laura will be the death of me."

"They quite literally were. It's a good thing I don't blame them, otherwise I wouldn't want them as our friends."

He propped himself up on his elbows and stared back at her, concerned. "Seriously? Jim's been my best friend for over twenty years. I'm not going to turn my back on that."

"Despite the fact he got you shot in the back twice, not to mention beaten, kidnapped, and God knows what else I've mentally blocked?"

Milton lay back down on the table. "Well, when you put it like that, I suppose you could make a case for cutting them out of our lives, but life isn't as black and white as that."

"And I realize that, which is why I said it's a good thing I don't blame them. I just wish sometimes that the two of them would decide they have had enough of it all, and just stay home for a change."

Milton laughed. "Have you ever actually met Jim? He's not the stay at home type."

"I know, he never has been. I had hoped that when he found a wife, he would finally settle down. Little did I know he'd just be marrying a version of him with breasts."

Milton snorted. "Don't make me laugh. It'll hurt too much."

"Mommy, I'm hungry."

Milton flipped his head to the other side and spotted Niskha in the door.

"I'll get you lunch in a few minutes, I just need to finish fixing Daddy's back," replied his wife as she continued working on him.

"How did he break it?"

"You remember when he hurt it long ago?"

"But I thought he fixed that."

"It is fixed, sweetie," said Milton. "But every once in a while it hurts, and Mommy has to tune it up like a car."

"Okay."

Niskha headed back downstairs and Sandra smacked his ass. "How does that feel?"

"The ass-smack or my back?"

"Your back!"

"Let's just put it this way, it's feeling good enough that tonight there'll be a whole lotta ass smacking."

She smacked him again, a little bit harder, and chills rushed through his body, suddenly making him curious.

He eyed her mischievously. "You're doing that again tonight."

She laughed. "You're terrible, and you're also cut off for twenty-four hours minimum until that back returns to normal."

He groaned. "Sure. Tease me with a little slap and tickle and then deny me." He became serious. "Don't worry, I'm not going to be in the mood until I see Jim and Laura safe and sound outside of China."

Sandra helped him from the table. "Me neither."

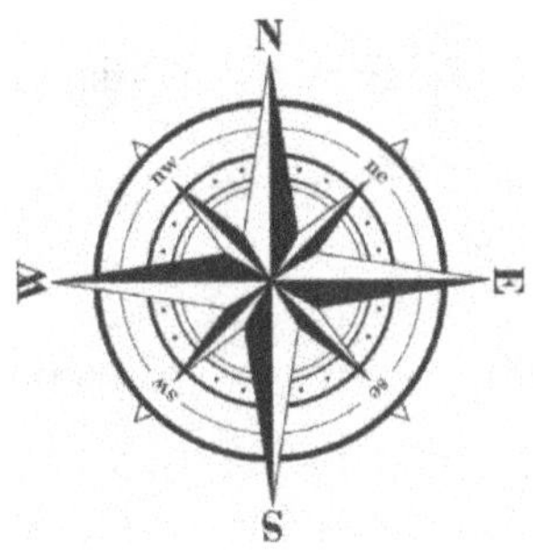

Operations Center 3, CIA Headquarters

Langley, Virginia

"What's the word, boss?" asked Child as Leroux walked into the operations center.

"The Chief says we can help the professors with soft intel—no assets, at least not yet. His recommendation is what we've already been thinking. Get the Aussies to their embassy, then Professor Palmer to hers, and then Acton to ours." He checked his watch. "What happened on the last check-in?"

"The Aussie, Kyle Rapp, had a good idea to avoid the cameras. He's now driving since nobody's after them. The professors are going to pretend they're asleep in the back seat so they can avoid the facial recognition cameras."

"Good thinking. When's the next check-in?"

"They're supposed to call in five minutes."

"Okay, any luck finding anything?"

Child nodded. "I just found some frame grabs that look interesting, but I can't tell if they're real or not. I'm still analyzing them. For all I know, they could have been taken out of a Hollywood movie."

"Show me."

Child put three photos up on the displays, one showing the helm of a ship heading toward another, the next one showing them much closer together, and the third one showing what appeared to be the aftermath of the collision.

"Interesting. Is it at least the USS Somerset?"

"I just began the analysis, I should know in a few minutes."

"Okay, do whatever you can to find the original video. Those are time codes in the corner."

"Will do."

Tong raised a finger, her other hand pressing her headset against her ear. "The Professors are checking in."

Leroux grabbed his headset and fit it in place. "Hello, Professors."

A young man's voice he didn't recognize replied. "Oh, umm, this is actually Kyle and Amelia."

Leroux's eyebrows rose. "Where are the professors?"

"They're crashed out in the back. I didn't want to wake them since nothing's happened. We've been driving for about half an hour and haven't had any dramas yet, so I thought I'd let them get some shut-eye. I can wake them if you want me to."

Leroux shook his head. "No, when they do wake up, just tell them that we've been authorized to continue to assist them in reaching their respective embassies, and that includes the two of you. Do you have your passports?"

"Na, they're at the dig site."

"Do you have any sort of ID on you that shows you're at least Australian residents?"

Amelia piped in. "I have my driver's license."

"Likewise," said Kyle.

"Then that should be enough to get you through the gates. I'm going to hand you off to one of my staff who's going to take down your exact names, addresses, and dates of birth, then relay that to the Australian Embassy in Beijing and let them know you're coming. That should get you through the gates, and then they can issue you temporary passports. That will hopefully have you safe and sound back in Australia once the crisis is over."

"Thanks, mate, appreciate your help."

"No problem. Here's my colleague." He pointed at Tong who took over the conversation. Leroux removed his headset and Child gave a thumbs down. "What?"

"It's the USS Somerset in those photos, but she's been edited in. They are fakes."

Leroux cursed. "Keep looking. We need to find something that proves the Chinese did this, that they won't be able to deny. It might be the only way we stop this thing from turning into an all-out war."

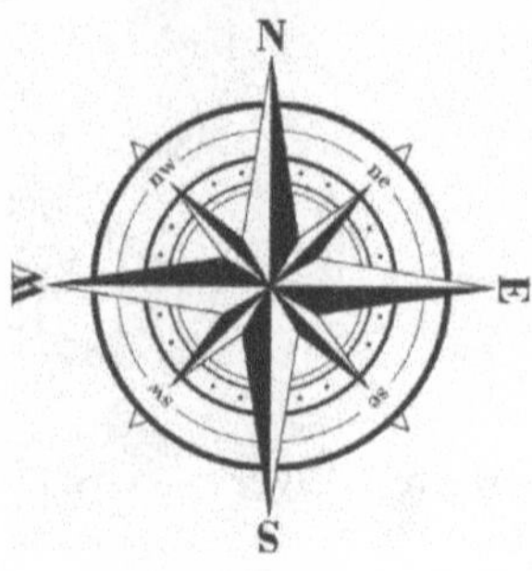

Ministry of State Security

Luoyang, China

Yan sat across from his prisoner, Professor Cao. He had let him stew for a while, and was about to begin his interrogation when a knock at the door had him bristling. He was tempted to ignore it, though it had to be important, for no one would dare interrupt him interrogating a prisoner. "Enter."

The door opened and his second-in-command, Shen, beckoned him outside. Yan stepped through the door, closing it behind him. "What is it?"

Shen held up two passports. "We found these at the dig site, sir. Two Australian passports. We interrogated the staff, and they confessed that the professors left with these two Australians, claiming they would take responsibility for them."

Yan scratched his chin, shaking his head slowly. "Why would two criminals volunteer to take responsibility for students they likely never met before today?"

Shen shrugged. "I don't know, sir. It doesn't make sense to me either. What should we do?"

"Add them to the list. I want their faces everywhere, along with the professors'."

"Yes, sir. At once, sir."

Yan stepped back into the room, closing the door. "Now, let's talk about these foreigners you had at your dig, including the two Australian students."

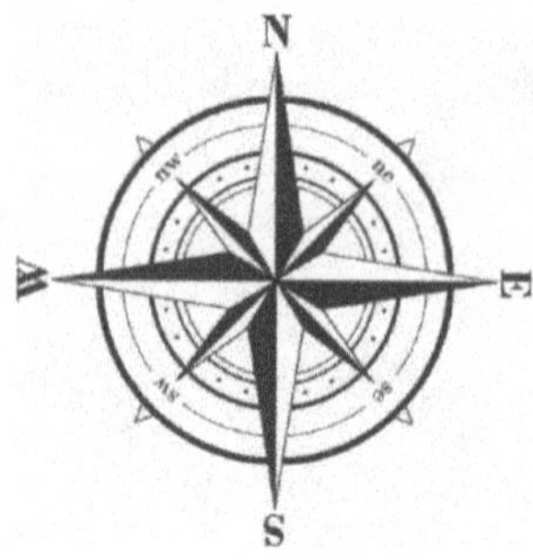

USS Somerset

South China Sea

Kidd lay in the infirmary, an IV in his arm. He was completely relaxed now, and had no doubt he was on a lorazepam drip or equivalent. And that couldn't stand. He reached over and yanked the IV from his arm. He had had a panic attack. He recognized the symptoms, and he also recognized the fact it was perfectly normal under the circumstances. Everyone reacted differently to combat, and this had been his first real taste of it. As he had lain there in a relaxed state, he had been able to think. Even if the Chinese had targeted him for his actions, what they had done was a war crime, and even if he had triggered their actions, those actions were illegal, and he wasn't to blame. The Chinese had rammed the ship, creating the incident in the first place, and he obviously had nothing to do with that. He and the others had been following orders to help rescue the Chinese, and the Chinese had opened fire on them.

And again, there was no way he could possibly be blamed.

No one had specifically told him he couldn't go over the edge to save his crewmates, though that was playing fast and loose with the rulebook. He had disobeyed orders, of that there was no doubt, but what had followed, though perhaps precipitated by his actions, should never have happened, and he was confident the powers that be would recognize that, though if they didn't, then so be it.

And then there was the fact that his ship had opened fire, as the Chinese shot at him and the survivors in the water. That wasn't an order he had given, and all things considered, that was the only hostile act taken by anyone on his side of things today.

He sighed.

Your career is sunk, but whatever happens isn't your fault. All blame lies with that Chinese moron of a captain.

"Chief, what are you doing down here?" asked the Doc.

Kidd's head lolled to the side and he spotted the Command Master Chief standing in the doorway of the infirmary.

"The Captain wanted an update." He nodded toward Kidd. "And I wanted to talk to the corpsman."

Kidd struggled up on his elbows and the Chief waved him off as he walked toward him. "How you doing, Kidd?"

Kidd dropped back on the bed. "Much better now, sir. Ready to return to duty."

The Doc laughed. "He's as high as a kite right now. He won't be returning to duty until he's off that drip for eight hours."

"What drip?" asked the Chief.

The Doc walked over and cursed at the sight of the IV dangling beside the bed. "Don't make me sedate you."

Kidd shook his head. "I don't need it. I'm okay now, I swear. I was just upset because of what I did."

"What did you do?" asked the Chief.

All his rationalizations were instantly forgotten, all blame once again squarely on him as his chest ached anew. "I started everything. This is all my fault."

Both the Doc and the Chief gave him incredulous looks. "What the hell are you talking about, Kidd?" barked the Chief. "Were you piloting that Chinese ship?"

"No, Chief. That's not what I meant."

"Then what the hell did you mean?"

"I mean, I'm the one who disobeyed orders and swam back to help the survivors. Because of me, they opened fire, and because of that, so did we."

"Bullshit. You did nothing that I wouldn't have done, Kidd. American soldiers were under enemy fire, and some ended up in the water, injured or worse. You took it upon yourself to try and save them. I doubt the Chinese even knew you were there. Those bastards opened fire on our people the moment our RHIBs were out of range. They were just looking for a new target. They would have fired whether you were there or not."

Kidd stared at him, wide-eyed. "Are you sure?"

"Absolutely."

"So, the Captain didn't open fire because of me?"

"No, the Captain opened fire to defend his men and women in the water. You just happened to be one of them." He leaned closer and lowered his voice slightly. "We just got the file on the Chinese captain. He's the son of a senior party official, and had no business being in command. Not only does he have no clue what he's doing, but he has a history of reckless behavior. There's only one person to blame here today, and it's that asshole. I don't want you giving a second thought as to this being your fault."

Kidd sighed in relief, sagging into the not-too-uncomfortable pillows. "Thanks, Chief. I really needed to hear that."

"So, you think you're fit for duty?"

"Absolutely."

"Absolutely not," interjected the Doc.

The Chief chuckled. "I mean, when he's down from his high."

"Let me reassess him in the morning. Physically, he's fine. Once the lorazepam is out of his system, I'm okay with him returning to duty. However, he should be referred for a psych eval."

Kidd groaned. "Oh, come on, Doc! I don't want to have my head shrunk."

"Standard procedure in these situations. It's just a formality. Tell him what you told us, and I have no doubt you'll be back to duty by lunch tomorrow."

Kidd frowned. "Fine, you're the doc, Doc."

The Chief and the Doc stepped away, a murmured conversation taking place before the Chief left. Kidd closed his eyes, a smile spreading as he drifted off to sleep, the intense pressure of the past few hours finally lifted from his shoulders.

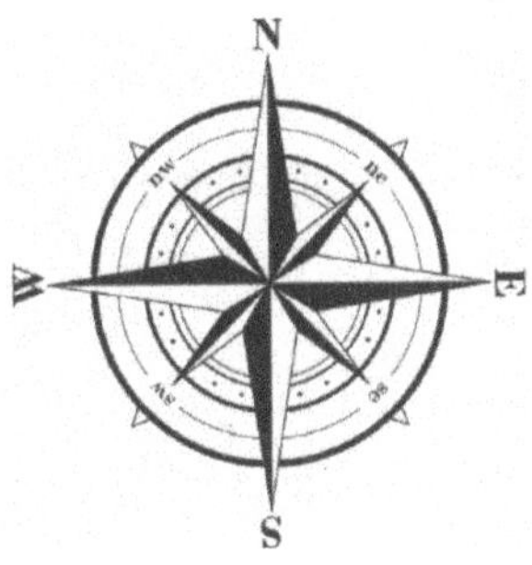

Imperial Palace

Luoyang, Han Empire

166 AD

"You're sure you want to do this?"

Jieyou wrapped her arms around Lucius, burying her head in his chest, and he could feel her nod. "Without a doubt. I couldn't go on living if I didn't."

"And you've written a letter to your father?"

"I have."

"What did you tell him?"

"I told him I've fallen in love with one of the palace guards, and we've left to live a humble life on his family farm. I've asked him not to look for me, but to know that I'm happy, and that I will always miss him and remain loyal to him."

Lucius embraced her as he felt her tears on his chest. "If this is too painful for you, then we'll find another way."

She propped herself up on her elbows and stared into his eyes. "There is no way we can be together as long as I am a princess. My father will scour the land for me, searching every farm within the realm. Our only hope of happiness is to leave this land far behind and live out our lives in Rome."

"It may be difficult for you. You would be the only one of your kind there."

"That doesn't bother me as long as I have you. And now that you've agreed, four of my ladies-in-waiting will accompany me."

"And we will have many children," he added.

She smiled broadly. "Many children. And they will fill our home with laughter and all the love and company that I will ever need."

His heart ached at the thought of the future that now lay before them. Tomorrow, the caravan would be leaving for Rome, and if everything went according to plan, her entourage would join it, disguised as peasants requesting protection during the shared portion of the journey, protection he could grant as commander of the mission. "I'll be departing first thing in the morning. When do you think your father will begin searching for you?"

"I already told him earlier that I wasn't feeling well, and not to expect me at the ceremony. He won't be looking for me until dinner at the earliest."

"That should hopefully give you plenty of time to get in position to meet up with us. And with his suspicions directed toward the household staff, there should be no risk to my father and the others, and no worry of pursuit."

She kissed him gently, her eyes closed, then pulled away. "May your gods and mine bless the future we are attempting to create."

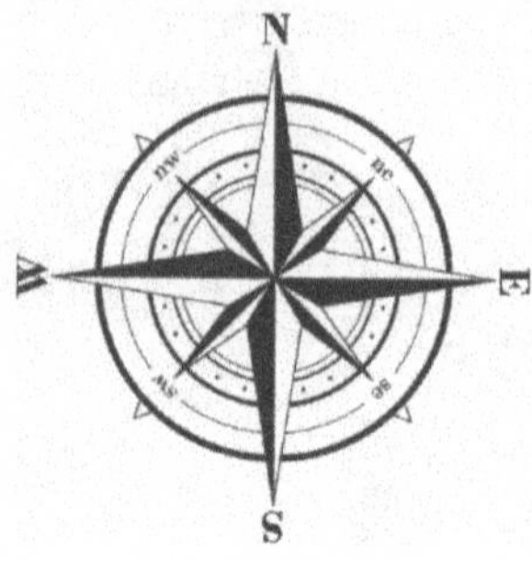

En route to Beijing, China

Present Day

Acton jerked awake at a car door closing. His startled reaction woke Laura, resting on his chest. He pushed the jacket covering their faces aside, though only slightly.

Kyle glanced over his shoulder. "Oh, sorry to disturb your slumber, Professor."

Acton moved the jacket a little more. "What's going on?"

"Just stopped at the servo to fill up."

"But I just filled it."

"Sorry, Professor, you two have been napping for almost six hours. We're only about an hour away from Beijing. I figured it was best if we had a full tank, and as far as I can tell from the radio, they're not looking for Aussies yet."

"What about the calls with Leroux?"

"We've been making them every thirty minutes."

"Anything new?" asked Laura.

"Na, not really."

"When's the next call due?"

Kyle checked his watch. "In about five minutes."

"Okay, hand me the phone." Amelia handed the phone back to him and he hit redial, deciding five minutes was too long, since he'd been out of the loop for hours. The phone rang and Leroux answered. "Hi, Chris, this is Jim Acton."

"You're a little early, Professor. Have a good nap?"

Acton chuckled. "Yeah, a little bit longer than we were expecting. The two of us just woke up after Kyle refueled the vehicle. Apparently, we're about an hour outside of Beijing. Do you have a plan for us?"

"I have a preliminary plan, though I have a feeling we're going to be changing that any moment now."

"Why's that?"

"Things have escalated on the South China Sea. Several missiles were fired at our ship, and we lost a chopper and crew."

Acton ached at the thought and Laura gripped his hand. He saw the change in demeanor of the kids. "My main concern right now are these two students. What can we do for them?"

"I've already reached out, and the Australians are expecting them. I'm texting you a set of coordinates. Enter those into your GPS. That'll provide you with the location where you can stop and let them out of the car. We're arranging a camera blind-spot for you. When they get out of the car, all they have to do is continue walking down that street, and they'll see the Australian Embassy directly in front of them. They just need to show their driver's licenses at the gate, and they'll be let through."

"Are the Chinese blocking the gate?"

"No, not yet."

"And after we've handed them off?"

"Then you'll need to head for the British Embassy. As soon as you've handed them off, call us."

"Will do." Acton ended the call and handed the phone back to Amelia who plugged it back into the charger as the phone vibrated. "Are those the GPS coordinates?"

She nodded.

"Okay, input them into the GPS."

She scrolled through the menu options, finding the proper one, then input the coordinates. The directions updated and she smiled. "Got it."

"Okay, when we get there, this is what's going to happen. You're both going to have your driver's licenses in your hand before we arrive. The moment you come to a stop, put the vehicle in park. You both get out without saying anything to us and just head straight to your embassy. Keep at a steady pace, hold each other's hands as if you're a couple. If you see police, try to avoid them without looking suspicious. If anyone says anything to you, just keep walking and get to those gates. If you're in trouble as you're approaching the gates, yell to the guards that you're Australian. Say your names and tell them you're expected, and just repeat that holding out your IDs as you run. They know you're coming, so they'll open the gates and sort things out after you're through. Whatever you do, don't stop unless they aim a gun directly at you. Understood?"

They both nodded, Amelia's eyes filling with tears. "But what about you two?"

"Don't worry about us. We've been in tougher situations than this plenty of times," said Laura.

Amelia shook her head. "If this is what you call a normal day for an archaeologist, I don't know if I'm cut out for that."

Laura laughed. "No, this isn't the normal life of an archaeologist, this just happens to be our lives. I'll give you one piece of advice if you want to lead a quieter life in your chosen profession."

"What's that?"

"Never go on a dig with us."

Acton laughed and Amelia smiled slightly, the tears finally flowing down her cheeks.

"Don't worry, Professor Palmer. I had already decided that almost eight hours ago."

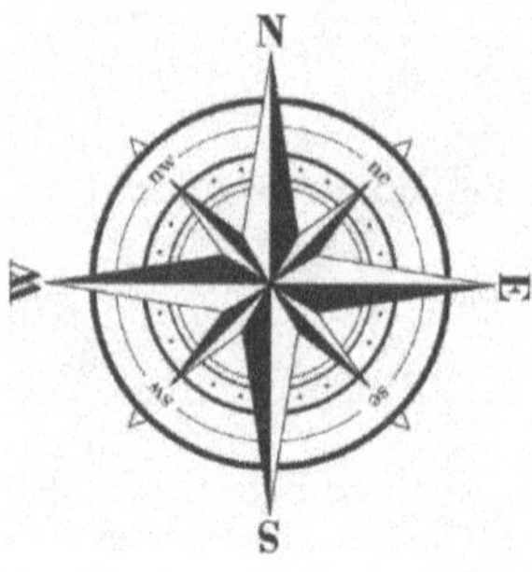

Ministry of State Security

Luoyang, China

Yan stared through the glass at his prisoner. Professor Cao had proven to be cooperative. In fact, too cooperative. It had been his experience that those with nothing to hide rarely volunteered anything, and those who wanted to appear innocent would often spout anything, including the most trivial of facts. This man had dumped his entire history with Professor Acton, providing a fountain of information should he desire to write a biography on the man, however nothing that might help in finding him.

It had him thinking the man was hiding something, and he was confident it had something to do with what had happened in that trailer. The delay wasn't caused by the man's dead cellphone. When he had picked it up, he had seen it had a nearly full charge. He had played along with him, however, letting him feel at ease, for sometimes those who chattered did reveal a critical piece of information involuntarily.

In the meantime, his team had been pulling apart Cao's life, reviewing every official piece of documentation associated with the man, and they had found something—a phone number that wasn't on the man's current official records.

There was a rap at the door.

"Enter."

The door opened and Shen stepped inside, handing him a tablet. "You were right, sir. A text message was sent while he was in the trailer."

Yan smiled.

I have you now.

Professor Cao sat in an interrogation room, facing a large mirror he had convinced himself was one of those two-way jobs with someone on the other side watching his every move. He had been here all night, and had slept for much of it, after it was clear he wasn't a priority. He now sat starving, thirsty, and with a full bladder, struggling to appear as calm and innocent as possible, yet every fidget had his pulse racing harder. Yan had asked him questions for perhaps an hour, the interrogator becoming increasingly agitated. He told him everything, everything he could possibly want to know, even volunteering information. The only thing he had kept to himself was the secret text message he had sent, and so far, Yan appeared to have no knowledge of it.

He had told him about the dig. He had told him how he had met Acton years ago. He had told him everything he knew about his guests, why they had asked to be on the dig, who Dean Milton was and why they had been added to the team roster at the last minute. He told him everything, for in reality, beyond the text message, he had nothing to hide. He had done nothing wrong, and if this international incident hadn't occurred, their visit would have been uneventful, and none of this would be happening. Yet despite all that, he was desperate to know why they appeared to be after his friend specifically, though he dared not ask.

That was the state's business, not his.

The door was flung open and he flinched, nearly wetting his pants. Yan stepped back in the room, a satisfied smile on his face as he held up some papers. "You said Dean Gregory Milton contacted you to have Professors Acton and Palmer added to your team?"

"Yes."

"And you spoke with him?"

"I did. Also, there were several emails exchanged."

"And when was the last time you spoke to him or communicated with him in any way?"

Cao's chest tightened as he was about to tell his first lie. "I guess it would have been yesterday or rather the day before yesterday. I'm not really sure what time it is. You took my watch when we arrived."

"And what was the nature of your conversation?"

"Merely confirming that I had registered them as part of the official team, and notified the proper authorities in Beijing."

"And was that through a phone call or an email?"

"An email."

"And what number do you have for Dean Milton?"

"I'm afraid I don't know. It's stored on my phone, however, which you have."

"And does anyone else at your dig have his phone number?"

"Not that I'm aware of, except, of course, for Professors Acton and Palmer."

Yan smiled smugly. "Then how do you explain that there was a text message sent by a foreign-registered cellphone at your dig site after I arrived?"

He was certain his cheeks paled, but he shook his head vigorously. "I have no idea." He had to save himself. "Maybe Jim or Laura were still in the area. Maybe they didn't go to their hotel."

"Oh, they went to their hotel. We have video of Professor Palmer arriving, going to her room, then bribing a hotel concierge to get her and her husband's passports, then that same concierge helping her escape my team. He's in the next room, being very co-operative."

Cao shrugged, attempting to maintain his picture of innocence. "I don't know what to say. The hotel isn't very far from the dig. They might have still been in the area. I just don't know."

"I think you do, Professor." One of the pieces of papers was laid out in front of him and his shoulders slumped as he recognized the documentation he had filed last year to attend a conference in Singapore. Yan placed a finger beside the contact info for while he was out of the country. It included the name and address of the hotel, the conference center, and his own personal cellphone that he used while out of country. "Would you be surprised to learn that this was the number used to contact Dean Milton while you were in your trailer, supposedly getting me the phone numbers for the professors?"

There was no denying it now. Any story he might concoct could only shift blame to one of his students or staff, and he wasn't willing to do that. He exhaled loudly, all fight gone from him. "No."

Yan folded his arms. "So, you admit you sent the text message?"

"Yes."

"And what did you say in this message?"

He quickly debated whether he could risk lying about the contents of the text message, and decided against it. This was China, and he had no doubt they already knew the contents, for everything was tightly controlled within these borders. There was no such thing as freedom, no such thing as privacy. This was a Communist dictatorship that had fooled the world into believing it was benevolent.

Yet it was anything but.

He had but one choice, and that was the truth. "I sent a message to Dean Milton, telling him that you were specifically looking for Professors Acton and Palmer."

"And why would you do such a thing? Why would you betray your country?"

"I didn't see it that way. These are my friends. Or at least Jim is. I've known him for twenty years. He's a good man. And I know by Professor Palmer's reputation, and the fact that my friend married her, that she's a good person as well. I believed that whatever reason you had for seeking them out had to be some sort of misunderstanding, and I wanted Dean Milton to be aware of what was going on so that he might be able to help clear up the matter from his end. I wasn't betraying my country, I was merely looking out for two people I thought were innocent."

Yan grunted. "If you knew what they've done to interfere in the affairs of your country, you never would have allowed them to join you, and you certainly never would have attempted to save them." The man took the papers then left the room, slamming the door shut, leaving Cao alone with his thoughts. He lay his head down on the table, emotionally and physically exhausted, and closed his burning eyes, picturing his wife and daughter, convinced beyond any doubt that they would never see each other again.

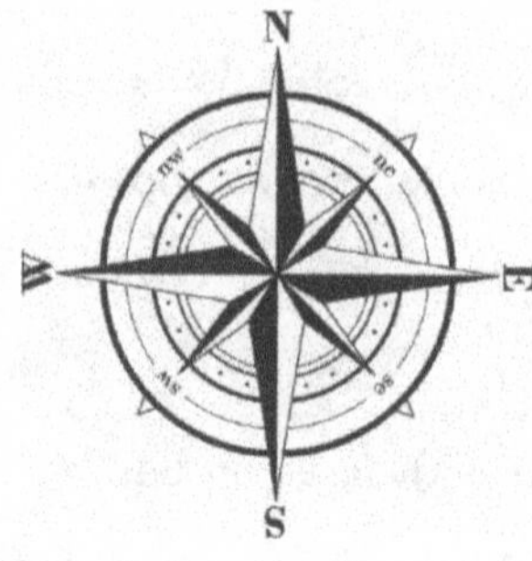

Luoyang Commandery, Han Empire

166 AD

Lucius rode at the head of the column. Ten soldiers of the Roman Empire accompanied him, along with a Han interpreter trained in Latin over the past months, an asset that might just save their lives should they encounter problems along the way. A large contingent of 100 of Emperor Huan's men also accompanied them.

And they weren't part of the plan.

It had his entire body tensed as he wondered how the plan could possibly succeed. He kept his eyes peeled for his love, who should lay ahead, and as they rounded a bend in the road, he spotted what must be her. Five women stood by a heavily laden cart drawn by two oxen, and at first, he didn't recognize her, for he had only seen her in the finest of linens or nothing at all. The rags she now wore would make her impossible for anyone who didn't know her intimately to recognize her.

The imperial soldiers ahead of them passed the apparent peasants, ignoring them, but as he approached, one of the women stepped out, blocking his path, a woman he recognized as a member of Jieyou's entourage, speaking rapidly. His limited understanding of their language allowed him to follow along, but he pretended not to comprehend a word, instead turning to his translator. "What does she want?"

"Just ignore her, sir, she's merely a peasant and means nothing to us."

He controlled his anger. "That's not what I asked. I asked you what she wanted, not your opinion on who she is."

The man cringed. "She asks if they can accompany us for protection."

He made a display of pondering the request. "I don't see why not. Put them behind the supply carts."

"But, sir, these are peasants. Why would you help them?"

He glared at the man. "We are Roman, and have no need to explain our actions to someone such as yourself."

The man's eyes diverted to the ground. "I'm sorry if I offended you, sir."

Lucius waved his hand, dismissing the apology. "Pay it no mind, but in the future, do not challenge my decisions."

"Yes, sir."

"Now, tell them they may join us."

"Yes, sir."

The man relayed the news and smiles spread through the young women, his love finally raising her head slightly, their eyes meeting for a brief moment. The caravan continued, the ox-drawn cart and its custodians pulling into the group, and Lucius relaxed for the first time all day. Their plan was working so far. He only prayed that back home, things were also proceeding according to plan.

And his thoughts betrayed him as he realized at that moment at least part of him no longer considered Rome home.

Home had become Luoyang.

If only we could be together here, life would be perfect.

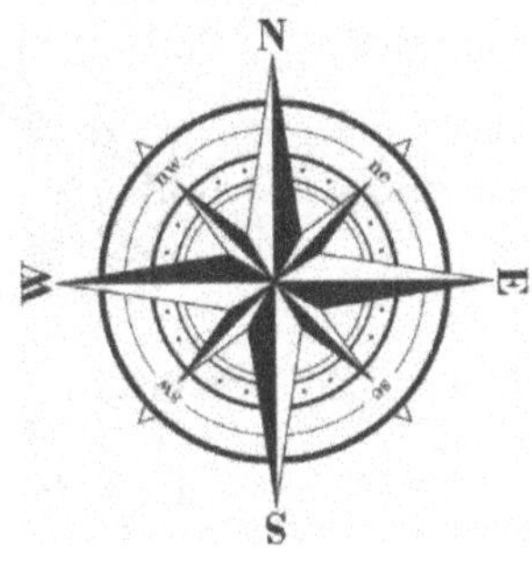

Ministry of State Security

Luoyang, China

Present Day

A knock at his office door had Yan flinching, then scrambling to straighten himself as he realized he had fallen asleep. He was exhausted, having been up for almost 24 hours straight. "Enter."

The door opened and Shen entered, a broad smile on his face as he wagged a tablet in the air. "I think we found them, sir."

Yan rose. "Where?

"Heading for Beijing. I've got footage of the Australian male refueling an hour outside of Beijing. The female is in the passenger seat. There are two people in the back seat, asleep, but none of the angles show their faces. It looks like they're intentionally covering themselves."

"That has to be the professors."

"That's what I'm thinking as well, sir."

"Get me a chopper, and notify Beijing that I'm on my way."

"The chopper's already been requested. I figured you'd want to go yourself."

Yan smiled. "Good work. Let's go." He headed out the door, confident he would soon have his assignment completed. If he played his cards right, he just might get a promotion out of this. He spotted Deputy Bureau Chief Wei approaching, a frown creasing his face.

Wei held up a hand. "Yan, I need to speak with you."

"Yes, sir."

He was guided into a conference room, Wei jerking a thumb over his shoulder, the occupants scrambling to vacate the room. The door closed and Wei pointed at a chair. "Sit."

Yan did as ordered, his stomach flipping, for he knew exactly what was about to be said.

"I've just been informed by Beijing that the ship that sank was the Yueyang. I'm afraid your brother is listed among the missing."

Yan's lungs burned and he forced himself to breathe as what he had feared was now true. His fingernails dug into his legs as he struggled to control the emotions that demanded release. "Thank you for letting me know, sir."

"Why don't you go home and be with your parents, then report back tomorrow morning?"

Yan shook his head, drawing a stinging breath through his nostrils. "No, sir. I'd rather do my duty for my country in its time of need. The best way for me to honor my brother is to bring these wretched foreigners into custody, so that whatever treachery they may be up to is prevented."

Wei nodded. "I understand. You're doing your country and your brother proud."

"Thank you, sir."

"Take a few moments before you join your team."

"Yes, sir."

Wei left the room, closing the door behind him, and Yan's lip trembled, then his shoulders shook as the tears finally flowed. His brother was dead. It was a pain that few he knew could understand, for with China's one-child policy in effect for so long, not many people had siblings if they were born within an urban center. He had been fortunate because he was a twin, and the bond between twins was like no other.

He drew a deep breath and held it, forcing himself to regain control. He wiped the tears from his eyes and cheeks, then stood, all the more determined to bring these foreigners to justice, and to avenge the death of his brother at the hands of the imperialist Americans.

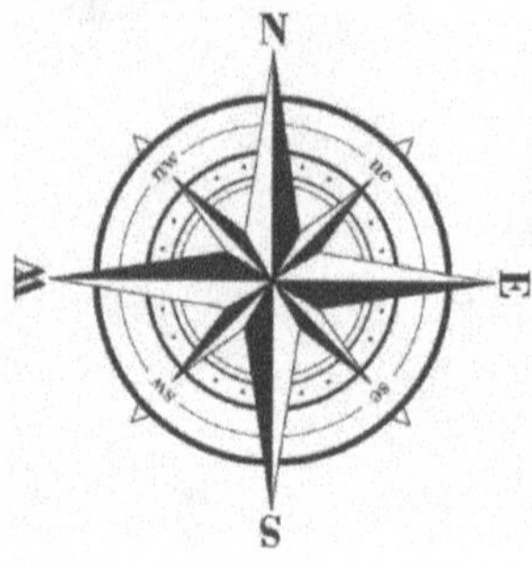

Embassy of the Roman Empire

Luoyang, Han Empire

166 AD

Ambassador Statius Seneca sat alone in his office, his chest aching with the knowledge he wouldn't see his son again for years, and perhaps never, should the journey prove fatal. Countless things could go wrong, not the least of which were the murderous seas. Yet he had to have faith in the gods and his son's abilities.

He picked up a ceremonial dagger sitting on his desk in a position of honor. It had been a gift from Emperor Trajan to his grandfather before the great shame his family had suffered, and it was a constant reminder of what had once been, and would be again. He unsheathed the blade and stared at his reflection in its polished metal, then pressed on the hilt, safely stowing the sharp instrument. It had never drawn blood, nor would it, if he had anything to say about it.

A commotion outside his window had him rising from his chair. He stepped over to the window and stared outside at the street. Scores of soldiers were rushing by, small groups stopping at each building, hammering on the doors then disappearing inside. He watched as this played out, quickly realizing they were searching for somebody as a group of soldiers stopped at the gate in front of the embassy. Two of his men approached them, though it was clear no one spoke the other's language.

He left his office and told the guard at the door to summon the translator. He strode outside into the baking heat toward the gate, raising a hand to calm the situation. "Stand down." His two men at the gate, who had been joined by several others, snapped to attention. This calmed the imperial guards considerably, and one of them stepped forward, bowing deeply before saying something. Statius understood enough to know they wanted to search the embassy for someone.

He held up a finger, and delivered a rehearsed phrase, telling them to please wait for the translator. The man bowed and stepped back, and the situation calmed for the moment. It would be against protocol to allow foreigners to search their embassy, yet they were too far away from the Roman Empire to use the threat of retaliation should the Han press their request. There would be little he could do if he wanted to stop them, though he needed to know what they were searching for, to judge the risk accordingly.

The translator, Nedum, rushed out the doors and was soon at his side.

"Find out what they want."

"Yes, sir."

A rapid-fire exchange proceeded, and Nedum's eyes bulged. He turned to Statius. "Sir, they claim Princess Jieyou is missing, and they request permission to search the embassy for her."

Statius kept his emotions in check, though his heart hammered at what he had just heard. He didn't believe in coincidences. If Jieyou was missing on the same day his son had departed for Rome, he had little doubt exactly where to find her.

And that realization meant there was no risk of allowing them to search the embassy.

He nodded. "Of course they may search, and please let them know that should they require any assistance from us, we'll be happy to provide it." The message was relayed as Statius indicated to his guards to open the gate. The soldiers rushed in and Statius pointed at two of his men. "Accompany them, and instruct the others to not interfere."

"Yes, sir."

The search party disappeared inside the embassy, re-emerging a short time later empty-handed. The commander of the small group bowed and thanked him before rushing off.

Nedum stared at him. "What do you think has happened to the princess?"

"I haven't the foggiest idea." He turned to his troop commander. "No one is to leave. Check the log, and if anyone is outside the gates, go find them. Until further notice, we're under lockdown."

"Yes, sir, at once, sir."

Statius turned on his heel and returned to his office, uncertain as to what to do. His son was young, and by definition foolish, yet he couldn't believe he would do something so irresponsible as to run off with the princess, leaving them all at risk of execution. Yet if they suspected him, if they suspected Roman involvement, then they wouldn't be searching all the houses, they would be coming to the embassy in force.

Whatever had happened, whatever Lucius and the princess had planned for the moment, appeared to be protecting the Roman contingent, though for how long, he had no idea. He feared that should they fail in finding the princess, a scapegoat might be needed. His men, so visibly different from anyone around them, could prove too convenient not to blame, for the Emperor could never blame his daughter, for it would show weakness, nor could he blame a citizen of his empire for the same reason.

But foreigners could be blamed with no shame to the Empire, or the Emperor.

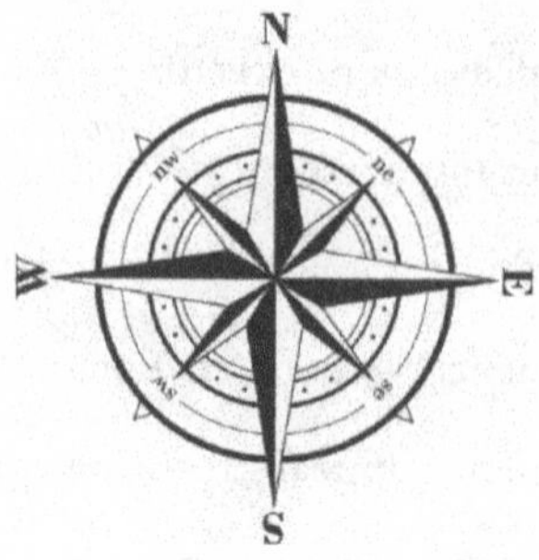

Beijing, China

Present Day

Amelia handed Kyle's sunglasses back to Acton. He fit them in place and turned up his collar. It was dawn now, and they were deep inside Beijing. They still hadn't encountered any roadblocks, and according to the GPS, they were only two minutes away from the coordinates provided by Leroux.

"Everybody ready?" asked Acton.

"Yes, sir," said Amelia, Kyle merely nodding, his knuckles white on the steering wheel, every bit as terrified as she was.

"You both have your driver's licenses?"

She held hers up along with Kyle's, holding on to his as he concentrated on driving. "Yes, sir."

"Okay. Remember, stop, put the engine in park, get out, walk hand-in-hand to that embassy. Don't look back, and ignore anything that anyone says."

"Yes, sir," she said, his voice somehow calming. She didn't know why this mild-mannered archaeology professor and his wife appeared so at ease during this entire situation, but it was comforting, and if it weren't for them, she had no idea where they might be right now.

Kyle pointed ahead as the GPS indicated they were less than 100 meters from their destination.

"Good luck," said Acton. He leaned forward and gave Kyle's shoulder a squeeze as Laura gave Amelia a quick hug from between the seats. Kyle brought them to the curb and put the vehicle in park. They both turned to face the professors.

"Be safe," said Laura.

Acton pointed down the road. "Go. Now."

Amelia wiped the tears from her eyes and opened the door, stepping out. The rear doors opened then slammed shut behind her, but she remained frozen. A hand pushed her forward, a hand that must have belonged to Laura, and she stumbled a few steps as Kyle rounded the front of the vehicle, his hand extended toward her.

She took it and he gently pulled her forward. After a few moments of indecision, he whispered, "Just breathe, it's gonna be okay."

She sucked in a breath, realizing she had been holding it, then nodded and gripped his hand tightly as the doors closed in the car behind them.

They walked briskly down the street, and goosebumps rippled over her body at the sight of the Australian flag flying proudly over the gates ahead. Then she cursed. There was a lineup of people desperate to get inside that stretched half the way there. Chinese police were on the opposite side of the road, though appeared not to be interfering, at least for the moment. For all she knew, however, she and Kyle might be on some watchlist now, because of their involvement with the professors, and the Chinese could be waiting for them to arrive.

"My driver's license."

She flinched. "What?"

"My driver's license."

She had forgotten she still had his gripped in her hand. She handed it to him as they approached the rear of the line. "What should we do?"

"I don't know."

"Should we go to the front, or just get in line and blend in?"

"If we go to the front of the line and they send us back, we'll stand out like dog's balls."

He had a point, though might be missing an important one. "Yeah, but if we get in line, it could be hours before we get in, and by then they could be looking for us."

Kyle looked at her. "Your choice."

She bristled. "Don't make me choose. That's not fair."

Kyle smiled weakly. "Let's just go with it?"

She agreed, though wasn't so sure it was the right decision.

Yan stood across the street from the Australian Embassy. He had teams positioned here as well as at the American and British embassies, though he suspected this would be their first stop. All three embassies were in close proximity to each other, but he suspected the professors would want to relieve themselves of the dead weight that were the students. He didn't particularly care about them, he merely wanted them for questioning should they not be with the professors anymore.

His comrades had tracked them into Beijing, but the cameras for this area had all gone dead simultaneously several minutes ago, convincing him even more that these professors were anything but innocent. He didn't believe in coincidence, and there was no way these cameras went down by accident the moment they entered the embassy district. This was being coordinated by enemies of the state from within, or by the CIA itself.

He scanned the long lineup of foreigners waiting to enter the Australian Embassy, holding his tablet in front of him to remind himself what these two students looked like. He had been here for half an hour, and the fatigue was getting to him. He had managed to get a little bit of sleep on the helicopter, the roar of the engines and the vibrations of the rotors soothing. But his mind was working against him as his thoughts continually drifted to his missing and presumed dead—at least by him—brother, part of him wishing he knew why the Politburo wanted these professors, for if he had his druthers, he would empty the magazine of his sidearm into both their heads as retribution for what the Americans had done to his brother and his shipmates.

"Sir."

Yan turned to see Shen pointing across the street at two young Caucasians walking quickly past the line. He held up the tablet and sneered. "That's them."

As they walked past the line, Amelia glanced over at the Chinese contingent, noting several of them were holding up tablets. "What do you think they're for?"

Kyle glanced over then quickly turned his head away. "I'm guessing they're comparing mugshots. Do you think they have ours?"

"If they're after the professors, then they will know we were at the dig site too, and probably know we left with them. They'll assume we know where they are."

Kyle frowned. "So, what should we do?"

A shout erupted from the Chinese side and she glanced to see one of the policemen pointing directly at them. "We run!" she cried as she let go of his hand and sprinted toward the front gate. She could hear Kyle following her, right on her heels. She glanced over her shoulder to see several of the Chinese police running across the street, dodging the traffic. She held out her license, remembering what Acton had said to do.

"I'm an Australian citizen! My name is Amelia Robinson. Please let us in!" Kyle shouted the same behind her, and she repeated her cry as they sprinted past the line. "I'm an Australian citizen! My name is Amelia Robinson! You're expecting us! Please open the gate!"

She could hear the Chinese getting closer, nearly across the street, yet she didn't dare look. Acton had said to ignore them, though the pounding of boots behind them as they ordered them to stop in Chinese and in English was impossible to ignore.

Especially the one distinct order that now resonated through her.

"Stop, or I'll shoot!"

Yan yelled the warning in English, though he had no intention of following through—it would be exceeding his orders. His only hope of capturing and interrogating them for clues as to where the professors were was to stop them before they crossed into the embassy grounds. He was almost at the other side of the street now, and they were only feet away.

He reached out for the arm of the young man, and to his dismay, he spotted a side gate opening. The girl was nearly through, but the boy was still within his grasp. He reached out, his fingers gripping the sleeve of the Australian's shirt.

Amelia pressed on. Acton had said to ignore everything unless a gun was aimed directly at her, and as far as she was concerned, if she didn't see a gun, then none was aimed in their direction. They were almost at the gate now, and she shouted her plea one more time, one of the guards finally noticing. A side door opened and a man stepped through, beckoning them. Kyle cried out behind her, but she couldn't stop now. She burst through the small gate and crashed into a guard, bringing her to an abrupt halt. She checked over her shoulder to see Kyle wrench free from one of the Chinese who had a grip on his shirt, then rush through. The gate shut behind them as several Chinese police slammed into it, shouting demands.

The man who had let them through held up a hand, walking over to the gate. "This is the Australian Embassy, and under international law, you have no right to pass without a recognized request from your government. Unless you can show me such a request in writing, and it is approved by the Ambassador, I'll kindly ask that you back off."

The police slowly fell back, clearly not pleased with this turn of events, and as the last fell out of sight, Amelia was gently pushed away by the guard toward Kyle. She embraced him, hard, the two of them sobbing uncontrollably in panic and relief.

And she prayed that the professors would be as successful as they had been in finding safe harbor.

Yan gave the gate one final shake of frustration, the law clear. He wasn't getting inside without the proper paperwork. It was a common misunderstanding that the grounds of an embassy were considered foreign soil. They were not. That was in the movies. The reality was the grounds were protected by international treaty, and that treaty made provisions for entry by the host country.

But protocol had to be followed.

He growled in frustration and spat through the bars before turning on his heel and marching back across the street. He waved a finger in the air, making a circle. "Everybody to the British Embassy." He climbed into the vehicle assigned to him, all the while muttering curses, determined more than ever to seek his revenge.

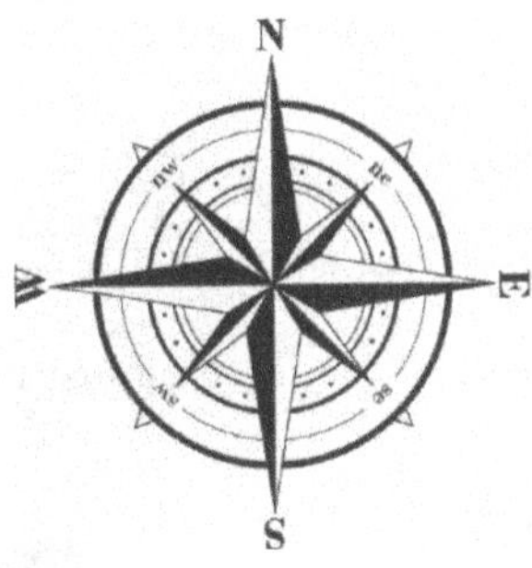

Operations Center 3, CIA Headquarters

Langley, Virginia

Tong raised two fists into the air in triumph as she leaned back in her chair, executing a Randy Child spin. "We've just received confirmation that the Australians are safe!"

Leroux smiled as cheers erupted around the room, high fives and fist bumps exchanged. "Excellent! Good work, people. What's the status of that camera outage?"

"We've got maybe two more minutes."

"Get me the professors."

Tong tapped at a keyboard then nodded as Leroux fit his headset into place. The phone rang and was answered immediately.

"Hello?"

"Hello, Professors, this is Chris. I just wanted you to know that the students are safe inside the embassy."

"Oh, thank God," said Laura. "Thank you so much for helping them. I know you didn't have to."

"No problem, Professor. Now it's time to get you two to safety. We've already spoken to the British Embassy and they're willing to give you priority access, Professor Palmer. You just need to get to the main gate. They're waiting for you."

"What about James?"

"Unfortunately, they're only allowing British nationals inside at this point. There are just too many people."

"That's okay," said Acton. "The priority right now is to get Laura to safety."

"Bollocks!" cried Laura. "The priority is to get *both* of us to safety."

"And just how would you propose we do that?" asked her husband. "The American Embassy probably has the same policy."

Leroux inserted himself into the spat. "It does, but there's no point in even attempting it. The American Embassy has been completely surrounded. There's no way you're getting in there."

"Then what will happen to James?" asked Laura.

"We're already working on something, but it only works with one person. We need you safe before we can help your husband."

Laura cursed. "Well, I don't like it."

"It's okay, hon, they've gotten us this far, they'll get us the rest of the way. Let's just get you to safety."

She sighed heavily. "Fine."

"What's the plan?"

Leroux exchanged a glance with Tong, frowning. "You're not going to like it."

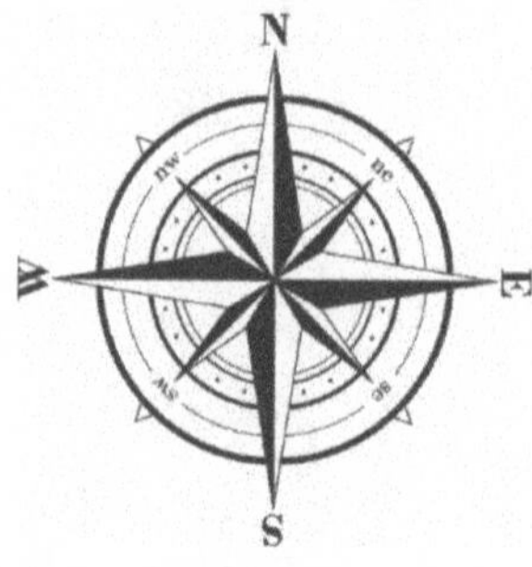

Luoyang Commandery, Han Empire

166 AD

Lucius slipped from his tent and slowly walked through the camp. The imperial contingent was set up around them, and he had instructed that the "peasants" be provided with tents and set up at the edge of the Roman area, as he feared the Han soldiers wouldn't protect people of their status. He had paid close attention, and knew which of the two tents into which Jieyou had gone. She wasn't alone, yet obviously there were no secrets between her and her ladies-in-waiting accompanying her. He walked over to the tent then examined his surroundings, making certain no one was watching before ducking down and climbing inside.

Jieyou lay curled up on the floor, one of her ladies-in-waiting opposite her, a lamp burning between them casting a dull glow. He reached out and gently squeezed her leg. She bolted upright, a dagger hidden under her blanket emerging. He held up his hands. "It's me."

She relaxed and lowered the knife, then threw herself into his arms. They held each other tight, and he caught the lady-in-waiting smiling at them. She turned over to give them some privacy.

"You shouldn't be here," said Jieyou.

"I know, but I couldn't resist, knowing you were so close yet so far. Did you encounter any problems?"

"No, we were able to get away easily. My people have become quite adept at moving in and out of the palace, what with our goings on."

He smiled. "Good. We'll be rid of this contingent of soldiers soon enough. They're just a ceremonial guard and are supposed to accompany us to the border of the commandery, and then we'll be able to relax a little bit. Just make sure people don't get a good look at your face, and that your people stay quiet and don't interact with anyone, especially the Han soldiers. Stay as close to my people as you can."

"Are they aware of what's going on?"

"No, the only people who know are you and me, and whoever you told. Once we're rid of the Han contingent, I'll make a show of taking a liking to you, then invite you and your friends to come to Rome with us. My men will accept that."

"It will take weeks before we reach the outer boundaries of my father's empire."

"Hopefully, nothing will go wrong between now and then."

"Trust in the gods."

He smiled. "I always do, though I find too often, they expect those under their dominion to help themselves."

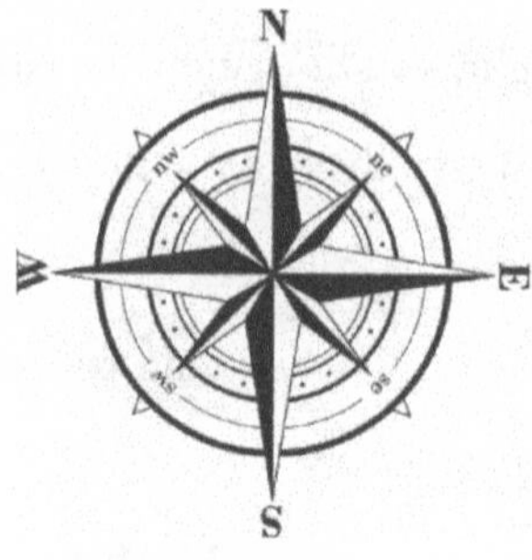

USS Somerset

South China Sea

Present Day

Kidd heard laughter and a smattering of Chinese, or at least what he assumed was Chinese, drifting down from the deck above. The rescued crew of the Chinese frigate were held topside, and he had to see for himself how many had managed to survive, and how they could possibly be in such good spirits after what had occurred. He climbed the ladder and emerged from the hatch. To his left, he could see several RHIBs conducting a recovery operation for the chopper crew lost in last night's attack. With the sun now up, he prayed they might find something they had missed in the dark, though he was certain they wouldn't, and if they did, anything they found would merely be body parts. He just prayed the helicopter had gone with a skeleton crew and not a full complement.

He rounded a corner and found what appeared to be thirty, perhaps forty survivors, all in orange life jackets provided by his ship, all sitting on the metal deck. Somebody laughed and his head spun toward the sound. One of the prisoners held a cellphone, playing what appeared to be a video of the stricken helicopter falling out of the sky. A pit of rage formed and he stormed past the guards, snatching the phone from the man's hand. He delivered a swift kick to the man's head, ending any laughter.

"You realize this is all your fault, don't you? None of this would have happened if you morons hadn't done what you did! Good people are dead because of you! You should be ashamed of yourselves! You should be ashamed of your country, you pathetic pieces of shit!"

He spun on his heel and headed back toward his quarters, one of the guards holding up a hand to stop him.

"Don't worry, Corpsman, nobody saw anything."

Kidd grunted, only at that moment realizing what he had done was probably a violation of some international convention. He headed back below decks, the phone still gripped in his hand, and then found a nook out of the way of the others rushing around. He watched the video, his stomach churning, his head shaking the entire time as if this were confirmation that what he had witnessed first-hand wasn't a cruel hallucination or dream.

He stopped the video then brought up the other files stored on the Huawei device. He tapped on the previous clip and his eyes shot wide as it showed a gunnery crew on the Chinese vessel opening fire on the rescue team, the man who had taken the video giggling uncontrollably as he said something in Chinese. The rage grew inside him as he brought up a third video that appeared to have been taken near the prow of the

Chinese ship, showing the entire sequence of their vessel ramming the Somerset.

And he finally realized what he had in his hand.

The proof that could stop a war.

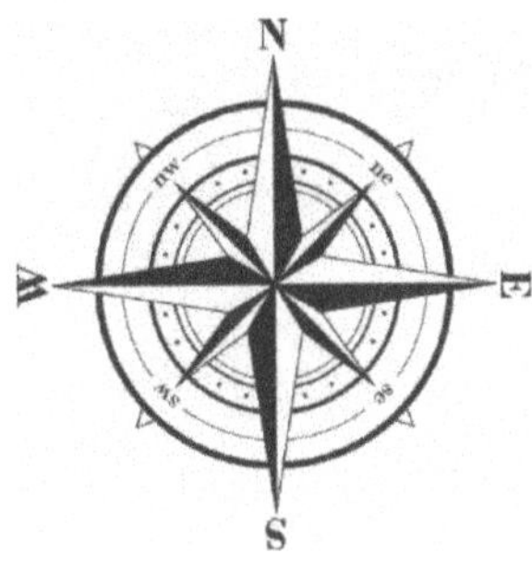

Approaching the Embassy of the United Kingdom

Beijing, China

Laura spotted the Union Jack flapping in the wind, relief and trepidation consuming her. She was perhaps only minutes away from safety, but also minutes away from leaving the love of her life behind, and she was torn. She didn't want to go. She didn't want to leave him alone. They had been in this together from the beginning, and she was willing to face whatever consequences that might lie ahead alongside her husband. But if the CIA had a plan in the works to save him that could only work for him alone, then her selfish desire to remain at his side could put the life of the man she loved at risk.

"Are you ready?"

She held up her passport. "Ready." She leaned over and gave him a quick peck on the cheek, her eyes pools of tears as her voice cracked. "Be careful."

He grinned at her, but she could see the pain and fear in his eyes. "You know me, I'm Mr. Careful."

She squeezed his leg. "I love you."

"I love you too." He nodded toward the windshield and she looked, the front entrance of the embassy just ahead, a long line of her fellow Brits desperate to get inside, queued on the street. "No matter what happens, you just go."

A single tear escaped from each eye, both wiped away swiftly.

"Here we go."

He was traveling at full speed with the traffic, the Chinese not having closed off the British Embassy yet, all their focus still apparently on the American. He hit his flashers and brought them to a swift halt, the traffic behind him protesting with honks of their horns. Laura threw open her door and jumped out, slamming it behind her. As she ran toward the front gate, somebody shouted and she turned her head, spotting a dozen Chinese soldiers racing toward her, an Armored Personnel Carrier pulling into the gap in the traffic created by James having come to a stop.

She checked over her other shoulder to see him with his hands raised, several soldiers with automatic weapons rushing toward the vehicle, aiming directly at her husband. He stepped out of the car and their eyes met.

"Run!" he shouted. "Run!"

It took her a moment, then she turned and sprinted the last few steps toward the gate, holding up her passport. "I'm Laura Palmer, a British citizen! You're expecting me! Open the gate! Open the gate!"

Somebody on the other side jogged down toward the gate, shouting orders. "Open it! Open it!" The gate slid open several feet, and as she was about to cross the threshold into United Kingdom territory, somebody grabbed her arm, their grip like iron.

She screamed and tried to yank her arm away, but it was no use. She reached across the barrier and the man who had given the order grabbed her hand, pulling on her, and she was now the rope in a tug of war between two nations.

"Let her go, you bastards!" shouted James, and his voice yanked her out of her state of panic, giving her a moment of clarity. Her foot snapped out, buckling the man's knee. He cried out, his grip loosening, and she spun her arm, breaking his hold, and yanked free as she was hauled inside the embassy gates.

"Close the gate! Close the gate!"

The gate rumbled shut, the panicked crowds still running away from the terror that had just happened. She pressed against the metal bars, sobbing as her beloved James was shoved to the ground, a boot pressed against his head as he was handcuffed and searched. He was hauled to his feet and their eyes met. She could see the relief on his face at her now being safe.

"I love you!" he yelled.

She reached out to him through the bars. "I love you too! I won't stop until we're back together!"

"Just stay safe!" he said as he was led away then shoved into the back of a police vehicle. She spun toward the man who appeared to be in charge.

"I need a phone. Now!"

Acton was shoved into the back of a police vehicle and the door was slammed shut. A man climbed into the passenger seat and peered through the grate that separated them.

"We meet at last, Professor Acton."

Acton stared at the man as he struggled to calm himself. He had to get the adrenaline pumping through his veins under control, otherwise he wouldn't think straight. He was under arrest in a communist country that might be in a state of war with his country at any moment. He had been arrested publicly and violently, which had him thinking the Chinese didn't care about optics. The fact the man knew his name also confirmed what Leroux had told him.

They were after him and Laura specifically.

He drew a deep breath and exhaled slowly, then stared at the man. "Do I know you?"

"No, Professor Acton. I'm Special Agent Yan of the Ministry of State Security, and before this day is through, you'll wish we never met."

Yan signaled the driver and they pulled from the curb. Acton leaned over to see Laura one last time, and caught a glimpse of her at the gate, still gripping the bars. And as he turned his head, keeping her in view as they drove away, he couldn't help but wonder if this were the last time that they would see each other.

Imperial Palace

Luoyang, Han Empire

166 AD

Statius was a bundle of nerves as he strode toward the Imperial Palace. He had convinced himself that his son was indeed behind the disappearance of Princess Jieyou, though he had no evidence to prove it. Either way, it was simply the coincidence of it, and the fact he knew his son had an eye for her from the moment he had spotted her in the palace.

And he had caught the young woman's reciprocal smile, her own interest evident.

He had been young once, and men that age thought with the wrong body part. If his son had carried on a clandestine relationship with this woman over the past months, he had no doubt the boy was in love with this woman, and if she had agreed to leave with him, the feelings were obviously mutual. While he couldn't fault young love, he could curse the boy for putting all their lives at risk. Sometimes one couldn't control who one fell in love with, but one could control whether one followed through with it.

And this was one instance where his son shouldn't have, as there was no hope of it ever ending well. This was a princess of an empire they had no formal relationship with, and little understanding of their culture. What was universal, however, was that the daughters of emperors were never meant to marry those so far beneath them as his son was.

He had been summoned by Emperor Huan, and wasn't certain as to why, though the fact he had been allowed to arrive unaccompanied, suggested no suspicion had yet fallen upon him or his people. He bowed deeply, and the Emperor flicked his wrist in acknowledgment. Statius rose. "How may I be of service, Your Highness?"

Huan spoke, his translator, now proficient in Latin, interpreting. "As I'm sure you are aware, our daughter, Princess Jieyou, went missing yesterday. We have conducted a thorough search of the city and the surrounding area, and have found no sign of her."

"Yes, Your Highness, I am aware of this, and please know that I pray for her safe return."

"As do we."

"Do you have any idea who took her?"

Huan listened to the translation, waiting several moments before he responded. "We are going to share with you something that few know of. Our daughter left a note."

Statius' eyebrows rose involuntarily, and his heart rate picked up a few notches, for if his theory of what had transpired had indeed occurred, this note could have revealed the truth. "And what did this note say?"

"It said she had fallen in love with one of the palace guards, and they had left to live a simple life on his family's farm."

Statius steadied the exhalation of relief that threatened to escape, and questioned whether his theory was accurate after all. "Have you been able to verify this? Have you been able to identify who this palace guard is?"

Huan shook his head. "No, and if it were true, then one of our guards should be missing as well, yet all are accounted for."

Statius' pulse thundered in his ears with the implications. Huan was implying that his daughter's note was a lie, and the fact he was being told, suggested the man suspected he or one of his people might be involved. He had to deflect any notion of that. "Could the letter have been forged?"

Again, a shake of the head. "We recognize our daughter's handwriting. It was written by her hand. There is no doubt."

"Then what do you think it means?"

Huan beckoned someone in the far corner with a finger. Two guards marched forward, hauling a young woman between them. They shoved her onto the floor in front of the Emperor. The girl's shoulders shook as she sobbed in terror.

"Tell him what you told me," demanded Huan.

The woman spoke rapidly, the translator struggling to keep up. "I am sorry for my betrayal, but the princess ordered me not to tell anyone, but she and the son of the Roman ambassador have been carrying on an affair since the night he arrived. They have run off together to be married in Rome."

Statius staggered back a step, the words shocking despite the fact they exactly matched what he had feared was happening. He had to tread carefully now, the fact he was still alive a shock, and perhaps temporary. He dropped to a knee and held his deferential position. "I can assure you, Your Highness, I had no idea this was happening. Please tell me how I can correct this situation."

Huan rose and everyone in the court bowed. "The damage is already done. The betrayal is complete. As we speak, all within your embassy are being executed. The walls will be knocked down, the remains of what you built buried. Any sign of the Roman Empire within our realm will be wiped from existence. You, your son, and his entourage are all that remain of Rome within the borders of this empire. We have already dispatched messengers to catch your caravan. All of your people will be executed save your son, who will be returned here. You will be executed before his eyes, so he can witness the consequences of his actions."

The words took a moment to register, and Statius' response was muted. "And what will become of my son?"

"He will endure a death so long and so painful, that it will echo through the ages."

"And your daughter for her betrayal?"

"She too will die alongside him. Today, because of your son, we all lose."

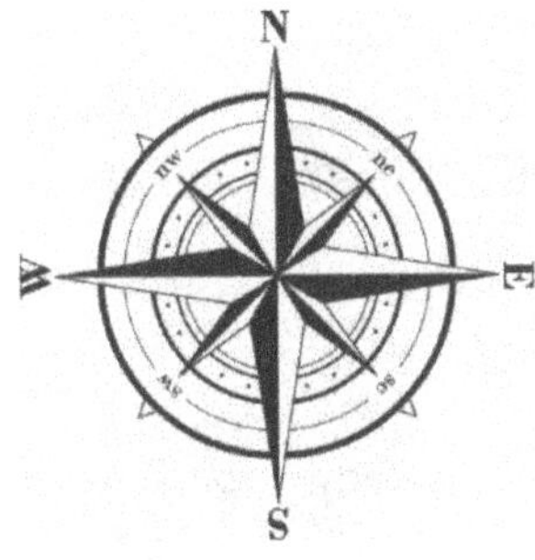

USS Somerset

South China Sea

Present Day

Kidd watched as the others in his assigned quarters stared at the video. Their shock and rage were obvious. Everyone on board now knew about the chopper crew that had sacrificed their lives to save them all from an anti-ship missile that had made it through their defenses, and revenge was on everyone's mind. Word that another crew was already out there if needed, prepared to sacrifice themselves like their comrades had, gutted them all. He would love to join those who wanted to go above decks and beat the living shit out of the Chinese prisoners then toss them to the sharks, yet what he had discovered could bring it all to an end.

He was handed the phone back.

"What do you plan on doing with it?" asked Reese, his best friend on board and fellow corpsman. "I'd be posting that shit on the Internet right now."

Kidd shook his head. "I can't. The Internet's shut off while we're under GQ."

Reese frowned. "When those Chinese get here, you won't have any chance to post it. And if they sink us, it means it's lost forever. You have to get it to the Captain."

It was a decision he had already come to, but he just needed someone else to say it. "Should I go directly, or up the chain of command?"

"To hell with the chain of command, go direct. What happens if just one person decides to sit on it? And even if they didn't, minutes are important here. Another missile could be on its way for all we know, another chopper crew could be about to die." Reese jabbed a finger at the phone. "That shit is important. The Captain needs to see it now."

Kidd drew a breath. "You're right." He left the quarters and headed for the bridge, confident he was ultimately doing the right thing, though still scared shitless. He had never been on the bridge, and wasn't sure how firm he should be in his insistence on seeing the Captain, as he had no doubt he would be challenged.

He was better than halfway there when a voice behind him had him freezing. "Corpsman, what are you doing here? I thought you were supposed to be going to your psych eval?"

He spun and his stomach was instantly a bundle of knots at the sight of the Command Master Chief. He had completely forgotten where he had been heading when he heard the Chinese crew laughing, but he figured what he had discovered during his detour would provide him a reprieve. He held up the phone. "Chief, I confiscated this from one of the Chinese prisoners. It has footage of them ramming us, and opening fire on our survivors in the water."

The Chief's eyes shot wide. "Show me."

He played the video clips for him, the Chief shaking his head the entire time.

"Where were you heading with this?"

"I was bringing it to the Captain. This is the proof the Chinese are responsible. If we can get the word out, then maybe we can end this before it's too late."

The Chief regarded him. "Why didn't you follow the chain of command?"

"I didn't think there was time, sir. I saw that chopper shot out of the sky for no reason. They didn't have to die, and I didn't want to be responsible for any more deaths. The Captain has to see this now."

The Chief agreed. "Follow me." He walked briskly toward the bridge and Kidd scrambled to keep up. "Make a hole!" ordered the Chief, sending the crew scrambling to get out of his way. Minutes later, they were on the bridge. Kidd gulped as the Chief whispered something in the second-in-command's ear, pointing at him. The commander nodded and the Chief beckoned Kidd over. "Show him the video."

Kidd played the clips, the commander's eyes widening with each one. He took the phone and walked it over to the Captain sitting in his chair. "Captain, you need to see this."

"What is it?"

"Exactly what we need."

The Captain watched the clips and cursed. "Where did you get this?"

Kidd snapped to attention. "I was topside and saw one of the Chinese prisoners playing the clips for some of his crewmates. I confiscated the phone and brought it immediately here once I saw what was on it."

"Good work, Corpsman." The Captain handed the phone back to the commander. "Get this to Seventh Fleet headquarters immediately."

"Yes, Captain." The commander headed to the communication station and the Captain turned to Kidd.

"We'll take it from here, son. Return to your station."

"Yes, Captain."

The Chief gave him a surreptitious thumbs up and Kidd grinned then retreated from the bridge, returning to his quarters as quickly as he could, praying his good deed could erase the damage he might have done earlier by having disobeyed orders and gone back into the water.

For no matter what the Chief had told him earlier, he still felt responsible.

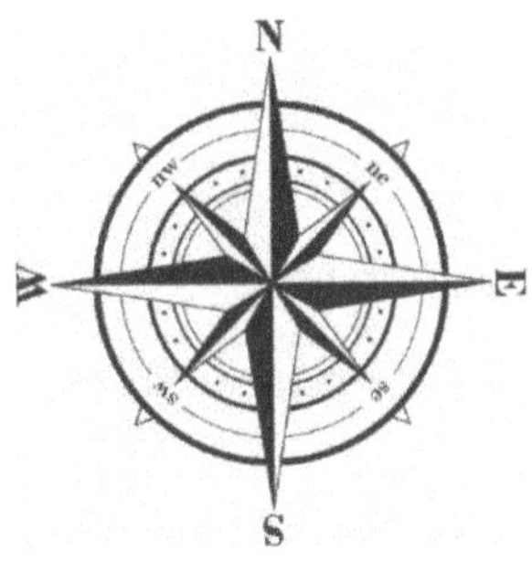

Embassy of the United Kingdom

Beijing, China

Laura's fingers trembled as she dialed the digits she had written on a piece of paper before getting out of their car. She had left the satphone with James and just prayed she hadn't written the number down wrong. It rang twice before a woman answered.

"Hello?"

"Hello, this is Professor Palmer."

"Hello, Professor. This is Sonya, are you okay?"

"I'm inside the British Embassy, but the Chinese just arrested James."

"Understood. Just stay put and don't do anything stupid. We'll work the problem from this end."

Laura decided objecting to the 'stupid' line would be pointless, and was arguably sage advice considering her and James' track record. "Can you help him?"

"We'll do whatever we can. I have to go now."

"Okay, I'll call you back with a new number as soon as I'm established here."

"Understood, Professor. Goodbye."

The call ended and she turned to the man, handing him back his phone.

"Who were you speaking with?"

"I'm not sure if I can say. Let's just say they're people who can help."

The man eyed her. "Very well. However, let me make something perfectly clear. That's the last call to the CIA you make from within these walls."

She tensed. "What do you mean?"

"I mean, if the Chinese think that we're in any way associated with the Americans, especially the CIA, they very well might come through those gates and arrest every single one of us."

Her cheeks flushed and her chest hurt at the realization. The man was absolutely correct. The call had been foolish, and she should have asked permission before making it. "Do you have any secure means of communication?"

"We do. I'll check with the Ambassador, however with the current situation, I wouldn't get my hopes up. Everyone's a little paranoid right now."

Laura frowned. "And rightfully so."

He held a hand out toward the main building. "Come with me. Let's get you cleaned up and some food into you, then we'll figure out what happens next."

She smiled weakly at him. "Thank you. Thank you for everything." She followed him into the building as she struggled to control her emotions. James was in the hands of a brutal regime that had no respect for human rights or international law, and if things didn't calm down soon, some hot-head might just mete out his own dose of revenge on the only American to which they had access.

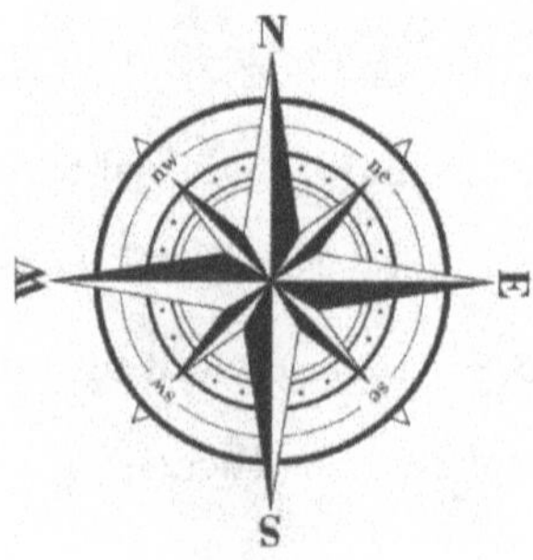

Luoyang Commandery, Han Empire

166 AD

Lucius rode at the head of the Roman contingent, still surrounded by their escort, when the entire procession was brought to a halt. He rode forward with his second-in-command, Valerius, and their Han supplied translator. He was greeted by the commander of the Han forces, who bowed deeply before delivering a rapid-fire speech that Lucius understood little of, even his translator struggling to keep up, leaving out far too many words for his liking. The gist of the man's message, however, was clear.

They had reached the border of the commandery, and they were on their own, the honor guard's orders fulfilled.

Another bow was executed, an order shouted, and the imperial soldiers of Emperor Huan turned around and briskly marched away. He suppressed his smile, for they had succeeded. They had managed to escape the capital, and with every step they took, they would be that much closer to the river that would swiftly carry them to the sea, and away from any further danger. He indicated for the column to proceed, but his translator raised a hand.

"What about the women?"

Lucius eyed the man, and if he didn't need his services, would have dismissed him for his continued impudence. "What of them?"

"Why are they still with us?"

"They asked if they could stay, and I granted them our protection."

"But they belong here with their people. If they leave, they'll be in more danger."

Lucius decided it was best to play the part he had discussed with Jieyou last night. "Not that it is any of your business, however I tire of these questions. One of the young ladies paid me a visit last night, and convinced me, shall we say, to allow them to continue to travel with us, perhaps all the way to Rome if my liking for her continues."

Smirks and snickers from his countrymen greeted this revelation, but the translator was appalled. "You would bed one of those creatures? They're filthy vermin, not worthy of our protection, and certainly not worthy enough to share the bed of the son of the ambassador of the Roman Empire. If this is what your empire feels is appropriate, then I question how we could possibly have any treaty with you."

Lucius bristled, his hand gripping the hilt of his sword. "You would be wise to mind that tongue of yours, lest it be removed. I think you would find your chosen vocation very difficult without it."

The man showed none of the fear Lucius would have expected, instead merely meeting his gaze. "You wouldn't dare touch me, as you require me more than I you. In fact, my instructions were to accompany you for as long as I felt my services would be helpful, and I have no desire to share the road with those who would consort with the likes of them." He spat at Jieyou and her entourage.

Fire burned in Lucius' stomach at the disrespect shown not only for him, but for Jieyou and her ladies-in-waiting. Yes, the man had no idea who they were, and perhaps his anger was merely irrational. But these women weren't slaves. They were citizens of the Han Empire, and at least deserved some modicum of respect. Even in Rome, the lowliest citizen had rights, and though he might ignore them in the streets that he walked, he couldn't imagine treating them the way this man did.

If this man had his druthers, the women would have been left defenseless on the road, vulnerable to anyone they might have come across. The very thought of anything untoward happening to a group of innocents, whether he knew them or not, whether they were Romans or Han, sickened him. His father had raised him to believe that all citizens were equal, and all people deserved respect—even the slaves that worked their household.

It had always been his family's policy that should a slave reach the age of 40, they would be granted their freedom. And what he had always found comforting was that almost every slave granted it, had happily remained under the household's employ as a freeman. Many of his father's friends felt similarly.

And if this vile man were any indication, such sentiments were rare in the Han Empire.

"I'll be leaving you now, and rest assured the Emperor will have a full report of what has transpired."

"It is your right to leave." Lucius drew his sword and plunged it into the man's belly, twisting the blade several times, scrambling his innards. "As it is my right to protect the interests of Rome."

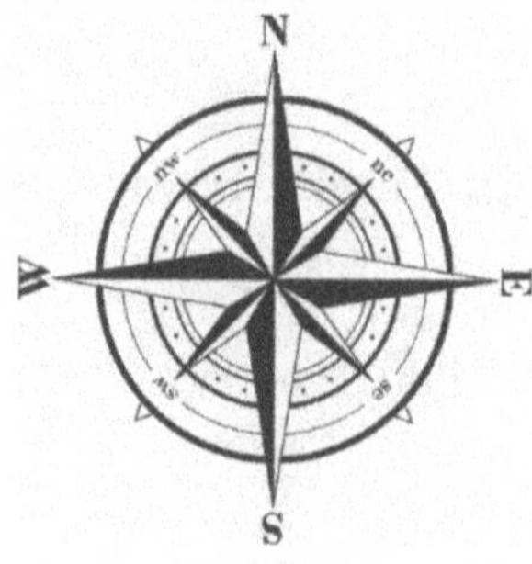

Ministry of State Security Headquarters

Beijing, China

Present Day

Acton gasped as yet another blow was delivered to his stomach. He was being screamed at in Chinese, the inflections suggesting questions were being asked, but even if he understood them, he was never given any chance to answer. The beating had begun the moment he had arrived in the police station and placed inside an interrogation room. Two police officers stood in opposite corners, staring straight ahead expressionless, while the man in charge, Yan, delivered on his promise Acton would wish they had never met.

As each blow landed, and Acton became weaker and weaker, he had the distinct impression that what was happening was personal. Something more was going on here. If the Chinese had been after him and Laura specifically, then why wasn't he being asked any real questions? He wasn't sure how much more of this he could take. He had been beaten before, and with the way his luck ran, he had no doubt he'd be beaten again, though that assumed he survived this one, which was particularly vicious.

If this were personal, then this man was out of control, and if someone didn't stop this, he very well might die. He thought of the vicious beating that Milton had suffered not too long ago, and how he had ended up in the hospital nearly paralyzed once again. He thought of all the pain and suffering that Milton's family and friends had suffered as they worried about him, and Acton was determined not to let this man win the day.

Yan stepped back, exhausted from his efforts, the hurling of fists physically demanding. Acton spat on the floor, a mixture of spit and blood splashing at his feet as he made a decision that might just cost him his life. He stared at one of the cops standing in the corner and prayed he spoke English.

"If he kills me, your government will hold you responsible, because they'll never get the information they're looking for. You better stop this now."

Glances were exchanged, suggesting at least one of them understood what he said. His interrogator screamed at him, a fresh flurry of blows landing, but out of the corner of his eye, Acton spotted one of the guards leave the room, and prayed relief would soon be at hand, as blow after blow, delivered in rage, not duty, continued to rain upon him.

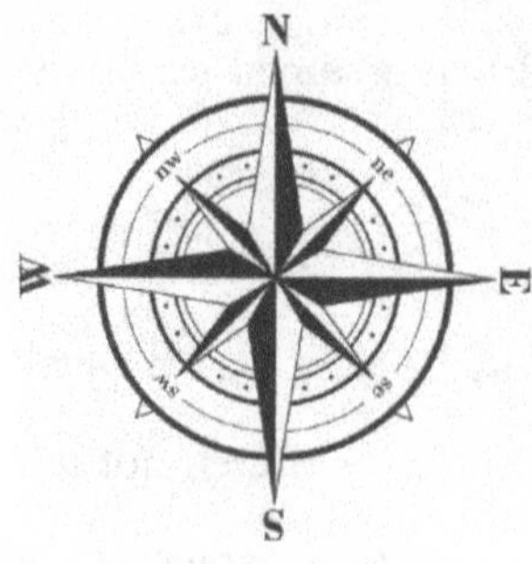

Operations Center 3, CIA Headquarters

Langley, Virginia

Leroux leaped to his feet as Director Morrison entered the operations center. "I just sent you a secure file," said Morrison as he joined him at the center of the room. "Bring it up on the main display."

Leroux nodded at Tong, whose fingers flew over her keyboard. A video appeared, then two more, spread across the displays. His eyes widened as he realized what he was watching. One showed the collision of the two ships from the Chinese perspective, another showed them opening fire on people in the water, and the third showed an American helicopter shot out of the sky. "Where did you get this, sir?"

"Apparently, a sailor on the USS Somerset confiscated it from one of the Chinese survivors. The Somerset captain sent it to the Seventh Fleet command, who passed it on to the Pentagon. They've asked for our help. The Chinese fleet is less than thirty minutes from our vessel, and ours are almost two hours. We need this pushed out, so it's all hands on deck.

Do whatever it takes to get this out to everyone. We need the world to know that the Chinese started this entire damned thing."

"Why can't the Somerset just leave the area?" asked Child.

"She's got a gash in her hull. She can make ten knots at best."

"We'll take care of it, sir." Leroux turned to Child. "Work your magic."

Child spun in his chair, a grin on his face. "With pleasure." He dropped a foot, killing the spin, then went to work.

"What's the latest on the professors?" asked Morrison.

"The Australian students are safe in their embassy, and Professor Palmer is as well. Acton was arrested by the Chinese in a pretty violent takedown. We've got some footage from the Brits on it, if you want me to send it to you."

Morrison waved a hand. "No need, I'll take your word for it. What's your plan?"

"We're trying to locate Acton, and with your permission, effect a rescue. I'll need to activate one of our assets."

Morrison pursed his lips, staring at the three videos playing on the screens, no doubt weighing the risks of authorizing the operation. If the dissemination of these videos had the desired effect, Acton might be let go without their involvement, however the opposite could also be true. Acton had been specifically targeted, and whoever was behind it might realize their window of opportunity was narrowing, and either brutally interrogate him, or simply eliminate him.

Morrison headed for the door. "Go ahead. But make sure whoever it is doesn't start World War Three just when we're about to prevent it."

"Understood, sir."

Minzhi Dynasty Hotel

Beijing, China

Jack—just Jack—lay on the bed of his underwhelming hotel room in central Beijing. There was nothing luxurious here whatsoever, and that was intentional. He had been in Macau when hostilities broke out, and had immediately left the administrative region for mainland China, then to Beijing, where should it become necessary, he might be of some use if things progressed to the next level.

And the authorities wouldn't be coming to this shithole seeking Americans.

His CIA issued TAG Heuer watch pulsed on his wrist, indicating he had a secure communiqué. He pressed a combination of buttons around the watch face, and the message was projected onto the crystal.

Check secure email.

He flipped open his laptop and logged in, then found the email from his handler. He read the message, his head slowly shaking. Professor

James Acton needed rescuing once again, though this time it appeared his wife had managed to save her own ass, and there weren't any students involved anymore, the two Australian students also managing to save themselves. Acton had been arrested outside the British Embassy less than half an hour ago, and he was now tasked to effect a rescue if possible.

Though he wasn't sure how the hell he could manage that. He replied back with the secure communications package installed on his laptop.

I will need a location.

The reply was instantaneous.

You'll have it as soon as we have it. Your regular supplier has been compromised. Use Chan Chao.

He frowned. He had used Chan just recently. He was normally Kane's point of contact in Beijing. His concern wasn't that Chan was competent or unable to assist him, his concern was more for the fact that the person he had dealt with for years, might be in trouble. He replied back.

Copy that, heading there now.

He opened the false bottom of his suitcase and pulled several items from the concealed compartment, then headed into the bathroom, preparing to head out into Beijing as a CIA spy during a time of crisis.

He stared into the mirror.

"What could possibly go wrong?"

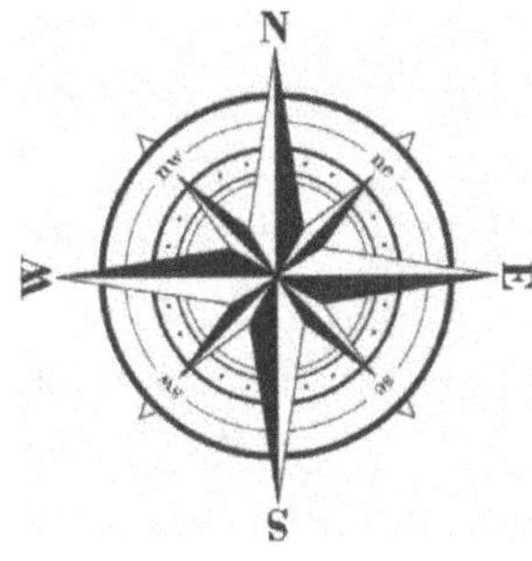

Ministry of State Security Headquarters

Beijing, China

The door to the interrogation room flung open and Yan spun, directing his rage at the interruption toward whoever had just entered. He gulped at the sight of his boss.

"Outside, now!"

Yan hurried into the hallway with his boss, who appeared none too pleased with him. He was surprised to see the man, unaware he had made the journey to Beijing, what with everything going on. It just added to his shame and fear for his future. And to the fact he had forgotten his mission—to bring in the two professors for questioning by the Politburo, not him.

"Just what the hell do you think you're doing?" demanded Deputy Bureau Chief Wei.

Yan stood at attention, his eyes directed at the floor, his chin pressed against his chest, his lungs burning from the physical exertion torturing a prisoner required—though that pain was easily overwhelmed by the aching in his fists. "I'm sorry, sir. I was interrogating the prisoner, but he refused to volunteer any information as to his activities or the location of his wife."

"Bullshit! I watched you in that room. You were asking questions, but you were doing so with no interpreter. And you never gave him an opportunity to answer regardless. You let your emotions about your brother overcome you. I thought you had been trained better than that."

His shame was complete, for Wei had witnessed his lapse in judgment. "Yes, sir, so had I. This was my failing, not my trainers', and I certainly hope would bear no reflection on you or your department. It was a frustrating manhunt, and with the news of my brother and the possible war with these vile Americans, I lost control. I apologize and surrender myself to you for any punishment you may see fit."

Wei regarded him for a moment before finally speaking. "Unfortunately for you, your life isn't in my hands. The Politburo member who ordered Professor Acton's arrest will be calling in five minutes to speak with the professor and decide his fate. Have him cleaned up and checked over. If he dies from the wounds you inflicted, there's nothing I can do to help you."

"Yes, sir."

"Dismissed."

Yan snapped to attention then pivoted on his heel, marching down the hall. He turned around the corner. "Get me some medics, now!"

The half-dozen men that stood there stared at him for a moment before one of them leaped to his feet. "Right away, sir." The man grabbed the phone off his desk and Yan returned to the door of the interrogation room, his chest heaving once again with the realization his actions might not only have ended his career, but ended his life.

I just wish I knew why the Politburo wanted Acton.

Acton sat slumped in the chair, uncertain how long his reprieve, granted with a single barked order by a man with a paunch and a clearly higher rank than Yan, would last. The new arrival poked his head back into the room and pointed at him, saying something in Chinese to the two guards before leaving again. The guards un-cuffed him from the chair he had been in since he arrived, then stepped back as what appeared to be two medics entered the room, immediately attending to him.

One cleaned up his bloody face as his female partner took his vitals, then began pressing on various parts of his body, each wince noted with a comment in Chinese. He could breathe, though with some difficulty. He was certain he had some cracked ribs, and he prayed none were broken. It was internal bleeding he was concerned with, so many of the blows focused on his stomach.

A light was shone in his eyes to check for pupil dilation as the man with the paunch stepped back into the room, a single question posed. The lead medic made a rapid report, and the paunch didn't appear pleased. A reluctant nod was finally given by the medic, and the man in charge left the room. The medic followed then returned with a gurney that must have been in the hallway.

With the guards' assistance, Acton was loaded onto it, and he sighed with relief that his ordeal was finally over, though what challenge he faced next might be worse. He suppressed a frown, instead paying attention to every detail around him, for if they were taking him to a hospital, the narrow window provided might be his only hope of escape.

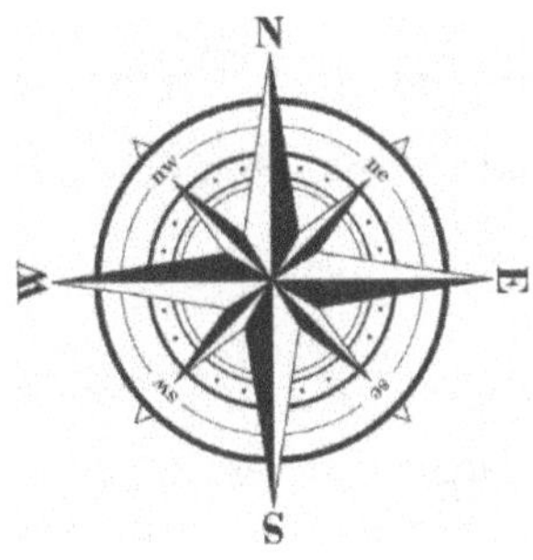

Embassy of the Roman Empire

Luoyang, Han Empire

166 AD

Ambassador Statius desperately wanted to weep at the sight before him, but he wouldn't give these murderers the satisfaction. His hands were shackled in front of him, though his feet had been freed for the tour in which the Emperor had insisted he participate. All of his people were dead, blood smearing the floors and walls. His guards had been slaughtered, though he noted with satisfaction at least a score of the enemy had been taken with them. He had no doubt his men had fought valiantly, and had merely been overwhelmed. If the numbers had been at par, he was confident his men would have prevailed.

Yet that was not to be. None had been spared, including the Han servants that worked at the embassy. All had fallen under the blade of the attackers. He thanked the gods that his son had had a change of heart, and hadn't been here along with the small contingent he had taken with him. Some of his delegation had survived, and he prayed they would escape Emperor Huan's troops, though if they did, they would return to Rome with a treaty meant to seal a pact with an empire that had shown it had no honor and no respect for the long-established laws of diplomacy.

Rome would send a larger contingent, and when they arrived at the end of their arduous journey, they would be slaughtered as well, including his son should he choose to return, though he had a sneaking suspicion that had never been the boy's intention. He had no doubt his son would be establishing himself with his forbidden lover in the family home, and beginning a family of his own, never to return, never to know the consequences of his selfish actions.

Yet knowing all of that, Statius still prayed his son succeeded, for no matter what he had done, he still loved him and wished him no harm.

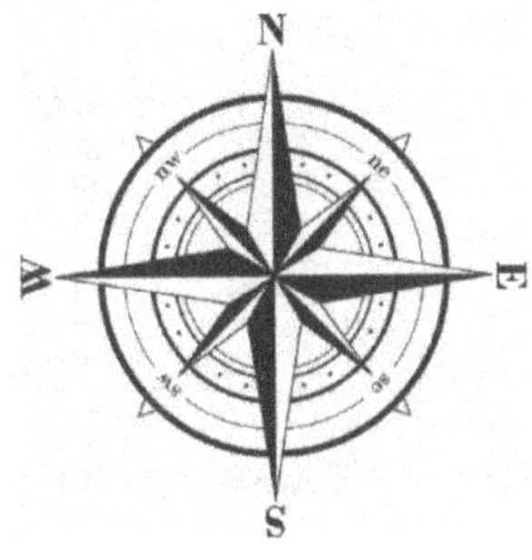

Li's Photo, Zhongguancun E Plaza

Beijing, China

Present Day

"Ooh, hot stuff on its way!"

Chan Chao paused from preparing the supplies Langley had requested for their operative, and eyed his wife, Bing. "Leave the poor kid alone. He's young enough to be your grandson."

Bing frowned at him, her lower lip puffed out. "You're so mean."

"Only because I've grown tired of you after forty years."

She batted a hand at him. "Nah, you love me and you know it."

"I'm a glutton for punishment. I only love the pain."

She walked over to him and patted him on the cheek. "Nah, you love me."

He groaned. "I suppose I do."

She grinned. "Good. Then prove it by giving me two hours alone with that young hunk. He'll keep my imagination fired up for another year or two, which will spice up our love life. And I'll pay it forward by teaching him a few tricks so he can satisfy the next generation of young women."

Chan shook his head as he doublechecked the list. "Do you see me fawning over the young female agents we deal with?"

"Of course not. You know I'd cut your nuts off."

"I'm sensing a bit of a double standard here."

Bing shrugged. "Men had the first hundred-thousand years, now it's our turn."

He laughed. "I suppose we did. But like they say, two wrongs don't make a right."

"They might not, but they do feel right sometimes." She grabbed her boobs and lifted one then the other. "What do you think?"

He became serious for a moment. "I think you're as beautiful as the day I married you."

Her eyes glistened and she dropped the girls. She embraced him and he held her tight, kissing the top of her head. The chime on the front door of their shop rang, and she pushed away, wiping the tears from her eyes. "I hope that's my stud."

He laughed. "You're incorrigible."

"Isn't that why you married me?"

"It was part of the reason. But it was mostly because you had a great ass." He smacked it and she squealed.

"Hands off the merchandise, I'm back on the market for the next two hours."

"Unfortunately for you, he's not going to be here long enough." Chan stepped out of the rear office and into the antiquated shop, the entire operation a front for the CIA. He received very few customers, mostly those wanting their old cameras repaired.

He sold nothing that wasn't at least a decade out of date.

The CIA paid him well, however he couldn't flash that money around. Most of it was held offshore in the event they required extraction someday. He loved his country, but he hated the Party. He and others like him, worked behind the scenes in the hopes that one day Chinese democracy would be a reality.

Chan smiled at the familiar face standing in the entrance. He pointed at the door. "Flip that sign, would you? And lock the door."

Jack—just Jack—flipped the sign indicating they were now closed, then engaged the deadbolt.

Chan regarded the young man. "I didn't think I'd be seeing you again so soon."

Jack shrugged. "My guy has been compromised, apparently."

"Well, let's hope it was something he did that was stupid and not you, otherwise you could compromise us."

Jack shrugged again. "I'm perfect at my job, so I'm sure it was nothing to do with me."

Chan laughed. "You're even cockier than Kane is."

"I do tend to overachieve."

Chan shook his head. "I think it's a prerequisite for people like you. You're all cocky, even the women."

"Langley told you why I'm here?"

"They did. I have all your stuff in the back. Do you know your target?"

"Yes, I do. A good man with a habit of getting in trouble."

"I read his file. That man shouldn't be allowed out of Maryland, let alone the United States."

Jack laughed. "You'll get no argument from me."

Chan led him into the back office and his wife straightened herself, batting her eyes at Jack, this not their first encounter.

"You couldn't stay away from me, could you?"

Jack's eyes widened in a combination of horror and confusion. Bing had been relentless the last time Jack was here, and the poor boy hadn't known what to make of her. And Kane wasn't any help, instead taking delight in the fact he was no longer the object of her desires.

Chan loved his wife, and knew it was just an act. She had always been flirtatious, and he wasn't the jealous type. She would never act on anything. It was just her own way of having fun and feeling young.

When they had met, she had been stunning. Every boy had wanted to be with her, yet he had prevailed in the battle for her heart. They had led a good, happy life, though when they had been recruited decades ago by the CIA, their life had become more complicated. It wasn't that their life-potential had been limited—they were never going far in this communist state—instead, it had led to a more reclusive one.

Friends of traitors tended to die along with them when caught.

Since they had no family or friends connected with the Party, whatever life they would have had without the CIA would have been even more difficult than the one they now led. He didn't fear dying, or rather, he no longer feared dying. When they were younger and had a life ahead of them, it had been a concern, though his was mostly for her. They had never had children, one of the two of them incapable, and neither of them had any desire to know who was to blame. They had chosen to be together, therefore the blame was equal.

Instead, they enjoyed the simple pleasures in life of being each other's best friend, and spending time together, whether that was in conversation, preparing meals, or simply watching television or listening to the radio. The only excitement were moments like these when secret agents came through their door, and, occasionally, he had to take action himself to save one of their asses. Just last week, one of the fools had used a certain notoriously unreliable British sportscar as a getaway vehicle. He didn't get far, and after Chan had rescued him, he had received a lecture concerning reliability over style.

Chan pointed at a table, the gear requested by Langley all laid out. "This is everything they thought you might need. Let me know if you think you need anything else."

Jack went to work, sorting through everything. He picked up the police uniform. "Do you have somewhere I can change?"

"You can change in my bedroom," offered his wife. "I'll help you."

Chan rolled his eyes at her. "Leave the poor kid alone." He pointed at a door. "Just go through there. The bathroom's the first door on the left."

Jack smiled and disappeared.

A machine beeped in the corner and Chan tossed his head back, sighing loudly. "Finally!" He stepped over and removed the facemask just printed according to the specifications provided by Langley. He gently placed it inside a case designed for this task. The mask was delicate at this stage, and normally would have been allowed to rest for at least half an hour, but there was no time.

Jack emerged from the bathroom, decked out in his police uniform indicating he was a colonel. It was a high enough rank that it would give him the respect and flexibility he would need, though not high enough that he might be recognized as an imposter, for many of the young officers desperate to climb the ladder made it a point to memorize all the faces and names of the asses needing kissing to achieve their goals.

"How do I look?" asked Jack foolishly.

Bing was immediately at his side with an answer. "Fetching. I love a man in uniform."

Jack stared down at her, his face serious. "And I love an older woman. Where did you say that bedroom was?"

Chan's chest tightened for a split second before he realized what was going on, though his realization came much quicker than his wife's. She stared up at Jack, her eyes wide, shock on her face as her bluff was finally called. Jack leaned in to kiss her and she quickly stepped back, wagging a finger at him as she laughed, finally catching on. "You're a clever one, you are."

Jack laughed and winked at Chan. "Hey, I was just checking to see if you were serious."

Bing stepped closer to Chan and he put an arm around her. "I'm a one-man woman, but don't tell anyone. It'll affect my reputation. Besides, I wouldn't want to ruin you for other women"

Jack chuckled then filled his pockets with the various tools of the trade. "Do you have my face?"

Chan opened another case, revealing a face that matched all the ID generated for Jack the moment he had received word the agent had arrived in Beijing and his usual contact was compromised.

Jack stared at it then compared it to the identification cards. "Doesn't really look like much just lying there, does it?"

Chan shook his head. "Of course it doesn't. It has no face behind it. That's just a lump of skin until it has some structure to go with it." He lifted it out of the case and gently applied the adhesive around the edges before pressing it into place. Within moments, Jack was transformed into a Chinese People's Armed Police colonel, carrying all the identification papers of a genuine officer who had gone home early with a case of food poisoning, if the CIA was correct.

Jack turned to her. "Now, how do I look?"

She shook her head, frowning. "Not nearly as good. I guess I like white boys."

Chan looked to the heavens, praying for strength, then pointed at the other case. "That's the face for the professor. It's still setting, but should be fine should you succeed in extracting him."

"Do we have a location for him?"

"Not that I'm aware of." Chan pointed at the set of comms on the table. "Langley is waiting for you to contact them."

"Who's Control?"

"Analyst Supervisor Chris Leroux."

Jack smiled. "Good. I know him. He has a competent team."

"Yes, he does."

"Is he white?" asked Bing.

Jack didn't play along. "Never met him. He could be purple for all I know." He fit the earpiece deep in his ear canal then clipped the tiny transmitter into a hidden slot inside his belt. "Control, this is Rawhide. Come in, over."

The response was immediate. "Rawhide, this is Control Actual, we read you, over."

"Control, do you have a location on the target yet?"

"We do. He's being held at the Ministry of State Security Headquarters."

Jack frowned as he looked down at his uniform. "Well, there's no way I'm getting in there, fake ID or not. That's one of the most secure buildings in the country."

"Agreed. We need you to set up some eyes so we can monitor the building for when they bring him out."

"Do you think they're going to?"

"They will eventually. I'm not sure if you've heard, but footage has been found proving the Chinese were behind the incident in the South China Sea. It's being broadcast all across the world."

Jack grunted. "Somehow, I doubt it's being broadcast here."

"Not officially, but we have our ways. It's making the rounds on Chinese social media faster than they can take it down. Enough people will have seen it before they shut the whole system down, but what the Chinese people think is irrelevant, it's what the world thinks. Assuming their leadership can react quickly enough, we're hoping to have this situation calming down soon."

"And if it doesn't?"

"Then don't stand near any fans."

Jack chuckled. "Good advice on any day in this job. I'll let you know when I have those eyes set up."

"Copy that, Rawhide. Be careful out there."

"I always am. Rawhide, out."

He turned to Chan. "I'm going to need the smallest cameras you've got."

Chan pulled a box from the shelf behind him then removed the false bottom, revealing a set of state-of-the-art cameras.

Jack smiled. "You'd never think you had cameras like these, judging from what you have out front."

Chan gave him a look. "That's kind of the point, isn't it?"

"I suppose so." Jack grabbed half a dozen of the cameras and stuffed them in his pockets, then fit his hat in place. "Time to save the world."

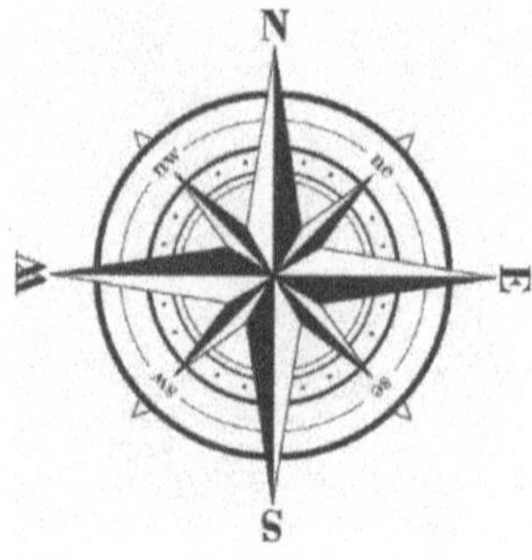

USS Somerset

South China Sea

Kidd was officially back on duty, the psych eval requirement waived by the Captain after he had proven his head was in the game by not only proactively confiscating the phone with the evidence that might stop a war, but having the balls to bring it directly to him. The bodies of the chopper crew had been recovered, and he was relieved to hear there were only two on board. The crew was subdued with the knowledge two more of their crewmates were dead, but they were also on edge as they scrambled to make repairs to the gash in the hull so they might improve their speed. They were in a race with the Chinese, who were steaming at full speed to their own ten knots.

The bulk of the Seventh Fleet, including the aircraft carrier USS Ronald Reagan, were at flank speed, rushing to reach them. However, they would arrive over an hour-and-a-half after the Chinese would catch up to them. Super Hornets patrolled the skies above them, ensuring air superiority should there be a battle, however the question was how far the Chinese were willing to go? He was just a corpsman, not privy to the intel that the admirals and the government were, and his only window into the mind of the Chinese came from his father, who claimed their way of thinking was completely different than the Western way.

There was no thought for the individual.

Everything was geared toward what was best for the state, the implication being that what was best for the state was, by extension, best for its population, and therefore, ultimately, best for the individual. And if individuals had to be sacrificed to achieve the goal of the state, then from what he understood, those individuals were sacrificed without hesitation.

That conversation from several years ago had him wondering whether the Chinese would be willing to sacrifice several of their ships just to eliminate the USS Somerset? Was this a face-saving game? An eye-for-an-eye operation? Would they come in firing, or would they merely surround them, making demands then bugging out when the fleet arrived?

He had no idea.

Nobody did.

All he knew was that the thought of a dozen Chinese ships closing in on them was a terrifying notion. He just prayed that the videos he had found would be enough to stop the thing before it was too late.

A lieutenant entered the infirmary and spoke to the Doc then left. The Doc pointed at Kidd. "Pick four corpsmen and head topside. They want you in position for when the Chinese arrive. Your responsibility is to treat any casualties among the Chinese prisoners."

Kidd's eyes shot wide. "Are you kidding me?"

"I don't kid, Kidd. They're our prisoners. Hell, they're not even prisoners, they're survivors. International law says they're our responsibility now."

"Do you think they'd actually do the same for us if the roles were reversed?"

The Doc shrugged. "That's not for me to say. All I know is I couldn't give a shit what they would do, all I care is that we do our duty and do it well, because the next time the roles might be reversed, and they're going to look back on what we do today when they decide how they're going to treat us tomorrow."

Kidd frowned. The Doc was right.

Do unto others as you would have them do unto you.

"Sorry, Doc. I didn't mean to question your orders. It's just been a rough day."

The Doc slapped him on the shoulder. "No worries, Kidd, even I have my doubts." He pointed above them. "Pick four and man your station."

"Yes, sir."

The GQ alarm suddenly sounded. "General Quarters! General Quarters! General Quarters! All hands man your battle stations!"

Kidd's heart leaped into his throat and he pointed at the four nearest corpsmen that weren't already tending to patients, including his friend Reese. "Let's go!"

They scrambled out of the infirmary then up the nearest ladder as the ship banked hard to port, the chase over, the Captain turning to face their pursuers for the battle about to ensue. As he came out onto the deck, he gasped at the sight of the dozen Chinese vessels on the horizon, rapidly closing the gap.

And swore to throw overboard any of the Chinese who dared interfere or even celebrate what was about to happen.

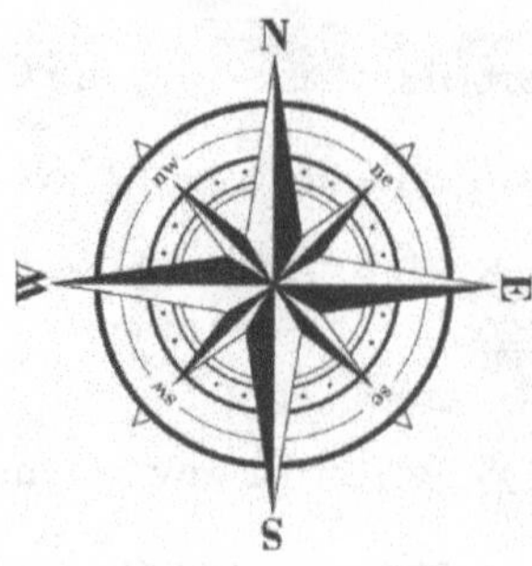

Milton Residence

St. Paul, Maryland

The doorbell rang and Milton put the remote control down, about to answer the door when Sandra waved him off. "I've got it. You stay put and rest that back."

The door opened and he could hear Sandra greeting their guests, Tommy and Mai. They had called earlier to find out if he had heard anything, and had sounded upset, so he had invited them over. Everyone was tense, not just in his household, but in the entire country and indeed the entire world. The Chinese were showing no signs of backing down, and even the commentators were only guessing as to why.

Few thought the Chinese wanted war. They had to know it was their own vessel that had caused the initial incident, so this wasn't a revenge operation. They were likely testing American resolve by threatening an American ship. Would America fire first and risk war? If they did, the Chinese would likely back down rapidly, but if America didn't, it would give the Chinese the answer they had been seeking to the ultimate question.

Did the American government fear the Chinese military?

And if they did, would they avoid conflict at all costs?

It opened an entire suite of options previously denied the Chinese, the biggest of which was laying total claim to not only the South China Sea, but in retaking Taiwan itself. America had vowed to protect Taiwan, however that was an old promise made in different times, and the Chinese would love nothing more than to take back a significant piece of their territory lost during the Communist Revolution.

Tommy entered the room followed by Mai. Milton smiled and waved at them. "Forgive me if I don't get up, my back's been bothering me."

"No problem, sir."

Mai appeared horrified. "If we had known, we wouldn't have accepted your invitation!"

Milton chuckled. "I *did* know, and I still extended it, so don't worry about it. Make yourselves at home." He gestured toward the couch.

Tommy held up a bag. "Do you mind if I set up my equipment?"

"Please."

Tommy sat on the couch and started yanking out laptops and tablets and various other devices, some of which Milton didn't recognize. Tommy was a computer whiz kid with a troubled history as a teenager, though he had pulled his life together. Milton believed in second chances, which is why he had allowed him to attend his university and pursue a graduate degree. His girlfriend, Mai, had saved the lives of his friends in her native Vietnam. Acton and Laura wouldn't be alive today if it weren't for her, and her actions had exiled her from her country. His friends had taken her under their wing, treating her like family, and with Tommy and Mai now dating, they were a package deal.

"I've got some snacks in the kitchen here, if you could give me a hand, Mai."

"Yes, Mrs. Milton."

Sandra laughed. "Please. Mrs. Milton is his mother. Call me Sandra."

"Oh, I don't know if I could."

Sandra shrugged. "Whatever you're comfortable with, dear."

"Thank you, Mrs. Milton."

Sandra gave her a hug. "You're such a sweet girl. I can see why Jim and Laura care so much for you."

Milton flinched as the phone rang. He grabbed it and answered. "Hello?"

"Hello, sir, this is Chris. I just wanted to give you a quick update. I probably won't be able to contact you for some time. The two Australian students are safe in their embassy, and Professor Palmer is safe in the British embassy. However, Professor Acton was arrested by the Chinese authorities just after he dropped Professor Palmer off."

He sank back in his chair as his stomach flipped. "Oh, no! Have we heard anything officially? I mean, what's happening?"

He felt Sandra's hand on his shoulder and he reached up, squeezing it as everyone stared at him, no one else privy to what he had just heard, though his tear-filled eyes and concerned tone no doubt gave them some clues.

"There's been no official word of his capture, nor do we expect any. It appears the Ministry of State Security is involved, which would be the Chinese equivalent of the CIA, though with the power to operate within their own borders. These are serious people, and they don't normally get involved in things like this unless there's some very specific motivation, or they've been directed by senior officials. Whatever is going on here might be personal."

Milton massaged his temples with one hand spread across his forehead. "Are you going to be able to help him?"

"No. Unfortunately, Professor Acton is on his own for now. All we can do is use official channels to see if we can effect his release."

He didn't like the sound of that. "Should I do anything? Should I start making calls?"

The response was definitive. "Absolutely not. The less attention we draw to Professor Acton while the crisis is still unfolding, the better. If they think they have somebody that's important to our government, it could be worse for him. Let's see what happens over the next few hours."

"I guess you're right. I'll leave it in your hands. If you hear anything, and you can find the time, please let me know."

"Yes, sir, you'll be the first to know. Goodbye."

The call ended and Milton leaned forward, hanging his head between his knees as his shoulders shook and his eyes burned.

"What is it, dear? What did they say?"

He took a breath and held it, struggling to steady his emotions. "The Australian students are safe, and so is Laura, but..." His voice cracked and she knelt in front of him.

"But what, dear?"

"The Chinese captured Jim."

Sandra gasped and Tommy's jaw dropped. Mai whimpered as she grabbed on to Tommy's arm, her tears flowing freely.

"What are they going to do?" she asked.

"Nothing. They said they can't do anything to help him. They're going to use official channels, but until the crisis is resolved, there's not much they can do, and he doesn't want us making any calls either, in case we draw attention to Jim."

Tommy's jaw snapped shut and he pointed at the television screen. "Look."

Milton stared as the headline appeared.

Chinese Navy about to engage stricken USN vessel.

He took the remote control and unmuted the television as they all set aside their individual problems, and turned their worry toward the most significant military threat to their country since the Cuban Missile Crisis.

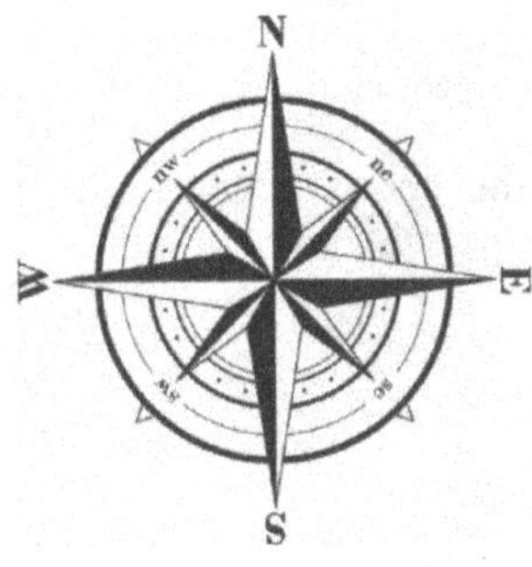

Outside the Luoyang Commandery, Han Empire

166 AD

Lucius rode beside the cart ferrying Jieyou and her entourage, no one now questioning why he would be paying her any mind, the story of a carnal relationship enough to satisfy his men. As each hour passed, his confidence in their success increased. The message would have been delivered to her father yesterday by her trusted servant, and a search of the city and countryside should have begun immediately. There should be no reason for anyone to suspect that she was with him, headed for Rome, yet he wasn't willing to ignore the fact something might have gone awry. In an abundance of caution, he had pressed on through the night, the men switching off in shifts, sleeping in the carts, no one questioning his orders as his power was absolute.

He wanted to put as much distance as possible between them and the capital. They were only days away from a river that would carry them quickly from the capital, and a good chunk of the way to the ocean. If they could reach that river, there would be no catching them.

Jieyou reached out and gently squeezed his arm. "What's troubling you, my love?"

"You don't know?"

She smiled. "Yes, I suppose I do, though we've come this far, perhaps there's nothing to fear now."

He patted her hand. "I'm sure you're right, though it's my job to worry about the one I love."

"And I love you for it, however it distresses me to see you so tense. If you share my tent tonight, perhaps I can help."

He grinned. "I would bring this entire procession to a halt just to spend a few moments alone with you, however I think it's best if we continue forward uninterrupted."

She looked at the rags she wore. "Perhaps if I weren't dressed as I am, you would find my offer harder to resist."

He tossed his head back and laughed. "I have no doubt that would be true, and I thank the gods that your fine clothes are packed away where none can see them."

A shout from the rear of the column had him turning in his saddle.

"Someone approaches!"

He turned his horse around, pointing at Valerius. "Don't stop unless I tell you."

"Yes, sir."

He headed for the rear of the column and found the rearguard blocking the road.

"Someone's approaching, sir."

"How many?"

"It's hard to tell. I spotted several torches. There could be two or three, there could be twenty or thirty, I have no idea, though they are traveling fast. What are your orders?"

He debated what to do. If this had nothing to do with him and Jieyou, and they were to engage, it could spell the end for them regardless of the purpose of those who approached. Yet if they were here for him and Jieyou, then they were all dead regardless. He stared up at the inky black sky, the only light from a scattering of stars breaking through the clouds, a new moon leaving everything bathed in black. "We'll take cover and see if they pass us."

"Yes, sir."

He turned his horse around and rushed forward, peering into the dark for some place they could hide. They were a much smaller contingent now that the Imperial Guard had left, and secluding themselves was at least a possibility. He spotted a path leading into a farmer's field thick with crops, and gave the order. The oxen-drawn carts were driven into the fields, his men following as the unknown potential enemy approached. The torches were numerous now, revealing more significant numbers, and that could play to their advantage, the flame blinding their pursuers to what lay in the darkness that surrounded them.

He was last to leave the road, and as he cleared it, two of his men rushed out and hid their tracks then attempted to disguise the disturbed edge of the field. He knelt in the tall grasses, watching the soldiers as they charged by. There was no doubt this was their escort that had left them earlier in the day, and there was only one reason they were now here.

They were searching for Jieyou.

The truth had obviously been discovered, and now not only were their lives in jeopardy, but so were the lives of those left behind, including his father. The last of the soldiers passed, and he was about to rise when a straggler approached. The man stopped and Lucius could hear him doing something. What, he wasn't certain, until the unmistakable sound of a stream of urine hitting the ground was heard.

And it presented an opportunity.

He motioned to Valerius and they both crept forward. The distinct sound of the final few spurts indicated the man's job was almost done, and he would soon be sprinting after his comrades. Lucius rose and rushed the man, tackling him and bringing him to the ground as he slapped a hand over the man's mouth, stifling any cry for help. Valerius stood beside them, scanning both directions of the road to make certain they were still alone.

"Was that wise, sir?"

"We need information."

"But won't he be missed?"

"I have no doubt he will be eventually, but not while it is this dark."

Lucius hauled the man to his feet then dragged him into the farmer's field where the others remained hidden. He shoved him to the ground and his men bound the man's hands and feet. Lucius regarded the others, all gathered, his men clearly nervous if not outright terrified.

And he decided it was time to reveal the truth.

He walked over to the cart. "Princess Jieyou, I require your assistance."

She rose from the ground that she sat upon with her entourage, all leaping to their feet along with her. She bowed. "I would be pleased to be of assistance," she said in perfect Latin, much to the shock of his men.

"What's the meaning of this?" asked Valerius.

"This is Princess Jieyou, daughter of Emperor Huan. You all now have the right to know what is truly happening here. The Princess has agreed to be my wife, and to accompany me to Rome where we will live out the remainder of our days together."

"With all due respect, sir, you've signed our death warrants, as well as all of those we left behind."

Lucius frowned, acknowledging his guilt. "It would appear so, if that is indeed why those troops are here. We thought we had planned this perfectly, but something must have gone wrong." He indicated the prisoner. "He can confirm our fears."

He led Jieyou to the man they had captured, and a rapid-fire conversation began that within moments had the man's eyes bulging, then an immediate struggle to prostrate himself in front of his princess. The conversation continued in an almost comic fashion until she appeared satisfied, and turned to report what she had discovered.

"I am horrified to say that our secret has been discovered by my father. I also regret to inform you that all at your embassy have been executed."

Shock cleaved his stomach as bile filled his mouth. "My father?"

"Apparently, he's still alive, but will be executed upon our capture."

"And their orders for my men here?"

"Their orders are to execute everyone except for you and me. We're to be returned to the capital, where we will be publicly executed."

His heart ached with the news. His selfishness had cost the lives of so many innocents, of so many of his countrymen. He turned to his men, gathered in silence in front of him, and he could sense their fear, their anger, their disappointment in him as a leader.

And he deserved it all.

"I apologize for what I have done, and I don't expect your forgiveness, as I do not deserve it. What I did was stupid and selfish, and now too many have paid the price."

Valerius stepped forward. "What do you propose we do, sir?"

"I think your best option is to split up. Rid yourselves of your uniforms and anything that would suggest you are Roman. We'll split up the valuables we have so that you can pay for your way back to Rome."

"Wouldn't it be safer to travel together?"

Lucius shook his head. "If you continue to travel as a group, you'll be too easy to spot."

"What about my ladies-in-waiting?" asked Jieyou.

He glanced over at the women, clearly terrified with this turn of events. "Could they return to their homes?"

"No. Because they left with me, my father will treat them as traitors as well. Most likely, their families have already been arrested, and perhaps even executed. There's nowhere for them to go."

Valerius cleared his throat. "We could take them, sir. There are only four of them. Each of us could take one. Perhaps we would look less conspicuous if people saw us traveling together, perhaps as husbands and wives."

Lucius turned to Jieyou. "What do you think?"

"I think it's the best hope. A woman traveling on her own wouldn't survive long. But with a man, she may survive, and may indeed help him to survive." She took his hand. "And what of us?"

"I must try to save my father's life. You go with Valerius, and I'll return to the capital."

She shook her head vigorously. "Absolutely not! We are in this together. We will both return and face the consequences of our actions, and perhaps my father, upon seeing me, will forgive us and allow us to live."

He squeezed her hand, knowing there was no chance of that, yet he forced a smile. "Perhaps he will be in a forgiving mood when he casts his eyes upon his daughter's face." He turned to Valerius. "Are you clear on your orders?"

"I am, sir."

"Then you are now in command. I hereby relinquish my authority over all of you, and pray that you reach Rome. Take the dispatches, but inform the Emperor of what has happened here, and that there is likely no possibility of a treaty. Tell him no further direct attempts should be made except through intermediaries."

"I understand, sir."

Lucius turned to Jieyou. "Say your goodbyes, and let your ladies know what is happening."

She wiped a tear from her face and joined the closest thing she had to friends. Sobs and hugs followed, all shaking their heads, clearly wanting to return with her. Yet they were sworn to obey her orders, and it was clear even from the smattering of words he understood, she was ordering them to go. Final hugs were exchanged, then the women paired up with his men as they stripped out of their armor and the vestiges that identified them as Roman.

He clasped each one of their wrists, wishing them well, his heart aching that his first command was ending in such a manner, and he had only himself to blame. "Take care of yourselves, and take care of these women. They are now your responsibility. And should you reach the Empire, do not abandon them. Make certain that you see to their happiness, for they have done nothing wrong. And perhaps during your voyage, you will grow to love them as I have grown to love the princess. I suggest you begin by teaching them how to speak Latin, for they will surely need it where they are going."

Valerius bowed. "I know I speak for all of us when I say you have my word that we will protect them." He stepped back and saluted, crying, "All hail Caesar! All hail Lucius!"

Lucius' eyes burned as he returned the salute, his voice cracking. "Now, off with you. Stay near the road, but out of sight. I am going to ride ahead to meet up with them and surrender. You'll see us return. When we do, then you should be free to pass unscathed."

"Should we not then be able to reunite?"

"No, it's too risky. We don't know how far word has traveled. They could send messengers ahead. Remember, their orders were to kill you, and those orders won't change just because the two of us have surrendered to them. Stay separated. Make your way back to Rome, but agree among yourselves to a time and place each year that you will attempt to reunite, for some of you may get home in a year, some may not get home for five. But if there's any chance of these women reuniting, all efforts should be made." He mounted his horse and extended an arm, hauling Jieyou up behind him. "We will see each other again on the Elysian Fields."

His men saluted him and he turned his horse around. He pointed at the captured soldier. "When his comrades are safely behind you, set him free. He's done nothing wrong. He's merely a soldier doing his job, as you have been."

"Yes, sir."

Jieyou relayed the man's fate in his native language and he visibly relaxed with the knowledge death wasn't in his future. Lucius urged the horse forward and they were soon back on the road, heading in the direction of the column of soldiers, and toward a future he feared would be all too brief.

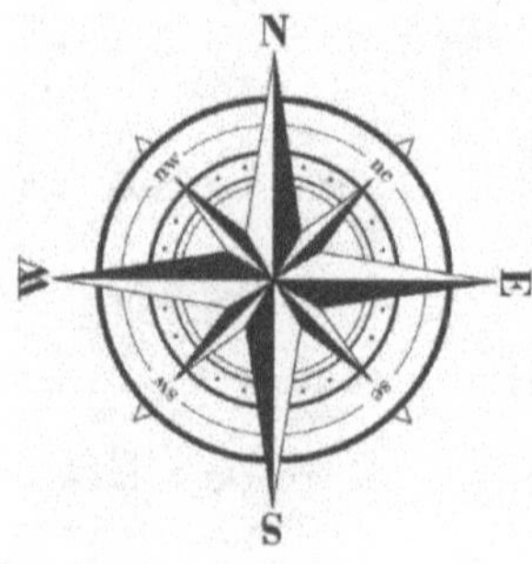

USS Somerset

South China Sea

Present Day

Kidd gripped a handhold, preparing for what was to come. The ship banked hard to port as it became clear the Chinese intended to surround them rather than sink them, at least initially. The engines roared, and as they emerged from their 180-degree turn, they eased off quickly. The gash on the starboard side hadn't been completely repaired yet, and there was no way they could outrun the Chinese, but the more they closed the gap with the USS Ronald Reagan's carrier group, the closer at hand help might be.

Reese pointed. "Look!"

Kidd's head spun to what had drawn his friend's attention, and his eyes bulged at the sight of a Chinese destroyer steaming past them, then turning to cut off their escape. With a damaged starboard side, there was no way the Somerset would outmaneuver the other vessels, which numbered at least ten if not an even dozen. The Somerset turned to port to avoid a collision, but at the same time, Kidd heard the engines cut, their flight over. The ship slowly came to a halt as the Chinese vessels surrounded them. If this were to turn into a fight, there was no way they would survive.

Cheers erupted from the Chinese crew the moment the engines fell silent as their victory was clear. Kidd's fists clenched as rage burned hot in his stomach. It was these people and their captain that had created this situation, and it was their government that was illegally laying claim to the seas upon which they now sailed.

This was China's fault.

All of it.

And what was sad, was that the only thing that might bring an end to actions such as these, would be war. According to his father, their economy was too strong, mostly because Westerners loved their cheap goods and didn't care that the reason they were cheap was because of a lack of labor and environmental laws. Manufacturing had to be shifted from China to other countries. Why things weren't manufactured by the hundreds of millions of poor in Mexico, and South and Central America was beyond him.

The West had put all their eggs in a single corrupt, communist basket, and gleefully so, politicians constantly touting new trade agreements with the communist state. It was ridiculous, and this was the result—death and destruction and possible war.

Engines screeched overhead and Kidd looked up to see dozens of F/A-18E Super Hornets screaming past their position, banking into two groups, left and right, before circling back. This was when he finally noticed something they had all missed in the excitement—a lone Chinese frigate steaming rapidly toward them.

He pointed. "Didn't they learn their lesson last time?"

Reese shook his head. "These Chinese are insane! What do you think the Captain's going to do?"

Kidd shrugged. "What can he do? If he takes any hostile action, there are a dozen Chinese ships that'll launch everything they've got at us, then claim we started it."

"Speaking of which." Reese pointed. "Look at the front of all those ships."

Kidd stared, his hand shielding his eyes as he squinted. "Are those camera crews?"

"That's what it looks like to me. Every damn one of those ships has a camera crew on the prow recording everything."

"My God! They're worse than Hollywood!"

"Yeah. Have you noticed how many movies out of Hollywood now have Chinese production companies behind them? Every one of those has Chinese stars that are the heroes, or it's the benevolent China coming to the rescue. They've already taken over. It's ridiculous!"

Kidd agreed. "Something has to be done to these people."

Reese wagged a finger. "No, something has to be done about their government. The Chinese don't know what's going on for the most part. Their news is so strictly controlled, they probably either don't know that this is happening, or think that we're the ones that started it. They can't be blamed for that."

The Chinese ship was close now, maybe a few hundred yards at best, and showed no sign of breaking off.

Kidd tensed. "He does know we can't actually get out of his way with our engines stopped, doesn't he?"

Reese shrugged. "The last guy didn't seem to know."

The collision alarm sounded and Kidd grabbed the handhold once again when Reese exclaimed, "Holy shit!"

A Super Hornet raced past, skimming the waves, coming between the two vessels, banking away from the Chinese, displaying its weapons pods that included anti-ship missiles.

Yet the Chinese continued forward.

And all hell broke loose.

Dozens of Super Hornets swarmed the area, cutting between the two ships just above the waves and buzzing the other vessels, coming dangerously close each time, their jet wash no doubt felt by the crews manning the enemy vessels.

Yet no one fired.

Plane after plane cut between the two ships as the gap narrowed, and Kidd resisted the urge to close his eyes, for he had no doubt that at any moment, the first shot would be fired.

And then somebody somewhere gave an order.

The Chinese vessel banked hard to starboard. The Super Hornets from the USS Ronald Reagan continued to buzz the Chinese ships as Kidd felt the engines of the Somerset start up, the slight surge indicating they were once again underway, albeit slowly. They steamed toward the blockade, the Captain heading straight for a narrow gap between two vessels. His heart hammered as they approached. The crew of the enemy ships leaned against their rails, staring at the oncoming Somerset as some of his own crew did the same. He rushed to the rail with the others and stared ahead as his captain attempted to thread the needle between the two vessels. The Super Hornets continued to buzz the enemy ships, reminding them that if they took any hostile action, every single one of them was forfeit, yet Kidd paid them no mind.

Less than 100 yards separated them now, and collision alarms sounded on the enemy ships as well as his own. Both enemy vessels turned away from the oncoming Somerset, but water wasn't asphalt, and there was a risk their bows might slide into the path of the 25,000-ton vessel. He gripped the railing tight as the prow of the Chinese ship on the port side passed them, its tapered design belying the fact the rest of the ship would come drastically closer. Kidd prayed they had a bridge crew as skilled as his own, as he doubted the Somerset could survive another collision.

And there was no way in hell he wanted to be rescued by these pieces of shit.

He'd rather stay in the water until the USS Ronald Reagan arrived, sharks be damned.

He stared over the railing then looked up at his enemy. He could spit on the Chinese crew, they were so close. Their Chinese survivors were screaming at their comrades. One of them climbed up onto the railing and leaped across, one hand catching the edge of the Chinese deck for a moment as the crew on the other ship scrambled to grab him. But it was hopeless. He lost his hold and slid down the side and into the churning waves below, curing the remaining survivors of any foolish thoughts at escape.

Kidd ignored them.

If they wanted to die, then die. He couldn't care less.

He remained focused on the hull of his ship and that of their enemy, and breathed a sigh of relief as the widest part of both vessels came abreast of each other, separated by perhaps 20 feet, the gap widening as the Chinese ship continued to turn gently to starboard.

The horrifying screeching of metal scraping metal had butterflies battling in his stomach as everyone turned toward the sound from the damaged side of the ship. The Somerset banked as the screeching continued for several more seconds before it stopped. Kidd ran to the bow as the Chinese vessel they had just hit continued past, and sighed in relief that the enemy had suffered minimal damage, mostly paint scrapings from the hull, and he prayed the Somerset had suffered similar.

Damage control parties were deployed over the 1MC, reminding him of his duty. He turned to check that the Chinese crew were fine, and could see no evidence that anyone was injured beyond the one that had attempted to leap between two ships at sea. The Captain continued to steam away from the Chinese vessels, though still at their crippled speed. Kidd stared off the bow, gripping the metal tight as he searched for any sign the Chinese were attempting to re-establish the blockade, but saw none as the Super Hornets continued to buzz the Chinese vessels.

And again, someone somewhere gave an order.

The fighter jets suddenly broke off and gained altitude, though didn't leave the area, still providing a deterrent should the Chinese become the aggressors once again.

"They're leaving," cried Reese, a smile on his face as he pointed.

Kidd peered through the ocean spray at the bow of the ship, and every tensed muscle in his body released at the sight of all dozen Chinese ships turning away, their show of force over, and the might of the US Navy over these waters re-established.

For the Chinese had proven that when challenged, they would back down.

"Why do you think they chickened out?" asked Reese.

Kidd shrugged. "Probably because they knew our boys would blow them out of the water."

"Or they got enough footage for their propaganda reels."

Kidd chuckled. "Yeah, but something tells me whatever the Chinese people see is going to be heavily edited."

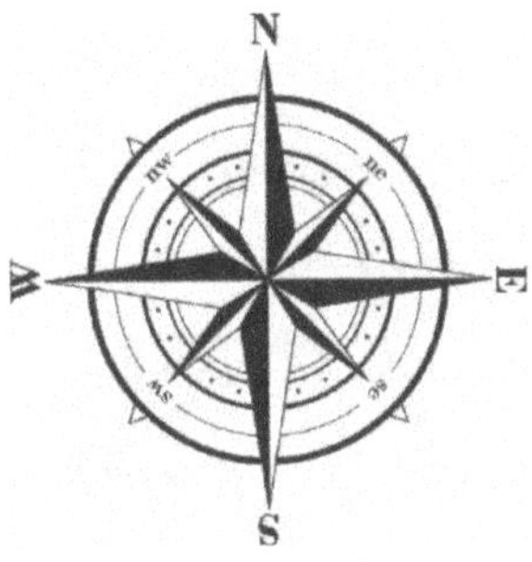

Luoyang, Han Empire

166 AD

Their capture had been relatively uneventful. Though they were both condemned to death, none of the soldiers had dared touch a princess. That courtesy hadn't been extended to Lucius, and he had been roughed up a bit. Jieyou rode in the back of a carriage that the column had met up with the next morning, and he was in the back of a prison wagon in chains and filth.

Yet he didn't mind, for he had spotted Valerius hiding in the grasses, a silent salute delivered, and he knew his men were safe, at least for the moment. The soldiers had asked him where the others were, yet he had feigned not understanding their language, and the soldiers likely had no idea the princess spoke Latin to act as a translator. And even if they did, they wouldn't dare speak to her, for under any other circumstances, addressing a princess of the emperor could mean death.

The journey back had been long and tiring, but word had clearly been sent ahead of their arrival, for as they entered the capital, the streets were lined with throngs of people throwing rotting vegetables at him, though carefully avoiding Jieyou's carriage. A point appeared to have been made by driving past the once proud Roman embassy, its colors stripped from its walls, and the bodies of all those who had once inhabited it hanging from the crisp white stone walls, now stained a deep purple from their dried blood. It was heart-breaking, yet he controlled his emotions, forcing himself to stare at the sight and honor those who had made the ultimate sacrifice because of his youthful impetuousness.

He deserved to die, and was willing to die.

He only prayed that the Emperor would accept his offer and spare the lives of Jieyou and his father.

They reached the palace and entered the courtyard, the massive gate slamming shut behind them, the crowds behind silenced not by the walls, but by the fact their orchestrated display was now concluded. His cage was unlocked and he stumbled out. Jieyou was helped down from her carriage and she was about to rush to his side when he slightly shook his head. She stared at him confused, but held her ground.

He still wore his armor and his colors, though the journey had certainly tarnished his appearance. He drew his shoulders back, inhaling deeply. He was a soldier of the Empire, he was a Roman citizen, and he was the son of an ambassador from a once wealthy, well-respected family. His dishonor had destroyed his family's future, yet he wouldn't allow these circumstances to diminish who he was.

Romans didn't cow to anyone.

He stepped through the massive doors of the palace, and toward what might be the final moments of far too short a life, a life ending in disgrace with his hands soaked in the blood of too many innocents.

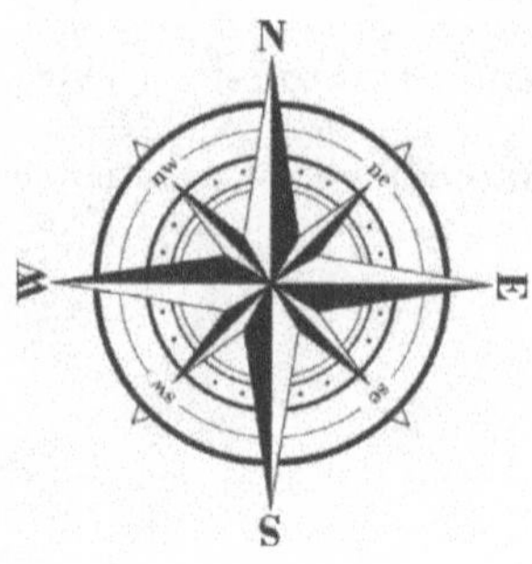

Ministry of State Security Headquarters

Beijing, China

Present Day

A door was opened and the gurney shoved through, and to Acton's dismay, he found himself in what appeared to be a stereotypical boardroom. The paunch who had stopped his beating stood against the wall, the bastard who had beaten him next to him. The medics swung his legs from the gurney and the woman pointed at a chair. "Please sit."

Acton did as he was told, wincing in agony with every movement. He noticed a timer on a computer screen, counting down for some unknown purpose, though whatever was about to happen would be happening in less than three minutes. One of the medics straightened his hair as another fit a hospital gown around him to cover his bloodied clothes.

That was when he spotted the webcam set up on a tripod on the boardroom table directly in front of him. This was a video conference, and his hosts were attempting to make him appear as presentable as possible, though judging from the way his face felt, only a fool would think nothing had happened to him. Ice packs were pressed against his face in an attempt to reduce the swelling, yet with less than a minute left, he had little doubt they would have no effect.

And their efforts confused him.

Who was he about to talk to that would care whether he had been beaten? If they were Chinese, they shouldn't care, and if they were American or some other foreign representative acting on his country's behalf, there would be little doubt about the type of treatment he had received.

The countdown reached ten seconds and the paunch snapped an order, sending the medics retreating out the door with the gurney. The screen flashed and a man appeared, perhaps in his late sixties or early seventies, wearing the stereotypical Mao-style suit and appropriately minimalist haircut—the ideal representation of the Chinese regime.

"Do you know who I am, Professor Acton?"

Acton shrugged, immediately regretting the motion. "I haven't the foggiest."

"My name is Chen Leji."

"Have we met?"

"No, we have not, but you met my grandson."

"I've met a lot of people."

"His name was Doctor Chen Qiang."

The name rang a bell, though Acton couldn't place it. The problem with Chinese surnames was that 87% of the population shared the same 100. "I'm afraid I don't remember the name. Where did I meet him?"

"In the Amazon jungle."

And suddenly everything clicked, those horrifying events that had taken place several years before rushing back. So many innocents had died, including the only woman his friend Hugh Reading had fallen for in years. It had been a tragic experience, and he had struggled for years to block those painful memories.

And he remembered the grandson.

Doctor Chen had been in charge of the entire operation in the jungle, and had died an appropriately gruesome death.

"Do you remember him now?"

Acton nodded. "Yes, I do."

"And do you admit that you killed him?"

Acton shook his head. "That's not how I remember it, though he's definitely dead."

The man's jaw clenched as he leaned closer to the camera. "You would dare speak of my grandson's death in such a cavalier way?"

Acton stared at the man. "You are aware of what your grandson was doing there, aren't you? Of how he imprisoned and forced innocent natives into slave labor? How his operation raped the land?"

"His actions were none of your concern, and you had no right to interfere in our operation. It wasn't your country. It wasn't even your continent!"

Acton spat. "As a member of the human species, I had a duty to interfere. What your grandson and your country were doing was illegal, not only environmentally, but from a human rights perspective. He was slaughtering innocent people, putting the survivors to work as slaves. As far as I'm concerned, your grandson deserved to die that day, as did everyone on his team."

The man growled, fists slamming on a desk heard through the speakers. Acton shouldn't have said what he did, but it was too late now to take it back. And besides, this man had gone to so much trouble to find him, Acton had little doubt the plan was for him to die so that this man's grandson was avenged.

"Professor Acton, you chose your final words poorly. I will be there in ten minutes to personally execute you for crimes against the state and for espionage."

Acton didn't bother replying—there was no point. The man had intended all along to kill him regardless of what he said, and the fact he was ten minutes away, meant his death would likely occur in the next fifteen. If he had any hope of surviving, he had to get out of this building.

And an idea occurred to him.

He began swishing his saliva, producing as much as he could, then rolled his eyes up and closed the lids partway so only the whites could be seen. As he continued to force the production of saliva in his mouth, he gripped the arms of his chair and shook his entire body as he did his best possible imitation of a seizure. He drooled from his mouth, the blood from his beatings mixed in, no doubt enhancing the effect.

Chinese erupted from the speakers as panic took hold of the room, and he continued to shake his entire body, praying this Hail Mary would work, otherwise he was dead before the hour was up.

Yan's jaw dropped and his eyes shot wide as Acton shook in his chair, bloody drool flowing from his mouth as his eyes rolled up into his head.

"What the hell is going on?" demanded Chen. Wei shouted for the medics and the door burst open, the two rushing in, going to work on Acton.

"If he dies, then whoever did this to him dies along with him," screamed the Politburo member.

Yan gulped, but said nothing.

"Understood, sir," said Wei. "I'll contact you as soon as I know what's happening."

"You do that, but I'm still going to be there in ten minutes."

"Of course, sir."

The video conference went dead and Yan prayed that Acton didn't do the same. The medics loaded him on the gurney as Wei stepped forward.

"What's going on?" he asked.

"He's having some sort of seizure, sir, probably from too many blows to the head," replied the woman.

"Will he survive?"

"Too early to say, but we need to get him to a hospital immediately."

"Do it, and tell the doctors that if they fail to save his life, they'll be answering to the Politburo itself."

"Yes, sir," replied the medic, her tone subdued, leaving little doubt she realized she and her partner would also be included in those who would be punished.

Acton was pushed out the door and Yan was about to follow when his boss grabbed him by the shoulder, spinning him around to face him.

"You do realize that you've likely ended all of our careers?"

Yan's head sagged in shame. "Yes, sir. I'm sorry, sir. I'll make it clear that you had nothing to do with it."

"That won't help. I chose you for the job, therefore I am to blame."

"I'm sorry, sir. There must be something you can do."

"He's a member of the Politburo. There's nothing anyone can do."

Yan lowered his voice. "But is he acting on behalf of the Politburo, or his own selfish reasons?"

Wei stared at him. "What are you suggesting?"

Yan sighed. He was dead already, or if he wasn't, life as he knew it was certainly over. And when one got on the wrong side of the Politburo, any life that might be allowed wouldn't be worth living, filled with either imprisonment, torture, or worse—rejection by the system, left to fend for himself.

He went for broke. "Sir. You're a Deputy Bureau Chief in the MSS. You can do anything." He lowered his voice even further. "*Anything*."

Wei stared at him. "I'm going to pretend I didn't hear that."

Yan snapped to attention, his stomach flipping as he realized he had crossed the line. "Of course, sir, I'm sorry, sir."

Wei pointed at the door. "Go with your prisoner. Make sure nothing else happens to him."

"Yes, sir." Yan fled out the door and down the hallway, his pulse pounding in his ears as he realized he had been a fool for suggesting they kill a member of the Politburo to save their own skins.

If Wei reports this, I might as well kill myself.

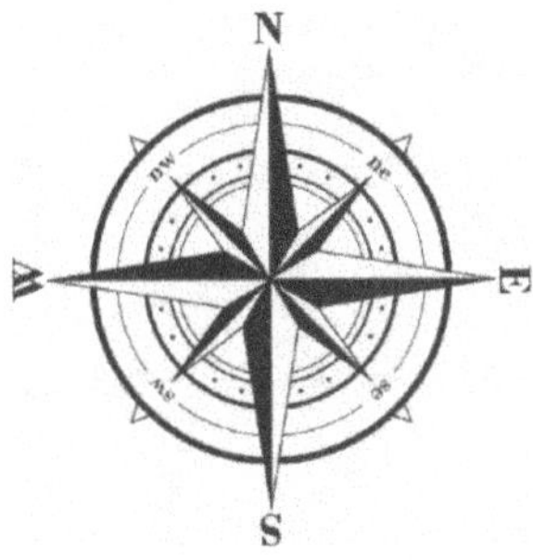

Outside the Ministry of State Security Headquarters

Beijing, China

Jack leaned against the wall of a building older than most countries, then reached up and pressed the tiny camera with built-in transmitter into a groove between the ancient stone and modern window frame. He stepped back and glanced at it to make certain his placement had been perfect, then walked toward his car, a rental arranged by Chan. He climbed inside and pulled away, tapping his comm. "Control, Rawhide, come in, over."

"Go ahead, Rawhide."

"I've just placed the last camera, can you confirm?"

"Copy that, Rawhide. We have six feeds, all five-by-five."

"Do you see him?"

Leroux laughed. "Yeah, I can see him through the window of the MSS gift shop. I think he's picking up one of those classic, 'I got tortured by the Ministry of State Security and all I got was this lousy t-shirt' type gifts. He should be out any moment."

Jack chuckled. "Why does Control always have to be a smartass?"

"I think they like us to keep things light and reduce your stress load."

Jack turned the corner. "You do know that bad jokes can be stressful, right?"

"So I've heard. But I've also been told by my team that my sense of humor is wonderful."

"It is, boss!" shouted someone, similar sentiments echoed in the background.

Jack smiled. He loved working alone, though there was something to be said about having a team that not only had your back, but that you could joke around with. "Well, if you see anything, let me—"

"Stand by, Rawhide."

Jack checked his mirrors, the change in tone suggesting something either dangerous or of interest was happening.

"Rawhide, we have an ambulance that's just pulled up to the building."

"You don't think that's for Acton, do you?"

"I think it's a definite possibility. You just try to keep yourself scarce, but close. And we'll…wait a second, he's being brought out. Zoom in on that."

Jack gripped the steering wheel, dying to check his phone, but accessing the images would get him into a car accident the way his day was going.

"Okay, it's confirmed. We just saw Professor Acton being loaded into the back of an ambulance. It looks like he's having some sort of seizure. They haven't left the grounds yet. When they do, they're going to be coming out of the southeast exit by the looks of it. Get yourself in position to follow, then act accordingly. It looks like he's with the driver and two medics, one male, one female, no guards."

Jack smiled. "It's like they're sending him out gift-wrapped. I hope he got a t-shirt for me."

"Be careful, Rawhide. I just had to lie to Professor Acton's best friend about this op not happening."

"Why'd you do that?"

"It was an unsecured line that had been compromised before. Just in case they were listening, we wanted the Chinese to think we were standing down. Let's do this right, and maybe I can call him back and make his day."

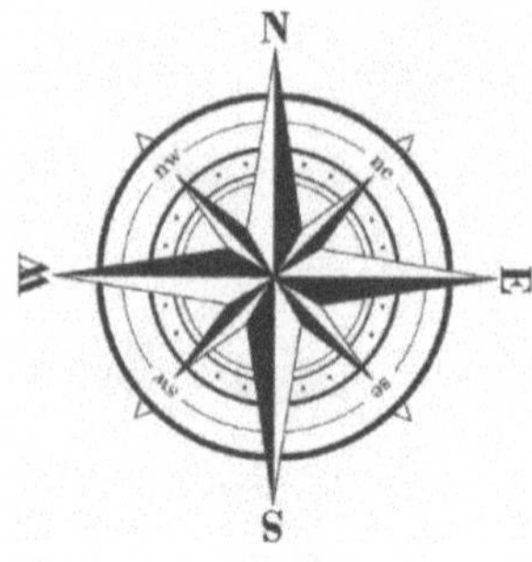

Ministry of State Security Headquarters

Beijing, China

Acton continued his act, though he had run out of saliva, and, frankly, that entire portion of his charade was rather disgusting. He eased off on the shaking slightly, so far successfully managing to prevent them from getting an IV into his arm that would no doubt knock him out. He was out of the building now and in the back of an ambulance. Once he reached wherever they were heading, he had no doubt security would be put on the door. At this very moment, he was with two medics, both of whom he had no doubt lacked his training.

Yet they also didn't have the cracked ribs and bruised and broken body he suffered.

This would be his only chance of escape. He opened his eyes halfway and assessed his surroundings, searching for things that could be used as weapons, but most importantly, how to open the rear door. He spotted the latch, and it appeared simple to operate, though there would be no point in attempting escape now—he was still on the grounds of whatever building in which he had been held.

But once they were underway, he should be able to judge by the traffic sounds when they were in the streets of Beijing, and that would be when he'd make his move. An elbow to the head of the man, then a simple shove of the woman into him, should have them tangled together on the vehicle floor long enough for him to make his escape out the back.

What he would find on the other side of the door, though, was the question. He might find himself on the freeway and trapped, or a city street with plenty of places to hide. There was no way to know, but anything was better than his destination, especially since they were merely saving his life so they could take it later.

The engine started and he reached down to the side, grasping for the clasp of the strap that stretched across his chest. He found it and waited as the medics attempted to hook up monitors as he continued to shake, though only in short bursts now, the effort painful and exhausting—he needed his strength for what was about to happen.

The ambulance moved then someone slapped their hand on the outside, bringing it to a jerking halt. The rear doors opened and all hope was drained from him as Yan climbed in the back, closing the doors behind him. Acton continued his fake seizure, though to what end, he wasn't sure.

There was no way he was overpowering three healthy people.

Yan grabbed him by the leg and shook him. "Don't die on me, Professor Acton. You've got an execution to live for."

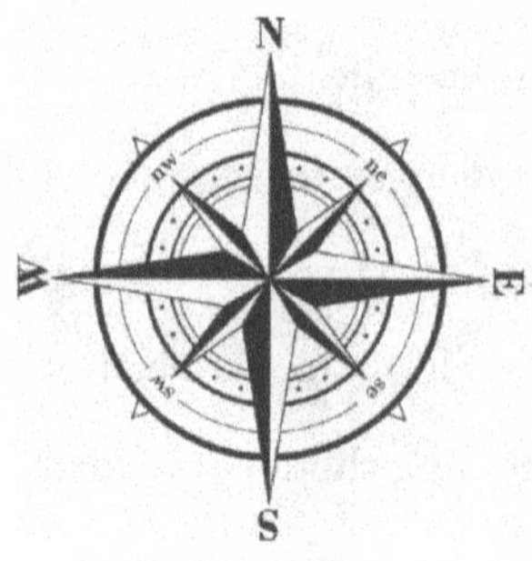

Outside the Ministry of State Security Headquarters

Beijing, China

Jack watched the ambulance pull through the gates, exactly as Leroux's team had predicted. He steered back into traffic as he formulated a plan. There would be no time for subtleness, nor was this the place for extreme violence—he'd have to figure out some middle ground, and unfortunately, the only ground he could find was shaky.

The ambulance's lights and sirens activated and the heavy traffic slowly parted to let it past. Jack glued himself to the bumper, then spotted an opening on the right-hand side. He gunned the engine and wedged himself in, then cursed at the sight of a stopped car ahead. A shoulder check revealed his spot had already been filled by someone else taking advantage of the ambulance's traffic clearing abilities.

He had no choice.

He hopped up onto the sidewalk, laying on his horn, sending the pedestrians scattering as he gunned ahead of the ambulance then back into traffic. He slammed on his brakes and was already out the door when the ambulance screeched to a halt. He left his front door ajar and opened the rear one as he walked by. The driver started shouting at him to get the hell out of the way, but he ignored him.

He rounded the rear of the vehicle and yanked open the doors, then climbed inside, tasing the last-minute arrival who clearly wasn't a medic, sending him shuddering to the floor. He pulled a gun on the two medics who held their hands up and retreated as far as they could into the back of the vehicle. In perfect Chinese, he asked, "Is he safe to transport?"

The woman shook her head. "No, he's having a seizure."

He turned to Acton, switching to English. "Are you having a seizure?"

Acton propped himself up on his elbows. "Actually, I was faking all that. Can we leave now?"

Jack eyed him. "So, you'll just run off with any old face?"

Acton laughed then winced, his ribs apparently in as rough a shape as his face appeared to be. "I'd recognize that voice anywhere."

Acton undid the strap over his chest as Jack did the same with the one over his legs. He glanced at the prone figure on the floor, noticing his bleeding knuckles. "Did he do this to you?"

"Yeah."

"Do you want me to even the score?"

Acton held out a hand and Jack helped him to his feet. "No, something tells me his superiors are going to be doing far worse to him than we have time for."

Jack climbed out onto the street and Acton hopped down. They headed for the car. "Get in the back and lie down."

"You got it."

Jack sprinted past the ambulance when gunfire erupted behind them. He glanced over his shoulder but kept going, the sight of at least a dozen uniformed men and women running toward them, all with weapons, urging him forward rather than stopping to gawk like Acton was. "Get a wiggle on, Professor!"

Acton continued forward. The driver of the ambulance threw open his door as he passed it, knocking the professor to the ground. He hit hard and cried out in agony, gripping his chest. The soldiers were closing in on them now, and there was no doubt they were both about to be captured. He gripped his weapon but Acton held out a hand toward him.

"No! Just get out of here! Tell them what happened. It's a member of the Politburo named Chen Leji, he's the one behind this. His grandson was in the Amazon when we took down their operation there. Tell Langley that, and maybe they can get me out diplomatically. Just save yourself. I don't want anyone else getting hurt because of me."

Jack regarded Acton for a split second. "I'll be back for you."

"And tell Laura I love her!"

Jack nodded then jumped in the car and hammered on the gas, surging away from the scene as the soldiers surrounded the ambulance, their guns directed at Acton. One of them raised their weapon to fire at the car and Jack cranked the wheel, disappearing around the corner.

"Langley, this is Rawhide, do you read, over?"

"We read you, Rawhide, status report."

"It was a Charlie-Foxtrot. I got him out of the ambulance but there were too many locals. We were overrun by a dozen armed police."

"What's your status?"

"I'm evading them now, but Acton was recaptured."

"Copy that. Get yourself to safety and we'll regroup."

"Will do. But Acton gave me a piece of intel he wanted passed on to you. He said that the man after him was a member of the Politburo named Chen Leji. His grandson was involved in some operation in the Amazon that Acton helped take down. I don't know what the hell he's talking about. Does that make any sense to you?"

"Yes, it does. We'll work that angle from this end."

"Sounds good." A police siren wailed too close for comfort. "I've gotta go and save my own ass right now. Hopefully, I'll see you on the flip side, Rawhide, out."

Acton was rolled onto his chest and handcuffed, then hauled to his feet. He groaned in agony but refused to scream from the pain, not wanting to give any of these bastards the satisfaction. Though right now, his concern wasn't for himself, it was for Jack. When the operative had entered the back of the ambulance, he had no idea who he was. The disguise was perfect, the face that of a middle-aged Chinese man. But the voice was something he recognized immediately, despite the fact he was speaking Chinese.

The first time he had heard it was in Mongolia, where the man had been instrumental in saving not only him and Laura, but Tommy and

Mai. He was CIA like Kane, and quite capable, from what he had observed. If anyone could get him out, Jack could.

Though not today, apparently.

The two medics were standing outside of the vehicle now, the woman stabbing a finger at him and screaming in anger. The only words he could understand were the lone two spat in English.

"You faker!"

His secret was out, so any time he had hoped to buy was now gone. He was loaded in the back of a police vehicle, which to his dismay, turned around and headed toward the building he had just left. And that meant only one thing.

He would be dead within the next few minutes.

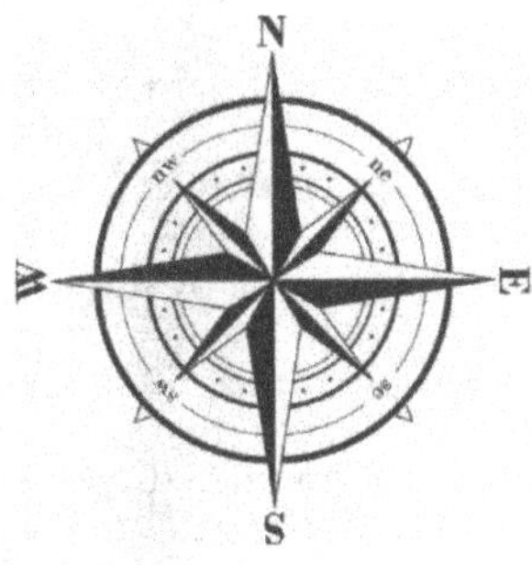

Ministry of State Security Headquarters

Beijing, China

Deputy Bureau Chief Wei stood in the conference room, pondering what to do next. The report had just come in of the rescue attempt on Acton. That meant the Americans were involved, and that this simple professor was far more important than Wei had imagined. The Americans wouldn't commit violent acts on Chinese soil for an academic. This man was either more powerful than they knew, or was better connected than he was aware. What it really meant, however, was that not only had Acton tricked them with his fake seizure, his people had almost allowed the Americans to rescue him, sealing Wei's fate.

His career was over.

There was no way he could survive this intact. He checked his watch. Chen Leji would be here from the Politburo any minute now. Acton would be killed, Yan imprisoned and tortured, and perhaps eventually executed. And his own career would be finished, and he might even face imprisonment himself. Life as he knew it was over, as it was for his family, all because of one man's personal vendetta.

He thought about what Yan had said. This was indeed a personal vendetta, so it likely wasn't sanctioned by the Politburo. If the Politburo were to discover what Chen was up to, the man could potentially get in as much trouble as he himself faced. The state frowned upon individualism, and there was no more individualistic act than revenge. But reporting a Politburo member would be a foolish act. Not only would it blackball him for any future promotions, it would likely end his career. And depending on how well connected that particular member was, perhaps end his life.

One never challenged the Politburo.

One never made trouble for the Politburo.

Yet what the Politburo didn't know...

Chen was acting alone, and he was old. And this was the Ministry of State Security. Everything Wei needed to save himself was located within these walls.

He breathed deeply, making a decision that had him terrified, though it was the only one available to him.

He headed out the door, sweat beading on his forehead, for what he was about to do was treason. And if something went wrong, he was guaranteeing his death, and perhaps the death of all those who worked for him.

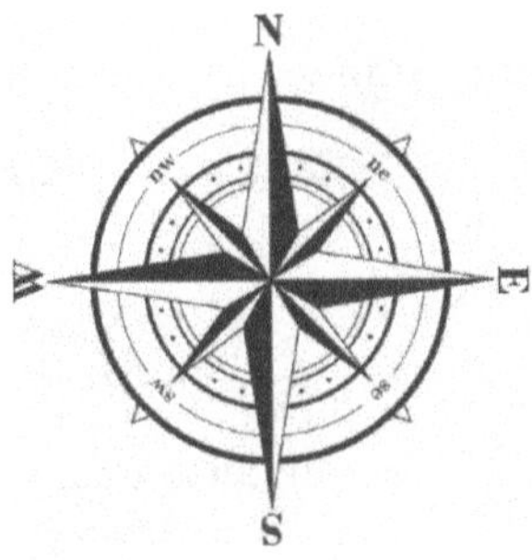

Embassy of the United Kingdom

Beijing, China

Laura sat in a chair in a conference room at the embassy. The complex was filled beyond capacity, but thankfully, the news was now reporting that the crisis in the South China Sea was over. War had been avoided, cooler heads prevailing. The details were sketchy, though she had no doubt both sides would claim victory, and perhaps this one time, that would be true, for avoiding war was a victory for all sides.

The man who had met her at the gate stepped into the room and beckoned her. She rose and walked toward the door, her seat immediately taken by someone else. She followed him out of the room, and he led her down a hallway and into an empty office.

"You'll want to sit." His tone was grave, his look somber.

And her chest ached as she collapsed into the chair, knowing nothing about to be said would be good. "Something's happened to James, hasn't it?"

He nodded, but held up a hand as if to preempt her presumptions. "We just received a report from the Americans. A rescue attempt was made, but failed, and your husband was recaptured. Beyond that, I don't know anything else."

Her eyes burned and she sniffed. "So, you don't know if he's alive?"

"No, I'm afraid not. If I hear anything else, I'll let you know."

"Thank you." She was about to stand when he waved his hand.

"No, this is my office, and I don't need it for a while. Stay here as long as you want."

She gave him a weak smile. "Thank you."

He left the room, closing the door behind him, and the torrent of emotions she had contained poured out of her. Her shoulders shook as she squeezed her eyes shut. She should never have left him, and though the thought was foolish, right now, she didn't care. She wanted to be with him, even if it meant that both of them would die. At least they would die together, and that idea was more appealing than the reality she now faced. The very thought of continuing on without him was simply too painful. What she would do without him in her life, she didn't know. All she knew was that it was a life she didn't want to live.

But he wasn't dead yet. There was still some hope, however slight. And for now, she would cling to that sliver of hope until she knew for certain he was gone. It was the only thing she could do trapped within this safe haven amidst a hostile city.

No matter how useless it was.

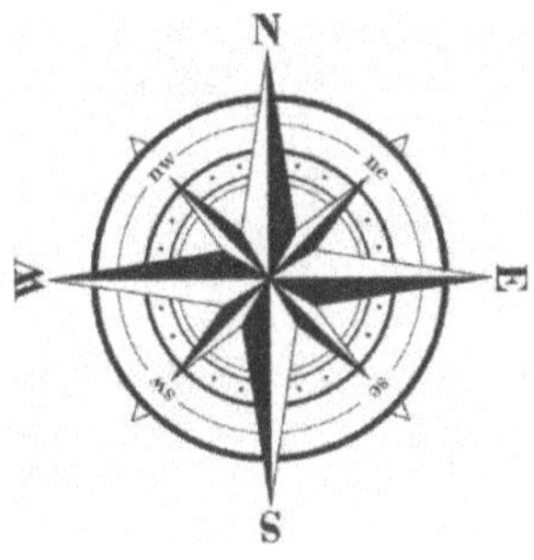

Ministry of State Security Headquarters

Beijing, China

Wei stood, his head dutifully bowed as Chen tore him a new asshole. He had just finished briefing the Politburo member about the escape attempt. The man who had attempted to free Acton was reportedly Chinese, though the medics claimed the assailant apparently knew the professor and said something about his face. It suggested a disguise.

And something that sophisticated suggested CIA.

Just who this professor was, he didn't know. The file had been classified and mostly redacted, likely by the man yelling at him right now. Beyond the photo and the tombstone data provided when the initial arrests were ordered, he knew nothing. Somehow Acton and his wife had been involved in the death of Chen's grandson, and he could understand the man's anger and desire for revenge. If someone murdered his child, he would go to the ends of the earth to deliver justice upon them.

And with the means at his disposal as a Deputy Bureau Chief in the Ministry of State Security, no one would be safe should he set his eyes upon them.

But at the moment, he couldn't care less about Chen's grandson—he only cared about his own son. Chen's tirade was all about blame. The man was obsessed with killing Acton personally, and the fact a nearly fatal beating had been delivered meant Wei was to blame, for he had chosen Yan for the job. He had also ordered Acton taken to a hospital, and hadn't provided the proper security to prevent the rescue attempt. Thankfully, it had been foiled by alert police in the area, but he would still be blamed for having put Chen's opportunity for revenge at risk.

"Your career is over! Your life is finished! Your entire department will be gutted, every single person replaced with more competent agents! I can't believe you managed to climb as high as you did, being as incompetent as you are!"

There was a knock at the door then it was pushed open. Yan entered, dragging a wincing Acton. He shoved the prisoner into a chair and the man cried out, gripping his ribs, his breathing labored. Wei pointed at the door and Yan left, closing it behind him. Chen's attention was now on the prisoner, his tirade finally halted, a new one beginning as he screamed at Acton, repeatedly slapping him ineffectually. Judging by the amount of pain Acton was already in, the slaps of a septuagenarian weren't going to affect him.

Wei tuned him out. Chen had confirmed what he had feared. The life he knew was over, and he faced either imprisonment or death, or perhaps something far worse—disassociation with the state. He would simply be left to his own means with no help in a country where all help was provided by the government. His family would be destitute, his wife's career would be over, as well as his son's. Any future grandchildren would be affected as well, all because Yan had been selected for the job.

The moment he had found out about Yan's brother, he should have pulled him off the case. It had been foolish to let him continue to chase down an American when Americans might have just killed his brother. He was to blame for what had happened, but his family wasn't.

Yet it wasn't just his family. Chen had threatened every single man and woman that served under him. It meant the end of their careers and their families' happiness. Thousands of souls had just had their lives ruined, their futures torn apart, and they didn't even know it yet. Chen was a member of the Politburo. There were only 25 of them in a country of 1.4 billion, and they controlled the Party, and the Party controlled the population.

Chen was untouchable.

The only person who could override an order he gave would be somebody more senior in the Politburo. And that rarely happened. The best Wei could hope for was that the personnel in his department might be spared, but that was just wishful thinking. The Politburo might decide that using them as an example could be worthwhile. If he let events continue to unfold the way they were heading, he would be responsible for the consequences.

He reached into his pocket and ran his fingers over the deliverance from this possible future brought to him only minutes before Chen's arrival. After Yan had left to join Acton in the ambulance, he had considered his underling's words. He hadn't yet come to a decision, but he had decided he needed to be prepared.

"Give me your sidearm."

Wei flinched as he realized Chen was now staring directly at him, his hand outstretched.

"Give me your sidearm, now!"

Acton's eyes were closed, as if he knew his fate was about to be sealed. Wei nodded and gripped the contents of his pocket as he pulled out his hand. He stepped toward Chen, pulling the cap off the syringe. He grabbed Chen by the hair, holding his head back, forcing his eyelid open with his thumb. Chen struggled but was no match for him. He jabbed the needle into the corner of Chen's eye, then pressed the plunger, injecting the concoction developed within this very building, before shoving the man to the ground. Chen gasped, staring up at him, his eyes questioning what had just happened as his mouth said nothing. He gripped his chest, the untraceable poison triggering a heart attack, and hopefully, saving not only his future and that of his family, but those for whom he was responsible.

"What the hell just happened?" asked Acton.

Wei continued to stare at Chen, not removing his eyes from the man until he heard the death rattle of a last breath taken. He put the cap back on the needle then returned it to his pocket. He locked the door to the main hallway to ensure no uninvited guests would enter. "He's had a heart attack. No one will ever know that it wasn't natural."

Acton eyed him warily. "Do you have another one of those needles for me?"

Wei shook his head. "It was never my intention to kill you, Professor Acton, just to arrest you under his orders."

"Then why are you helping me now?"

"I'm not helping you, Professor. I'm helping myself. You just happen to be a beneficiary of my need." He pointed at another door that led to another conference room. "Go out that door. One of my people is waiting. Do everything she says without question. Understood?"

Acton eyed him. "You expect me to trust you?"

"You can stay here, Professor Acton, in a room with a dead member of the Chinese Politburo. I will claim that you injected a poison given to you by the person who tried to rescue you earlier. Or, you can leave now, and take your chances on the other side of that door."

Acton struggled to his feet. "You don't have to ask me twice." He limped to the other side of the room then stepped through the door. As it closed, a Taser deploying could be heard, then a loud thump as Acton hit the floor.

One less problem to deal with.

His trusted operative reached in and closed the door. The moment it clicked shut, Wei unlocked the main door and yanked it open. He stepped out into the hallway, an appropriate amount of panic on his face for public consumption, and pointed at Yan.

"Comrade Chen has collapsed! Get the medics now!"

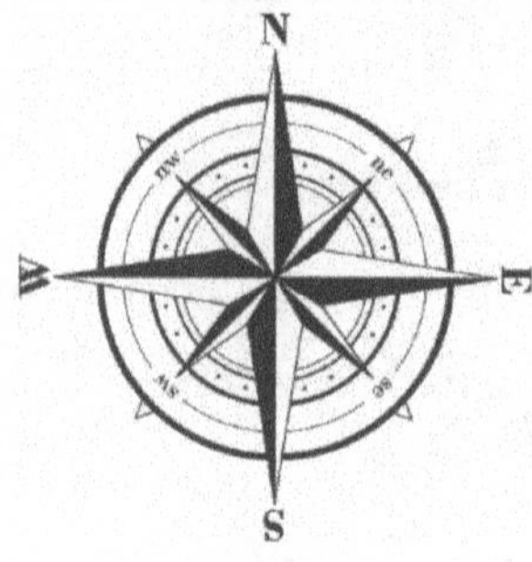

Beijing, China

Jack struggled to control the anger he felt toward himself. He had screwed up. In his eagerness to bring the ambulance to a halt, he had neglected to examine his surroundings. If he had taken a few moments to do so, he would have noticed there were too many police in the area, and could have simply stayed ahead of the ambulance until the right moment.

And now, because of his negligence, Acton was likely about to die, or was dead already.

Whatever would happen to him would happen within the walls of the Ministry of State Security Headquarters, and the only way he could save him now would be to get inside.

But he'd have to do it now.

He activated his comm. "Control, Rawhide. Come in, over."

"Go ahead, Rawhide."

"I need a way in."

"What do you mean?"

"I need a way into that building. Acton probably only has minutes. If this entire thing is about some guy's dead grandson, then it's a revenge operation. They don't intend to keep him alive, and judging by the beating he received by the guy I tased, the torture portion of the program is finished. If I don't get him out now, he's not going to be alive an hour from now."

"You might be able to get in there, but there's no way you're going to be able to get out with him. It would be a suicide mission."

Jack slammed his fist against the steering wheel. Leroux was right, and he had to be smart about this. "What if we create a diversion? Can you cut the power to that building?"

"We might be able to take down the grid for the area, but to what end? They'll just be on even higher alert. You'll never get in there."

He gripped the steering wheel then flexed his fingers, struggling to control his emotions so he could think clearly. "No, but it might delay things long enough for us to come up with a plan."

"It's a possibility, but we'd be tipping our hand that we can actually do that. I'll have to…stand by…oh shit!"

Jack detected the change in tone, the expletive laced not with anger, but pain. "What's wrong?"

"Another ambulance arrived. They're bringing somebody out on a gurney."

"Is it Acton?"

"I can't tell, the body's covered by a sheet."

Jack's shoulders slumped. "You mean they're dead?"

"Yes, it would appear so."

"Is there any way to tell if it's Acton?"

"No, the body's completely covered, and there are no visible markers to be able to tell. But I…I don't think it could be anyone else."

Jack cursed and slammed the back of his head against the seat. Leroux was right. It couldn't be anyone else—the timing was far too coincidental. Acton was dead and he had failed in his mission. "What do we do now?" he asked, his voice somber.

"There's nothing we can do. The South China Sea crisis appears to be settling down. Once things are back to normal, we'll request his body through diplomatic channels, though I doubt we'll ever see it. For now, just get yourself secure, and your handler will contact you should there be another assignment."

Jack sighed. "Copy that. But listen, if you can, let Professor Palmer know that her husband died a hero. I could have gone back to try and save him, but we both would have been caught. He told me to leave him. He didn't want anyone else getting hurt because of him. If he hadn't said that, I would have gone back and I'd be dead now too. Also, tell her that the last words he said to me were, 'Tell Laura I love her.'"

"I'll make sure she knows that."

"Thanks. Rawhide, out."

Jack yanked the comm out of his ear and tossed it on the passenger seat. He had failed before, and he had no doubt he would fail again, though for some reason, this time the ramifications cut deeper than usual. Most civilians would have begged that he come back for them, but that wasn't this man. This man had told him to leave him, had given him the critical piece of intel they would need if help were possible, and then had delivered a final message to the woman he loved.

Not for a moment had he given a thought to his own needs.

The world needed more people like Professor James Acton, and today, because of his failure, it was a worse place for it.

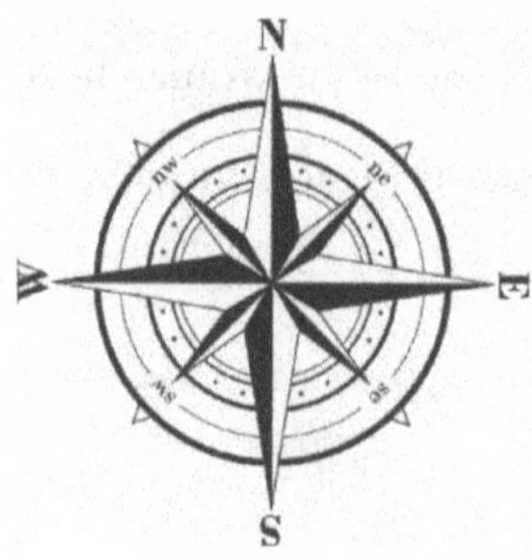

Imperial Palace

Luoyang, Han Empire

166 AD

Lucius strode into the court of the Imperial Palace of the Han Empire, and was surprised at how many were inside. On the few occasions he had been here in the past, they had been greeted by only the senior members of the Emperor's Court and his personal guard. Today, it appeared anyone of importance to the Empire was in attendance. And as they passed through the cleared center of the court toward the throne upon which Jieyou's father sat, all those present turned their backs on them.

Though that wasn't entirely accurate.

They were turning their backs on her, for he was of no importance.

She stared up at him, her eyes pools of tears that finally let loose, and it broke his heart. He never should have looked at her that first day, he never should have shown her any interest, and he certainly never should have followed that map. And though there was enough blame to share between the two of them, all he would have had to do was say no.

And he had had all the reasons to do so.

If she were unhappy in her role as a princess who would be married off at some point to a man she might never love, that was her cross to bear.

But he was Roman. He was supposed to be above all of this. He was supposed to put his family and his empire first, beyond all other considerations of self. He had betrayed his father, he had betrayed the expedition, he had betrayed his Emperor, all for love.

She sniffed, and all his thoughts were forgotten. These past months had been the happiest of his life, and should they die here today, he would have no regrets beyond the innocents that had died, and the damage done to the Empire.

They came to a halt in front of the Emperor and orders were barked. Jieyou dropped to her knees and prostrated herself in front of her father, and Lucius followed suit, remembering his father's admonishment that first day they had arrived. Another order split the silence of the court, and he turned his head slightly to see his father in chains, severely beaten, being led into the court.

And it gutted him.

Seeing the bodies of the embassy staff hanging outside for all to see as a warning to any who dared challenge the Emperor's will, had been heart-wrenching. But seeing his own father, with perhaps mere minutes left to live, went beyond any sense of grief and shame he had ever before experienced. The physical pain on his father's face, and the wounds his body bore, betrayed the fact the past days had been brutal agony for the man.

Jieyou turned her head, pressed against the floor to face him, her eyes red and her cheeks flushed as she stared at him. "I'm so sorry, it's all my fault," she whispered.

He met her gaze and shook his head slightly. "I could have said no."

She closed her eyes, all control lost as her shoulders shook with her sobs. He bit down on his lip, the salty taste of blood barely enough for him to maintain control over the tears and the anguish he was so desperate to express. A man was talking, reading from a scroll, the translator interpreting, his voice barely a murmur as a list of charges were read. He ignored them all, as they were of no importance. He knew they would die, and there was only one last thing he could do.

The interpreter uttered his final words, the only ones registering. "How do you plead?"

Lucius rose. Jieyou moved to join him, but he held out a hand, indicating she should continue her display of subservience to her father. "I plead guilty."

His father gasped. "No! No, he doesn't! He doesn't know what he's saying!"

Lucius turned to his father, his pulse racing as he struggled to control his emotions. "I know exactly what I'm saying, Father. I am guilty, but please let me explain."

The Emperor waved his wrist and Lucius stepped forward, physically separating himself from Jieyou.

"I plead guilty, Your Highness, but let me please make it clear that only I am to blame here. My father knew nothing of what was going on, and on our first day here, when I met your daughter, he gave me explicit instructions to pay her no mind, as I was beneath her, no matter how attracted I may have been to her. I gave him my word that I would heed his orders, but I betrayed him. For that reason, I am the only guilty party among the Roman contingent. My father had no reason to believe that I would betray him, as I never had before. I consider myself a man of honor, as did he, and unfortunately, I betrayed that honor.

"That first night, I snuck into the Imperial Palace and compelled one of her ladies to bring me to your daughter. It was I who initiated contact, and it was I who forced her to carry on a relationship with me. I knew it was wrong, and she continually protested, but I told her that if she informed you of what I had done, I would claim it was her that had contacted me, and she was terrified of what you might think of her should the lie be told. I blackmailed her the entire time, and then when the opportunity presented itself for me to return to Rome, I once again used the power I had over her to force her to write a note to you indicating she had fallen in love with a palace guard, and had left to live a simple life on his family's farm.

"As I'm sure you know, the very notion was ridiculous, and in retrospect, I believe she agreed to write that note because she knew you wouldn't believe it, and would seek the truth. You must believe me, Your Highness, that everything your daughter did was against her will, and she did it in an attempt to preserve her family's honor and her own virtue. I alone am to blame, not my father, not your daughter. Punish me, but not them. Execute me, but let them live."

Jieyou sobbed behind him at his words, but wisely said nothing. His own father stared at him, his chin trembling, his chest swelled with pride, for he knew every word spoken was a lie. Some in the court were sobbing as well, though he had little doubt it wasn't for him, but for what had happened to Jieyou against her will.

And it gave him hope.

If these people believed his story, believed that she was the victim, then perhaps there was a chance the Emperor might as well. He dared not look at the man to get a sense of his mood, for at this moment, respect was all that mattered. Emperor Huan finally broke his silence, and the interpreter, his eyes wide, spoke.

"Your words are eloquent, and we believe them, for we know our daughter, and she would never betray us willingly. As your father is well aware, parents are responsible for the actions of their children, and while we believe your father knew nothing of your treachery, he not only is your father, but he's the ambassador, and is responsible for the actions of all those under his command. Therefore, we find that as a father, and an ambassador, he is ultimately responsible, and must be executed before the sun sets."

Lucius opened his mouth to protest when his father cut him off.

"I accept Your Highness' decision, and accept full responsibility for all of the actions of my son, and I willingly offer my life as punishment and payment from the Roman Empire for this betrayal. All I ask is that you do not punish your daughter for my son's coercions, and that you do not blame the Roman Empire for the actions of one young man and the failings of a father who could see nothing evil within his son."

The tears threatening to escape finally flowed down Lucius' face, yet the rest of his body remained still, his Roman stoicism mostly intact.

"And what of your son, what would you have us do with him?"

The words from his father's mouth were heart-wrenching, though they were the only words that could be spoken. "As a father, I would beg you to spare his life and let him return to Rome, and have my life and those of the others from my contingent be all the payment required to right this wrong. However, it is not for my place to say. This is your realm, this is your court, and it was your daughter who was wronged. Whatever decision you make here today, I know will be wise and just, and will be supported by all those involved."

Huan regarded Lucius' father, saying nothing, the entire court in a hushed silence. "Your words are wise, and we accept the offer of your life as final payment for the sins committed here today that we demand satisfaction for. However, we are not the only one who suffered this affront, and as such, we will leave it to our daughter to decide the fate of your son. Rise, Daughter."

Jieyou rose, her entire body trembling. Lucius tore his eyes away from her, terrified the love they shared could never be hidden should their eyes meet.

"What is your decision, Daughter? What punishment should your abductor face?"

He could hear her sniffling behind him, then an inhalation that steadied her nerves. "Father, I apologize to you for fearing what you may think of me. If I had only gone to you when this Roman first committed his horrific betrayal, all of this could have been avoided, and I apologize to you and the Court for any disappointment or embarrassment I may have caused in my weakness. I do believe this boy, for that is all he is, is in love with me in his own foolish way, and his only sin is acting upon it, and me not trusting that you would believe me over him. If I had been more firm, and more courageous, all of this could have been avoided. I ask that you let him leave with the message, should you so desire, that no further Romans are to come here, and if you see it in your heart to let his father join him, I would be forever grateful. All I wish is that the pain and suffering that my weakness has caused be over with, and that I resume my position at your side to serve whatever purpose you have planned for me."

"Wise words, Daughter." Emperor Huan rose and the court swiftly dropped to a knee. "Many wise words have been spoken here today, and much truth has been revealed. Let this be a lesson to us all to never jump to conclusions, and to never assume the worst. Quite often, the truth is somewhere in the middle of the rumors and the gossip. Our daughter is both wise and beautiful, qualities this young man no doubt found irresistible. And we too were once a young man, and on occasion gave in to temptation, though we were never foolish enough to do so with the daughter of an emperor. We believe that ultimately, no harm has come to our daughter, and we trust the words she has spoken here today. If it is her wish that her captor and betrayer be set free and returned to Rome, then it shall be so."

Lucius' heart pounded as his eyes widened, his jaw dropping with the possibility he might survive the day. It was a stunning turn of events, yet he resisted the urge to look back at Jieyou to reveal his elation, for it would reveal all that had just been said were lies.

"And if we are not to execute the son who committed these acts, then we shall leave his future punishment to that of his father, who will also be banished from the Empire. No Romans will be permitted to enter our borders for the next one-hundred years, long enough to ensure that these two never return."

His father bowed his head even deeper. "Thank you, Your Highness."

Lucius immediately echoed the sentiment.

"Then this is a joyous day. Our daughter has been returned safely, her honor restored." He pointed at Lucius and his father. "You two will leave at once."

"Yes, Your Highness," he and his father both said simultaneously.

A commotion at the far end of the court had everyone turning. The doors burst open and two guards entered, hauling in a man, his feet dragging on the floor, his head sagging between his shoulders. He was dressed as the lowliest soldier, and appeared half dead. He was carried forward then thrown on the floor in front of the Emperor.

"Explain yourself," demanded Emperor Huan, the translator continuing to interpret.

One of the soldiers jabbed a finger at the prisoner. "This soldier claims to have news about the abduction of the Princess."

"That matter has been settled. The truth has been revealed. Our daughter was abducted by this man against her will, and appropriate punishment has been decided."

"Your Highness, you must hear what this man has to say." The soldier reached down and grabbed the man by the hair, pulling his face up, and Lucius gasped as he realized it was the soldier they had captured and interrogated.

The soldier who had been witness to everything that had happened.

The soldier whose account would contradict everything that had just been said.

Jieyou rose and walked over to Lucius, her hand extended, resignation to their fate in her eyes. He stood and took it, and she embraced him. He returned it, then looked at her father, whose eyes were wide with shock. His face turned red, his fists clenching at his sides, his arm finally darting out a long finger, more powerful than any weapon man had ever created.

"Execute them all!"

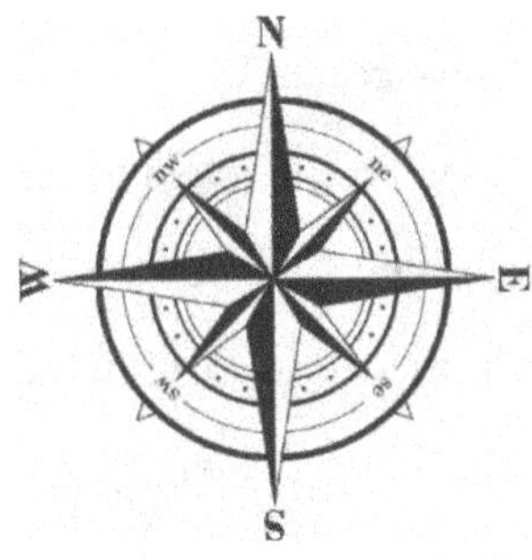

Director Morrison's Office, CIA Headquarters

Langley, Virginia

Present Day, One Week Later

Leroux entered Morrison's office and his boss pointed at the door. Leroux closed it and took a seat as Morrison shook a piece of paper.

"I got a rather cryptic message from Kane."

Leroux's eyebrows shot up. "I thought he was deep."

"He is, but apparently he came up for air for a few minutes."

"What does it say?"

Morrison handed him the paper. "See for yourself."

Leroux read the message, his eyes narrowing. "Send friendly faces to meet JA at midnight tomorrow, local time." He looked up from the page, his heart racing. "JA? Does that mean what I think it does?"

"What do you think it means?"

"The only JA I can think of at the moment is James Acton, but he's supposed to be dead."

"We never really confirmed it, did we?"

"No, there was no way we could. When we handed back the Chinese sailors we rescued, the Chinese were asked to return Professor Acton as a gesture of goodwill, even if he were dead, but they claimed they never had him, and Washington decided it wasn't worth pressing the matter if he was already dead." He held up the page. "This message says to send friendly faces tomorrow midnight, local time." He indicated a set of GPS coordinates under the message. "Just where is this?"

"The GPS coordinates included are on the Vietnamese side of their border with China, only a few miles from the coast. It's as if it were chosen so we could insert forces and get them out undetected."

"Do we still have friendly faces in the area?"

"I already checked, and yes, we do." Morrison pointed at the door. "Go get our man."

Leroux smiled. "With pleasure, sir." He paused. "Should I tell Professor Palmer?"

Morrison firmly shook his head. "Absolutely not. That woman is going through hell right now, and the last thing we need to do is give her false hope. We're assuming this is James Acton we're picking up, but it might be someone or something else, though I doubt that. My biggest fear is that he doesn't make the rendezvous. There will be lots of opportunities for him to be captured or killed between now and then."

Leroux rose. "You're right, of course. Let's just pray for her sake that whoever is getting him out knows what they're doing."

"From your lips to God's ears."

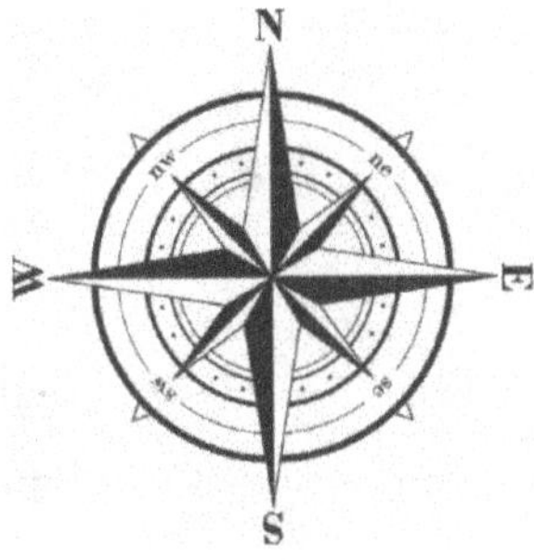

Vietnam-China Border

Dawson peered through his binoculars at the Vietnamese side of the border crossing. Their insertion had been uneventful, and their mission not entirely clear. They had received word through channels a week ago that James Acton was presumed dead at the hands of the Chinese. Once the crisis had de-escalated, Laura Palmer had evacuated to Japan and then home to mourn the loss of her husband, and he wished he could be there with her.

They all did.

The past week had been difficult for him and his team. Acton was like an honorary member. He had shed blood with them and for them. He had saved their lives on multiple occasions, and Dawson only prayed that the debt they all owed the man because of the events in Peru, had been repaid.

"Someone's coming," said Niner.

Dawson adjusted his binoculars, zooming in on a beat-up transport truck as it came to a halt. A short conversation was had, then something was handed over to the Vietnamese guard, who smiled broadly then waved the truck through.

"I think somebody was just paid a bribe," said Niner.

"And judging by the thickness of that envelope, I'd say it was one hell of a bribe," rumbled Atlas.

The truck cleared the small checkpoint, the gate closing behind it. Dawson tracked it through the binoculars, chewing his cheek as he debated what might happen next.

"So, what do we do now? Do we stop it?" asked Jimmy.

Dawson shook his head. "They're the ones that gave us the coordinates. I would think if they want to meet up with us, they'll be the ones doing the stopping."

"Can we be sure this is who we're meeting?" asked Niner.

"Nope." Dawson rose. "Let's get to the road, just in case."

They weaved through the trees, making their way to the road, then crouched in the ditch. Dawson flipped down his night-vision goggles, the jungle instantly alive around him, searching for any hostiles who might interrupt the party. He found nothing.

The truck rounded a bend in the road, showing no signs of slowing down, when the engine knocked then cut out, the truck slowly rolling to a halt.

"You don't think that's a coincidence, do you?" asked Niner.

Atlas punched him on the shoulder. "If you don't have anything smart to say, keep that trap shut."

Niner gave him the stink-eye. "I can tell you I certainly don't have anything *nice* to say."

The truck driver opened his door and stepped out, lighting a cigarette. "Are there any friendly faces out there?"

Dawson smiled and rose. "There's a couple if you have a JA to deliver."

The man slapped the side of the truck and a hissing sound was heard from underneath. Dawson watched as a hidden compartment lowered, a figure rolling out onto the muddy ground. He raised his weapon, activating the tactical light as the others did the same. The man gained a knee and raised a hand to shield his eyes.

"How about we ease off on those, okay?"

Dawson grinned at Acton's voice.

"Holy shit, Doc! We thought you were dead!" exclaimed Niner as he stepped forward and offered a hand. He yanked Acton to his feet and the man yelped in pain. "What's wrong, Doc?"

"I think I've got some broken ribs. I've been having a hard time breathing since this damn journey began."

The truck driver pressed a button underneath the wheel-well and the hidden compartment hissed once again as it rose back up inside. "My job's done. I suggest you get out of here quickly."

Acton shook the man's hand. "Thank you so much."

"Hey, it's what I get paid to do." The driver climbed back in his truck and fired up a perfectly functional engine, then continued on.

Dawson turned to Acton. "Can you walk?"

"I'll walk back to the United States if I have to." Acton examined his surroundings. "Just where the hell are we?"

"Vietnam."

"Shit. That can't be good, can it?"

"Not if we're caught."

"I'm going to slow you down. That's all I can tell you."

Atlas stepped forward. "I'll carry him."

"Thanks, buddy, but even you can't carry me that far."

Atlas yanked apart the stretcher he had been carrying. "This is the Army. Like the Boy Scouts, we're always prepared."

Acton laughed then winced. They helped him onto the stretcher, Atlas and Niner each grabbing an end.

Dawson took point. "Okay, let's get a move on. I don't want to be in Vietnam any more than Vietnam wants me in her."

Niner gave him a look. "That sounds kind of dirty, Sergeant Major."

"Only to a twisted mind like yours, Sergeant."

Niner shrugged. "Twisted is more interesting." He stared down at Acton, their reborn friend's head at his end of the stretcher. "So, Doc, what happened? Everyone thought you were killed over a week ago."

Acton's jaw dropped. "A week! It's been that long?"

"Yup."

"Holy shit! How's Laura? Is she okay?"

"Devastated, I'm sure," replied Dawson. "We haven't had any contact with her. We've been deployed since the South China Sea fiasco."

"What happened with that?"

"The Chinese backed down, though you wouldn't believe it from their newscasts." Dawson glanced over his shoulder at Acton. "How did you escape?"

"I didn't. The guy who wanted to kill me got himself killed by one of the ones who captured me. I don't know what the hell really happened. Almost everything was in Chinese, but I got the distinct impression that some old Politburo guy who blamed me for his grandson's death, also threatened to kill somebody who had the capability of fighting back. He jabbed a needle in the old guy's eye and gave him a heart attack. It's the scariest shit I've seen in my life."

"Then what happened?"

"The guy had me go through a door, I got tased by some bat-shit crazy woman who then chloroformed me or something, and then the next thing I know I'm in the back of that truck with some bottles of water, some protein bars, and not a pot to piss in. I have to shit so freaking bad, that at some point we're going to have to stop so that an American can once again bomb this godforsaken country."

Niner and the others snickered, the noise stifled quickly by a raised hand from Dawson.

"Let's just put some distance between us and that border checkpoint," said Dawson. "Then you can drop your deuce."

Acton nodded. "Sounds like a plan. Do you have any way I can call Laura?"

"Not while we're in hostile territory. We've got a nice submarine sitting offshore to take you home. You'll be able to make a call as soon as we're on board."

"Thank God. I can't wait to hear her voice. I can only imagine what she's been going through."

"I'm sure she'll be happy too, Doc."

"Yeah," said Niner. "You're lucky you surfaced when you did. I was only a few days from making my move on her."

Acton groaned. "Lucky me."

Niner grinned. "No, it would have been lucky her."

Atlas gave Niner a look. "Don't make me put this man down and teach you a lesson in respect."

"I learned everything I know from you. And besides, this man has a lot to look forward to."

Acton eyed him. "What do you mean?"

"I hear 'coming back from the dead sex' is the best of all."

Acton laughed as Atlas shook his head. "I can arrange the dead part, but the coming back from it, I'm not so sure about. How about we give it a try anyway?"

"If my hands weren't full, there'd be all kinds of gestures happening back here."

Acton chuckled. "So, you mentioned the submarine. Please tell me we don't have to swim to it."

"Don't worry, Doc. You just have to hold your breath. We'll drag you the rest of the way."

Acton laughed then groaned. "Okay, that's it. You guys have to shut up. If I laugh anymore, I'm going to puncture a lung."

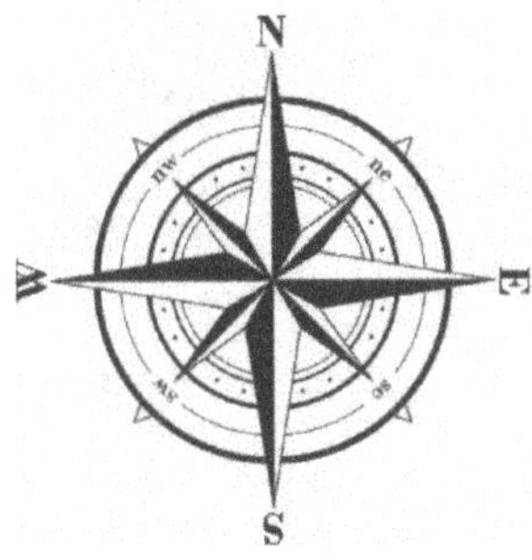

Acton/Palmer Residence

St. Paul, Maryland

Laura lay on their bed, curled in a ball, her entire body exhausted from a week of crying. They say time heals all wounds, but no one ever put a number to it. All she knew was that today, the pain hurt just as much as when she had received word through a personal call from Chris Leroux about what they had seen, and the conclusion to which they had come.

Her beloved husband was dead.

It had been over a week, and there was no longer any doubt. If they had been mistaken, she would have heard by now, and each day that there wasn't any word was another nail in a coffin she would never see.

Yesterday, she had received a message from Professor Cao indicating he had been held for questioning then abruptly released, asking if they were safe. Her reply had been heart wrenching to write, and the response from him to the news tearing open the wound yet again.

She would never see James again, would never get to bury him, would never have a grave to visit. The only man she had ever truly loved was no more, and her only regret was that she had survived. If she could turn back time, she would have stayed in the car with him. She would never have crossed through those gates and into the embassy. She would have been arrested with him and shared his fate, for she couldn't see how she could possibly go on without him.

Life simply didn't feel worth living.

And despite the fact he wouldn't want her to feel this way, that he would want her to move on to lead a long, full, happy life, at this moment, she simply didn't care about anything.

Sandra was sitting on the bed with her, gently rubbing her back. She could hear voices downstairs. Tommy and Mai were here, as well as Milton and his daughter Niskha. Terrence and Jenny had arrived yesterday, blaming themselves for the entire situation.

The phone rang and she heard Hugh Reading's voice on the ground floor as he answered it. She couldn't make out the words, but whoever it was had the closest thing to a father she had in years rushing up the stairs then knocking on her door.

"Come in," said Sandra. The door opened and Reading entered.

"Laura, I think you need to take this."

She buried her head a little deeper in the pillow. "Not now, Hugh."

"It's Chris Leroux. I really think you need to take this."

She groaned then rolled into a seated position. She took the phone, pressing it to her ear. "Hello?"

"Hello, Professor Palmer, this is Chris Leroux. I have somebody here who wants to talk to you."

She pressed the phone tighter against her ear as she heard a crackling sound.

"Hey, babe, is that you?"

She gasped at her husband's voice. "James?" She could barely say his name, her mouth so dry, her body spent. Sandra jumped from the bed and hopped up and down before rushing into Reading's arms. "I thought you were dead!"

The laughter she had thought she would never hear again filled her ear, bringing tears of joy to her eyes. "So did everyone, apparently, but I'm safe now. I'm with Bravo Team on a submarine. I should see you in the next few days. I just wanted to hear your voice and let you know that I was okay."

The tears she thought she had spent flowed freely once again, and she could barely speak. Her heart was racing with excitement, and threatening to cause her to pass out. She sucked in a breath then laughed with relief. "I can't believe you're alive!"

"Are you happy?"

She laughed. "Of course I am! I thought I would never see you again!"

"I'll be there in a few days. Let everyone know that I'm okay, and that I expect all kinds of expensive gifts."

She giggled. "I'll see you soon. I love you!"

"I love you too, babe. Talk to you soon."

The call ended and Reading sat beside her. "Please tell me that I didn't misinterpret what I just heard. Was that Jim?"

She smiled, wiping away her tears. "He's alive!"

Reading's eyes welled, and he hugged her hard as they both sobbed in relief while Sandra rushed down the stairs screaming, "He's alive! He's alive!"

Laura closed her eyes, all the pressure from the past week lifted as cheers erupted downstairs with the news her beloved James was coming home, and their life together would continue.

Until someone else decided once again to terrorize their existence.

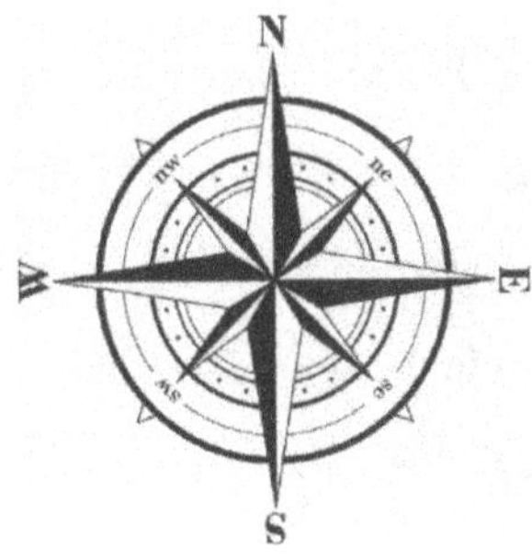

Outside Rome, The Roman Empire

168 AD

Valerius gasped at his first sight of Rome in over four years, the massive city stretching across the horizon. He wrapped an arm around Xijun, the woman he had been assigned to protect, and the woman who had become far more than just a responsibility.

"Is that it?" she asked.

He nodded. "It is. We're finally here."

"Home?"

He stared down at her. "My home, and our home, if you will have it."

She hopped up on her toes and gave him a kiss on the cheek. "Our home."

It had taken two years for them to arrive. The journey had been long, and he had taken Lucius' advice and taught the woman under his protection his language, and during the process, they had fallen deeply in love. She was to be his wife, yet he knew the prejudices of Rome. They could never be happy within its walls, though they could be happy elsewhere in the Empire. He had friends in Londinium, and had been stationed there at the beginning of his career and knew it well. It would be a tough life, but with her at his side, they could be happy.

Yet leaving here would take time. He still had the dispatches for the Emperor, and would likely be debriefed for some time after what had happened. They would also have to remain for at least several more years, as they had all agreed to meet at the Pantheon at midday of the summer solstice each year until all of them were reunited, or five years had passed since their departure from the Han Empire.

He had no idea whether they were the first to have reached home, the last, or if they were to be the only. Yet they had to know. Not only did he want to find out what happened to his brothers-in-arms, but they both needed to know if any of the other women had survived. If any had, life would be much easier for all of them if they at least had a companion from their native land who understood their ways and their traditions. And perhaps they could all travel together to Londinium, and live out their lives in peace, forgetting the horrors they had left behind.

He took her hand. "Ready?"

She smiled, though her eyes betrayed her fear. "Ready."

"Then let us begin our new lives together."

THE END

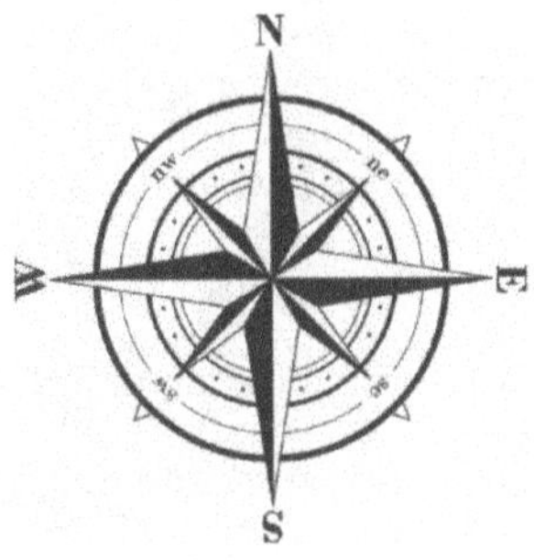

ACKNOWLEDGMENTS

While finishing this novel, a court case was unfolding in Canada with potentially far-reaching ramifications. On December 1, 2018, the American government requested the Canadian government arrest Meng Wanzhou, the Chief Financial Officer of Huawei, a massive telecommunications company based in China, founded by her father. The Canadians arrested her as part of the extradition treaty between the USA and Canada, and chaos ensued.

Two innocent Canadian businessmen, Michael Kovrig and Michael Spavor, were arrested ten days later in China. They were essentially accused of being spies, and have been kept in detention since without regular access to consular assistance, and from all reports, undergoing psychological torture every single day since.

In contrast, Meng Wanzhou has been living in one of her mansions in Vancouver with an ankle monitor and a curfew.

The Chinese also retaliated by punishing various Canadian farming interests, essentially indicating everything would stop if Canada were to ignore international and domestic laws by setting Meng free.

And this is the problem with China. We in the West have ceded too much control to a communist dictatorship that doesn't believe in the rule of law, in human rights, or common decency. This is not a commentary on the Chinese people, but on their unelected leadership.

Recent events from COVID-19 to Hong Kong will hopefully wake the governments and populations of the West to the dangerous situation we now find ourselves in, and compel them to act once and for all, cutting ties with this brutal regime. Our manufacturing should be shifted out of China, and their ambitions checked, as we did with the Soviet Union.

Only then might we have a chance at winning against an economic and military behemoth that within the next several decades, will be more powerful than the United States.

And unstoppable.

A terrifying thought for our future generations.

And that court decision to which I referred? It went against Meng Wanzhou, with the Chinese vowing further action. It was the correct decision legally, though I fear what happened to the two Michaels after the decision was handed down.

As usual, there are people to thank. My dad for all the research, Greg "Chief" Michael for some US Navy info, Michael Toma for some gun range info, Chris Kalle for the Aussie slang, Sherrie Men for some Chinese cultural help, and, as always, my wife, daughter, my late mother who will always be an angel on my shoulder as I write, as well as my friends for their continued support, and my fantastic proofreading team! Also, a special thank you to the winners of a character naming contest on my Facebook page, Pete Rosendahl and Chris Kalle. Follow me on Facebook to participate in these things.

To those who have not already done so, please visit my website at www.jrobertkennedy.com, then sign up for the Insider's Club to be notified of new book releases. Your email address will never be shared or sold.

Thank you once again for reading.

CPSIA information can be obtained
at www.ICGtesting.com
Printed in the USA
LVHW042119220723
753132LV00007B/229

9 781990 418532